INTRODUCTION

Cindy and the Prince
Forced to share her father's muffler shop with her bitter step-mother, Cindy is determined to make the best of a difficult situation. Eligible bachelor Luke Princeton admires Cindy's spunk and fortitude. He isn't interested in anyone but her. . .even though she's not interested in him. But as Luke tries to win Cindy's heart, her stepsisters, Annie and Zella, try to keep them apart. Will Luke's annual banquet be the perfect setting for a fairy-tale romance?

Love by the Books
When Annie fills in for the regular accountant at Brent and Luke's car rental business, she has no idea what she's getting into. . .until she finds some alarming discrepancies in the books. Annie is hesitant to speak up. Brent doesn't trust her, so why would he believe her about it, or anything else? When all fingers point to her, convincing everyone of her innocence seems hopeless except for the help of the most unlikely man—Brent.

Till Death Do Us Part
With her first name starting with a *Z* and her last with a *W*, Zella Wilson has always been last. And now she's the last to get married, but she's in no rush even if her mother is. When a book club brings Trevor into Zella's life, her mother is thrilled. . .until Zella's behavior starts to worry her. Could this new mystery man in Zella's life be using her love to cover up his life of crime?

Never Too Late
The one love of Farrah's life ended in tragedy, and she never got over it. Even though she is sometimes lonely, her life is busy and full without love, especially now that she is helping teenage Kat and her friends with animal rescue projects. Fellow volunteer Matt quickly falls for Farrah. . .but he struggles to convince her that age means nothing when it comes to love.

SEATTLE CINDERELLA

FOUR-IN-ONE COLLECTION

GAIL SATTLER

BARBOUR
PUBLISHING

Published by Barbour Publishing, Inc., P.O. Box 719, Uhrichsville, OH
44683, www.barbourbooks.com

 Member of the
Evangelical Christian
Publishers Association

*Our mission is to publish and distribute inspirational products offering exceptional
value and biblical encouragement to the masses.*

Printed in the United States of America

CINDY AND THE PRINCE

Dedication

Dedicated to all romantics and lovers
of the eternal happily-ever-after.

Chapter 1

L uke Princeton pushed open the door to the muffler shop and walked inside.

Ignoring the sign saying customers weren't allowed in the work area, he forced a smile at the young woman seated at the desk in the corner of the small service office. "Mind if I go in? I need to talk to the boss."

She jerked her head toward the shop window, where three people wearing blue coveralls stood together under a car raised on a hydraulic hoist. One of them pointed upward and the others nodded. "You know the drill," she mumbled, not missing a keystroke.

Indeed he did. He also knew which one of the three he wanted—the one who was six inches shorter than the other two.

He stepped into the shop, stopping with his toes on the yellow line. "Hey! Cindy!" he called out quickly before they fired up the welding torches and no one could hear him.

All three of them raised their welding masks and turned toward him.

Cindy laid her torch down, pulled off her safety gloves, stuffed them in her pockets, and walked toward him. "What can I do for you, Luke?"

"You can join me for lunch." He gave her his best and, he hoped, most charming smile.

She didn't smile back. Instead she lowered her head and wiped her hands down the legs of her coveralls. "No, seriously."

He was completely serious—as serious as he'd been the last dozen times he'd asked.

Luke rammed his hands into his pockets. "I have a reservation on the blue van this afternoon, but when it came back this morning it sounded a little noisy. I think the last people who rented it did something to the muffler. Can you fit it in before four thirty?"

She nodded. "We certainly can. All you had to do was make an appointment with Annie."

"Right. Annie." One of Cindy's two sisters who worked at the muffler shop part-time. He could never remember their names. "What's the other one's name again?"

"Zella. Annie comes in on Mondays, Zella comes in on Fridays, and they alternate Saturdays."

A and Z, first and last. He'd remember that. "Annie seemed too busy, that's why I asked you myself."

For a second Cindy smiled, but it wasn't a happy smile. "I'll just make that appointment for you."

Her lack of an answer about lunch didn't go unnoticed.

While Cindy penciled him into the appointment book, giving him the last empty time slot of the day, he fished the key for the van out of his pocket.

"Since you're busy, I could run and get a couple of coffees, and we can sit and have a little break without going out."

She pulled a white tag to attach to the car's keys, and wrote *Prince Rentals* on it. "Sorry, I really don't have time to stop today. Maybe another time, though." She tied the string to the key ring and hung it on the wall with the rest of the keys. "See you at four thirty."

Luke smiled in acknowledgment then turned around and his smile dropped. He tried not to let yet another rejection get him down as he returned to his building across the shared parking lot.

"Struck out again, huh?"

He glared at his partner and soon to be ex–best friend. "Don't you have some work to do?"

Brent raised a cup from the coffee shop a few doors down then set it back down on the counter. "Nope. Break time." However, Brent had the file open for a fleet quote they were going to make and was writing, despite his alleged coffee break. "I told you that you should have taken her a latté or something. Then she would have had to stop and talk to you, just to be polite."

"You're probably right, but it would have been rude not to bring one for her sister."

"Try when she's over there alone then."

"But I can't ask her when she doesn't have one of her sisters there to answer phones or deal with customers. She can't take the time."

"Did you ask her out for lunch again?"

"Yes, and she turned me down again. Too busy."

"Or you can't take a hint." Brent sipped his coffee. "She's obviously not interested."

Luke rammed his hands into his pockets. "She doesn't say she's seeing someone. I'd respect that. She always says 'another time,' so that makes me think one day she's going to say yes."

"She's just being nice because you're a good customer. You've been trying to get her to go out with you for at least six months. I think it's time to move on."

Hoping to catch a glimpse of Cindy through the window of the muffler shop, Luke turned to look outside. "I can't. There's just something about her that gets to me."

Brent snickered. "Right. You gotta love a woman who knows how to work a welding torch."

Luke turned to give Brent the evil eye. "I know it sounds strange, but that's a part of it. After her dad died, she stepped right into his footsteps. She does the same work Dave did."

"Even puts up with those lazy sisters like Dave did." Brent didn't look up from his quote. "Yeah, she's good all right."

"You've got to admit that running a brake and muffler shop isn't a typical job for a woman. She's got guts."

Brent's snicker turned into a belly laugh. "There's a line

you can use to impress a lady. I like you because you've got guts. Now I know why she won't go out with you."

Luke picked up a clipboard with an inspection form on it. "You're not helping. If you were in my place, what would you do?"

"Ask her to go out to a movie or something."

"If she won't go out with me for a short lunch, what makes you think she'll go to a movie?"

Brent shrugged his shoulders. "How about sending her flowers?"

"I don't think she's the flowers type."

"All chicks like jewelry. Give her a necklace with your initials on it."

"You're so funny." Luke made no attempt to keep the sarcasm out of his voice. He sighed and turned back to the window. "I've never seen Cindy wear jewelry. Not even earrings. Besides, isn't there a workers' comp regulation about jewelry and power tools?"

"Point taken. How about church?"

Luke shook his head. "She doesn't go to mine. But I think I know where she goes. When I took Kat to her friend's youth group a couple of weeks ago, I saw Cindy's pickup in the parking lot."

At the mention of Cindy's truck, both men turned their heads to look out the window. There it was: a large black 4X4 with orange flames painted on the sides, parked in the back corner of Mufford Brake and Muffler's area of the lot.

"There can't be too many of those around town," Brent muttered.

"Maybe that's what I should do. Kat won't go to church on Sunday morning, but that friend of hers has taken her to youth group a few times. Maybe I should check it out."

"Good idea." Brent raised his empty cup and tilted it toward the garbage container. "Coffee break's over. Back to work."

Cindy Mufford watched Luke return to his office from her vantage point beside lift three. The large windows were great for letting the natural light in—and for keeping an eye on her handsome neighbor.

As happened often, Luke and his partner were involved in a lively discussion. Cindy smiled as Brent smacked Luke in the back of the head with his empty cup before tossing it into the trash. Those two had a special relationship to be able to share a business partnership for so many years and still be good friends. Cindy glanced at her stepsister Annie and thought of her other stepsister, Zella. Unlike Luke and Brent's, hers was a partnership not made in heaven.

As she worked, she couldn't get it off her mind. When she couldn't stand it anymore, she sucked in a deep breath, put her wrench down, returned to the office, and approached Annie's desk. "Why didn't you make an appointment for Luke this morning? He shouldn't have come into the shop just for that."

Annie shrugged her shoulders and kept typing. "He wanted to see you anyway. He always does."

Cindy held her breath while she counted to ten. "I was working. Unlike you." She swept one hand through the air, encompassing the papers spread on the desk. "You're doing your homework. You're supposed to be closing off month end."

"Mom said it would be okay. The assignment has to be turned in tomorrow." Cindy tamped down her anger. Annie was still going to college to follow her dream, while Cindy had to drop out and take over the business when her father died.

"Your mother doesn't have the right to say that. I have a business to run."

"Your father gave Mom half interest, so that means she has every right. I'll finish the month end tomorrow at home. By the way, be quiet when you get home tonight. Mom is going to a seminar tomorrow and has to be in bed early."

"What about supper? If you're going to throw the half interest in my face, my half interest in the house means supper every day, not fending for myself. And please don't tell me Zella is cooking."

Annie's eyes narrowed. "Your supper will be in the fridge. There wouldn't be a problem if you'd gone out with Luke."

"He asked me out for lunch, not supper." Cindy opened her mouth, about to tell Annie that her personal conversations were none of her business, but stopped before the words came out. She didn't have a good relationship with either of her stepsisters as it was. Snapping back would only make it worse, if that were possible. If Melissa ever said something good about her in front of Annie and Zella instead of the constant criticism, things might be different. But that wasn't going to happen, so it was best just to keep quiet. Since she only had half interest in the house and half interest in the business, she couldn't sell either one to get a house of her own, and she didn't earn enough money from half the business to live on her own and pay rent. So she was stuck with them. Or they were stuck with her.

Annie leaned back in the chair and ran her fingers through her hair. "If you're not going to go out with him, maybe I will. He's hot."

As Annie spoke, the school bus stopped in front of the car rental, and a girl hopped out.

Cindy watched the girl run to Luke and give him a big hug. Luke might be hot, but he was also a single father. And Cindy had experienced enough misery with her own blended family to not get involved in someone else's.

"You go right ahead."

Annie pulled a flash drive out of the computer, scooped up her books, and stomped out without another word.

Cindy stared blankly at the clock. All day long Annie had been doing her homework for college on company time. Hopefully she would keep her promise and catch up on the company's accounting work on her own time.

Melissa had poisoned so much between them, but at least integrity remained. At this point, it was the best she was going to get.

Cindy gritted her teeth and got caught up on the paperwork until everyone scheduled to pick up cars today had done so. She worked on the next parts order until her two employees left then flicked on the CLOSED light and locked up.

Tonight she was spared from more drama from her stepmother and stepsisters because she wasn't going home, she was going out.

After she cleaned up, she was going to the church to join the youth group for a hockey game in the parking lot. She was normally a good player, but after the day she'd had, she pitied the goalie.

She hopped into her truck, slammed it into first gear, and roared off.

Chapter 2

Luke pulled into the church parking lot, stopping beside the tallest vehicle there—a large black truck with flames painted on the sides.

Before Kat opened the door, Luke turned toward her. "Are you sure you want to do this? Why don't you just go to the normal meeting on Wednesday?"

"Because they're starting something new. I hate starting in the middle of something. I want to start at the same time as everyone else."

He couldn't argue with that. He wanted to help Kat fit in and make friends—the right ones. There was no better place than here, at a church's youth group. He just wasn't sure this specific activity was right for Kat, who was short for her age and a bit frail—especially after all she'd been through.

He opened his mouth to tell her to be careful, but she grabbed her duffle and hopped out the door before he had a chance. Instead of escorting her to join the group, he took his time locking up the car then walked to join the crowd.

It had been years since he'd been to a youth group meeting—not since he'd been that age—but not much had changed. Except for those who were already coupled, the boys and girls stood in separate groups, chatting and glancing back and forth at each other.

He knew the routine well, except that this time he wasn't here as a youth; he was here as a parent, something he didn't know if he was ready for but hadn't been given a choice.

Slowing his pace, he walked past the circle of boys, checking out the group of young studs from a different perspective than when he'd been one of them. The oldest in the group appeared to be about seven or eight years younger than Luke and about three inches taller. Although he was talking to the boys, his eyes never left the girls and, Luke noticed, lingered on Kat.

He'd keep his eye on that one.

Luke continued on toward the group of parent volunteers. From a distance, he judged most of them to be at least ten years older than he was. As he joined them, a few of the mothers looked at him, crinkled their brows, glanced at the teen boys then back to him, probably wondering why he'd joined the wrong group. Most guys his age didn't have teenage children.

This felt more awkward than when he'd gone to the high school and registered Kat for classes and once again come face-to-face with Mrs. Pendegast, the mean secretary from his youth. She still hadn't retired.

"Hi, I'm new here, I'm with—" A green blur with a hockey stick streaked past him, the clatter of in-line skates drowning out his words.

Instead of finishing his sentence, he turned to the blur. All he could see was the top of a silver helmet with blond hair sticking out as the skater bent at the waist to sort a collection of red and blue vests into piles.

"Everyone who's playing, line up!" a female voice called out. "We're dividing into teams. You have three minutes to get your skates on."

Most of the girls stayed behind, but a few skated to the designated area and lined up with the boys, from shortest to tallest. The tall boy leaned on a light pole to put on his skates. Which meant he'd soon be even taller.

Kat waited at the front of the line, the shortest in the group.

The light-speed skater glided in front of Kat and stopped. The light-speed skater was curvy.

A woman.

She turned to the parent group. "We don't have enough to make two teams," the blond called out from across the marked-off area designated as the rink. "We need one more person. Who else brought skates?"

Luke's breath caught in his throat.

Cindy...

Kat raised one hand. "My uncle did. I told him to. Just in case."

"That's great, Kat. By the way, it's good to see you again." Luke could see her bright smile even from the distance. Which was good. Kat needed the reassurance of other adults besides him. "Where is your uncle?"

Kat pointed to him, so Cindy turned in the direction of Kat's finger. The second they made eye contact, he smiled. Cindy's smile dropped and her mouth fell open.

Her voice came out in a squeak. "Uncle Luke?"

The cylinders in Cindy's brain fired in a million different directions, high octane.

The tiny girl who got off the school bus every day for the last couple of months was Kat. And she wasn't a daughter. Cindy hadn't made the connection between youth-group Kat and the girl she'd only seen from a distance.

Maybe it was time to get a new prescription for her contacts.

Since Luke looked about the same age as she, he'd be about twenty-six or twenty-seven. Cindy had assumed— wrongly, it would appear—he could have had a daughter out of wedlock who could be as old as ten; Kat was that petite. Cindy had given him the benefit of the doubt and credit for taking some responsibility to care for a child. But a niece brought more relatives into the dynamics of whatever had gone wrong in his family. It was so much messier. She couldn't—wouldn't—get involved in a situation as bad as, or maybe worse than, her own.

But here he was, just like at work, giving her doe eyes. Or buck eyes. Or whatever that look was that men did when they were interested.

With an adorable niece between them.

Who might be just as messed up in the head as Cindy had been when her mother died.

If it hadn't been for Farrah, her mother's best friend and Cindy's godmother, Cindy didn't know how she would have made it. But at least until three months ago she'd had her father.

Poor Kat. Did she have a woman to guide her and help her when it felt like the world was against her? If Cindy had grown up with a mother, maybe instead of putting cars back together and having a journeyman certificate for welding she would be doing something feminine with her life. Like a ballerina or a beautician or a model.

Or not.

She cleared her throat. "Luke, if you've really got your skates, get them on. We don't want to run out of daylight."

Luke nodded then jogged to his car, which she noticed was parked beside her truck. He tossed his shoes into the backseat, yanked on his skates, secured the laces in record time, and was soon on his way back.

He wasn't a half-bad skater, which meant she would put him on the other team.

Luke waited at her side while she counted everyone off

by ones and twos as they stood in line, making the teams as evenly matched as possible. Then she suited up team one with red vests and team two with blue.

"The rules are what we discussed last Wednesday. No bodychecking. There have to be two girls on the ice on each team at all times. I don't count as a girl. We can't paint lines in the parking lot for practice, but we will draw chalk lines for a game. Until then, the white pylons show where center line is, and the orange ones mark the blue lines. Our first game is in two weeks against Blessings Fellowship. Pastor is the ref, so behave. Time for face-off!"

As Pastor skated to center ice, or rather, center parking lot, on wobbly ankles, Cindy caught sight of Luke gliding backward on his skates until they were side by side.

"You're wrong, you know," he said so only she could hear.

Keeping her attention on the pending face-off, Cindy spoke to him without actually looking at him. "Those are the rules. We were very clear at the last meeting. But I know you weren't there."

"Not about the rules." He smiled. "You definitely count as a girl."

She didn't want to hear that.

Fortunately Pastor dropped the puck, setting the game in motion.

Like her, Luke stayed back and let the teens play, including the girls, who were weaker and less aggressive than most of the boys. Whenever the puck was passed to him, also like her, he passed it back to one of his teammates quickly and kept himself out of the action.

Except for when Tyler, the oldest and tallest boy on her team, had the puck. It was like flipping a switch: Luke changed from a playful pup into a grizzly bear. At times, Cindy bit back a grin at the look of fear on Tyler's face, something she thought good to tame the kid's ego. Whenever he got the puck, Luke went after him. But as soon as Luke won the battle, he gently passed the puck to the nearest girl on his team and slipped back out of the limelight until the next time his team needed him.

Of course, he was probably just working all the tension out of his system after being nice to cranky customers all day. Whenever she had to deal with unreasonable customers— or worse, her lazy stepsisters—she had the option to go into the shop and break things.

Cindy had no idea how long they'd played because they agreed the game would be over when daylight began to fade. Her team won, which didn't matter because next week the teams would be different based on her system of dividing the players. Then the week after that, everyone would be on the same team against Blessings Fellowship.

While the teens threw their vests into the box, Cindy skated toward one of the nets to put it back into the church's storage area.

As she approached the net, a rattle of skates came from behind. She knew whose they were without turning around.

Luke zoomed in front of her then spun so he was skating

backward. Without missing a beat, he took off his helmet and smiled at her.

Cindy felt her breath catch. With his dark-brown hair and coffee-colored eyes, he was movie-star handsome, except for his big nose—but in her opinion it only added to his masculine appeal. At work his hair was always neatly combed, but now after a workout, it hung in disarray, flopping over his forehead. His killer smile nearly made her lose her balance; Annie's comment about Luke being hot didn't even come close to reality.

He jerked his head toward the crowd. "Everyone's going out for coffee. Are you coming?"

Usually she did, but this time she wasn't sure it would be a good idea. "I can't. I have to get up early for work tomorrow morning."

They stopped at the net. She picked up one side and Luke picked up the other. "I'm sure all the other adults do as well, and the kids all have to go to school. We won't be long."

She opened her mouth to tell him that she still didn't think it was a good idea, but he spoke before she did.

"Kat really wants you to go."

Cindy turned to the crowd, where everyone was either talking in groups or sitting on the ground taking off their skates.

Everyone except Kat, who was standing alone to the side, watching them.

Cindy gulped. "Sure. I'll go. As soon as I get everything all packed up."

Chapter 3

"Y ou like her, don't you?"

Luke tried not to grit his teeth. "Yes."

"But she doesn't like you, does she?"

"Katherine. . ." Of all the things he needed to discuss with his fifteen-year-old niece, his love life, or lack thereof, wasn't on the list.

Kat's eyes widened then began to go glassy and her lower lip quivered.

Luke's stomach dropped to the bottom of his shoes. His mind raced for something to say, except he didn't know what he'd done wrong.

Tears rolled down Kat's cheeks, and her breath came in short gasps. She swiped her arm across her eyes and turned her face to the car window.

"Kat. . .I'm sorry. . .I. . ." He let his voice trail off. He was the first to admit he didn't know much about women, much less pre-adult women, but one thing he did know was that saying sorry first usually was the key to finding out what he was supposed to be sorry for.

"Please don't be mad at me." She gulped. "I didn't mean it."

He gripped the steering wheel until his knuckles turned white. He didn't know whether to keep going and play it casual or pull off to the side and give her a hug. Then Kat moved her body closer to the door, which told him that she wouldn't welcome a hug right now.

He kept driving but thought maybe he'd go the long way to the coffee shop so they would have more time to talk.

"I'm not mad at you. Why do you think I'm mad?"

She gulped in a deep breath, and her voice cracked as she spoke in gasping breaths. "Mom used to call me Katherine—when she was mad at me—and that last night she called me Katherine—and I went out without talking to her—and then I went straight to bed when I got home—and then Mom and Dad were in that car accident in the morning—and I never got to say I was sorry—and now she's gone and I'll never see her again—and I never told her I loved her—and my last words were that I hated her—and I can't take it back." She covered her face with her hands and began to sob.

Luke pulled off the road and turned off the car. He unbuckled his seat belt and Kat's and gently rested his hands on her shoulders. She didn't resist, so he pulled her in for a hug.

He hadn't known that the last time she'd seen her mother they'd had a fight. He couldn't imagine anything worse for a last memory. *"Don't let the sun go down on your anger."* Words he would never forget, especially now.

He held Kat while she cried, gently stroking her back, not quite knowing her loss. He'd been devastated by the loss of his brother and sister-in-law, but she'd lost her mother and father, and she was still a child. "She knew you loved her," he said, feeling his own voice start to crack as memories of that day came crashing down on him, of getting the call telling him that both Andrew and Susie had been killed in a car accident on their way to work. He'd never forget the numbness that enveloped him, going to his brother's house to be with Kat, knowing they were gone.

When Kat finished crying herself out, she pulled away and swiped at her face, for all the good it did. Even in the muted light from the streetlamps, he could see her eyes were red, her face blotchy, and her nose shiny.

He gave her a weak smile. "I think we can forgo the coffee shop tonight and just go home." Aside from Kat being a wreck, he didn't feel very sociable either.

Kat shook her head. "But Cindy is expecting you, and I know she only went because of me. I'm so sorry."

He didn't want her to be sorry. He especially didn't want her to start crying again. After the waterfall of emotions, he wasn't far from a few tears himself. "Don't worry about it. I'll see her tomorrow and explain."

Kat sniffled then pushed away from him. "Call her now. Then we can go home."

"I don't have her phone number."

"Are you serious?"

"It's true. I see her nearly every day. Even if I don't go in, we wave at each other across the parking lot. I've never needed to phone her."

Kat sniffed again. "Then maybe we should go. I know you like her."

Luke picked up one hand and gave it a gentle squeeze. "That's not important right now. What's important is to get you home. Maybe we'll make hot chocolate and watch a silly movie, and we'll both go to bed real late and be tired in the morning together."

She pushed his hands away and wiped her eyes with the back of her hand. "I don't want her to worry when we don't show up. How about if you go in to buy a couple of hot chocolates while I wait in the car, and then we go home?"

Luke fastened his seat belt and started the car. "Deal. Buckle up and let's go."

Cindy checked her watch then took another sip of her coffee.

It was nearly cold, half-gone, and Luke still wasn't there.

Just in case, she checked her cell phone. There were no missed calls.

As she flipped open the phone to search for Luke's number, she realized she only had his business listing. Kat was too new to the group to be in the group's directory, but

Cindy hoped the girl would join. Not only was the group good for her, but for a little thing, Kat was pretty good with a hockey stick. Because she was small, most of the boys on the other team treated her like she might break—which was their mistake and her team's gain.

While she tried not to worry, Cindy repositioned her chair to avoid being obvious about looking toward the door every time it opened, even though she should have been paying attention to the conversation at her table, which was about the postgame social activities the parent volunteer group was planning.

She'd nearly given up hoping they were going to come when Luke walked through the door.

Alone.

Luke stepped to the side of the entrance and slowed, glancing around the room until they locked eye contact. He paused, ran one hand through his hair, and approached her.

Cindy stood and guided him away for a private conversation. "Where's Kat?"

He ran his hand through his hair again. "She's feeling a little out of sorts right now so I'm just going to pick up a couple of hot chocolates and go home."

Cindy turned to look outside at Luke's car parked beside the building. Kat was sitting in the front passenger seat, blowing her nose.

It was probably none of her business and probably not smart to get involved, but she had to ask. "What's wrong?"

"Kat needs some downtime, I think."

She waited for him to say more but he didn't.

"Is she going to be okay?" The second the words left her mouth, she knew the answer. Cindy didn't know the whole story, but she'd figured out enough to make a good guess. The girl had lost both her parents, and now Luke was trying to pick up the pieces.

Cindy had been younger than Kat was now when her mother had died, but she still felt the loss and the heartache every day. Living with Melissa and her two daughters made Cindy miss her mother even more.

One day Kat would be okay, but that wouldn't be for a long time. No matter how good Luke could be, he would never replace her mother.

Cindy wanted to help but didn't know how much to get involved.

"I should get the hot chocolates and get going. Kat didn't want you to worry, so I came in instead of using the drive-through. I guess I'll see you at work tomorrow—if you've got time to squeeze in a couple of oil changes."

"Uh. . .sure. . ."

Before she could come up with something more intelligent, Luke turned and headed for the counter.

While he was being served, Cindy sank back into her chair and watched Kat. She didn't spend a lot of time with teenagers—she had only agreed to help the youth group short-term because of the hockey tournament. She did know that when left alone, most teenage girls went into texting frenzy, catching up on the precious minutes they'd been out of contact with their friends.

Kat sat still, staring out the window at nothing on the dark side of the parking lot, every once in a while swiping her arm across her face. She wasn't texting—just staring out the window. The girl probably hadn't seen any of her friends since she moved in with Luke.

The girl needed more than just a cup of hot chocolate.

But Cindy had needs, too. And one thing that she didn't need was to get involved in someone else's family troubles when she was drowning in her own.

She watched as Luke got into the car and handed Kat one of the cups. The girl nodded then continued to stare out the window.

Cindy stood. "I have to go home; sorry I can't stay. I'm sure whatever you decide will be fine." She tossed her cup and half-eaten muffin into the garbage can and headed for her truck, hoping once she got home she would be able to just sneak in quietly and go to bed. Whether sleep would come would be another issue.

Chapter 4

Luke had almost finished the paperwork on an insurance claim when the bell above the door tinkled. He did a double take when he caught sight of Cindy walking in.

He grinned. "This is a surprise. Welcome to Like a Prince Rentals." He looked up at the rack where they hung the keys. "Did Brent take you something that I don't know about?"

"No." She glanced at the street then back to him. "I came over so we could talk before the school bus arrived."

Automatically he turned to the direction of the bus route. "Kat's feeling better today. We watched a chick flick last night with cold hot chocolate and burnt microwave popcorn. It wasn't my kind of movie, but Kat enjoyed it—something about Chihuahuas and Hollywood and some number in the title."

"That's *Beverly Hills*. . ." Cindy shook her head. "Never mind. I was just wondering about something. I'm sorry if I'm sticking my nose where it doesn't belong, but I was wondering if Kat might want to come with me and a few of the kids from the youth group to Pike Place Market on Saturday. They're doing a fund-raiser lunch after church on Sunday and want to buy all the fruits and vegetables from the market."

"Pike's Place is kind of far. Can't they get good vegetables locally?" Ever since Kat had come to live with him he'd tried to buy more healthy stuff, like salad in a bag, already cut, with carrots and everything, at the local supermarket. He certainly didn't have to go across the city to fight the crowds and pay a fortune for parking just to buy rabbit food.

"I think they asked me to go so they don't have to carry big bags home on the bus."

He couldn't help but look at her hulking truck. "Just how many vegetables do they plan to buy?"

She grinned. "They're going for the adventure. This would be a good way for Kat to make some new friends." Her smile dropped and her expression became serious. "I'd like you to come, too. If you can."

He turned back to Cindy, unsure of the reason for her request. He couldn't count the times he had wished, even prayed, for exactly this to happen. Before he'd become Kat's legal guardian, except for running his business, starting a relationship with Cindy had been foremost on his mind. But after last night that had changed. He'd thought Kat was doing okay, but all he'd done was call her by her name instead of her nickname and she'd fallen apart. With Kat sobbing her guts out and breaking down like she had, he'd almost lost it, too, and that wouldn't have done either of them any good. For now he needed to help Kat, which meant concentrating all his time on her, not pursuing something that wasn't likely to happen.

But Cindy was right: Kat needed to make some new friends. Texting her friends back home in Portland wasn't the same as having someone close by. And she was doing less of it.

He nodded. "Sure."

She watched him, waiting for him to say more, but no more was needed. Kat needed to make some new friends.

"'Sure'? That's it?"

"Yeah. Would you like to pick us up, or is it better for us to meet you at the church?"

"I guess it depends. Do you live between the church and downtown?"

"Yes. Here's my address." He scribbled it down on a scrap of paper and slid it across the counter.

"Great. I'll pick both of you up on Saturday afternoon, if Kat says she'll come. Let me know, okay? I need to get back to work."

Cindy pulled up to a large house in an upscale neighborhood.

It appeared the co-owner of Like a Prince Car Rentals really did live like a prince, at least compared to her humble abode.

Just as she turned off the engine, Kat and Luke stepped outside.

Kat didn't hesitate; she ran to Cindy's truck, opened the back door, and hopped inside. Luke waited for a few seconds and looked at the back door then slowly opened the front door to get in.

Cindy didn't know if she should be insulted.

"Hi, Cindy. I hope we didn't keep you. . . ." His voice trailed off as his attention turned to the backseat.

"Luke, I'm sure you met Tyler at the practice on Wednesday. A couple of the girls were going to come, but at the last minute they got called in to work. Tyler has the list of everything we need, so it's just us."

Tyler sat in the back beside Kat, grinning like an idiot.

Luke's eyes narrowed, telling Cindy that Luke did indeed remember Tyler from Wednesday evening. But today Cindy didn't think that Luke was quite so scary, probably because he didn't have a hockey stick in his hand.

Cindy turned the key to restart the engine. "I know you haven't been in Seattle very long, Kat. Pike Place Market is a Seattle landmark and a lot of fun." She put the truck into gear. "Buckle your seat belt and away we go."

Chapter 5

Cindy did her best to bite back a grin at Kat's wide-eyed look of wonder as they approached the main entrance to the market. The throng of people, more going in than coming out, was normal for this time of day.

Having grown up in Seattle, Pike Place Market had always been a part of Cindy's routine with her mother. After her mother died, her father preferred Bellis Fair Mall, but when Cindy reached her teenage years and was old enough to take the bus across town with her friends, they went to the market often.

Just like then, every time she was there she bought something. Seldom what she went for, but she always bought something.

Today was going to be no exception.

"I think we should go to the shops first and the market last. Let's go this way."

Before they stepped inside, Kat took a picture of Rachel the Pig with her cell phone.

"Stay together," Cindy warned as the crowd jostled them. "It's really easy to get separated." While Luke wasn't short, he was about the same height as most of the men and therefore wouldn't stand out in the crowd—at least not from the back. On the other hand, they'd never lose Tyler; he stood taller than everyone in the area. But Kat was tiny and apparently easily distracted, already stopping to check out the fish, neatly displayed at the fish vendor. They would lose her in an instant.

"Wait. . ." Cindy tugged the back of Luke's jacket. "Stay here." She took off after Tyler, got his attention, and they returned to the fish counter. "This place is famous for its flying fish. The fish don't fly, but when someone buys one, they throw it from the outside display to the staff at the cutting block, who will weigh and wrap it."

They waited for a few minutes, but no fish were flying through the air. She turned again to Kat. "Probably no one's buying any fish yet because it's so early. I know I sure wouldn't want to carry a fish through the market all day while I shopped, wrapped or not. We'll come back this way when we're done and ready to go home."

They had barely walked a few steps when a female voice called out. "Cindy! Over here!"

Cindy turned to see Farrah trying to wend her way through the crowd to get to her.

"What a pleasant surprise to see you here," Farrah said as she reached them. She turned to Kat. "How's our new hockey star?"

Kat looked at the ground and blushed.

Cindy smiled. "Luke, this is Farrah Tobias, my god-mother. She usually helps out with the youth group, but she couldn't make it last week when you were there."

Farrah turned to Luke and grinned ear to ear. "So you're Luke. I've heard about you."

One corner of Luke's mouth tilted up. "Really? I hope it was good."

Farrah smirked. "Apparently not as good as the real thing. Tell me, what—"

"Gosh, Farrah," Cindy blurted, stopping Farrah from repeating what she feared Farrah might say. "Isn't that your friend Elsie over there? Waving at you? Did you lose your friend?"

Farrah checked her watch. "We were supposed to meet half an hour ago. I'm glad she finally made it. I guess I'll see you next Wednesday."

"She seems very nice," Luke said as Farrah gave her friend a hug.

"The nicest. I don't know how she does it, but she's always there when I need someone. I hope I can be the same for someone else one day."

As Farrah and her friend turned and walked back to the produce, Cindy directed Luke, Kat, and Tyler past the food markets to the craft shops. Cindy headed for her favorite boutique to pick up her favorite herbal hand cream, since the degreaser soap at the shop dried out her hands. Before they got there, Kat had already slowed multiple times then stopped completely at one of the specialty jewelry boutiques. Luke waited outside while Kat browsed, but Tyler went right in to help Kat pick out the perfect pair of earrings.

So they wouldn't get separated in the crowd, Cindy guided Luke to wait inside the store. He followed her with obvious reluctance to a rack of beaded necklaces while Kat nearly squealed with glee as Tyler picked up the ugliest earrings Cindy had ever seen.

"I'm not very good at this girl stuff," Luke muttered. "I never had any sisters. Do you and your mother and sisters come here often?"

Cindy forced herself to hold back an impolite snort. "They're not my sisters; they're my stepsisters, and Melissa is my stepmother."

"Oh..." Luke's voice trailed off as he looked into her eyes, making her feel obligated to explain.

She looked down and pretended to examine a bracelet while she spoke. "The relationship between us is very strained." Strained being an understatement. "Melissa keeps threatening to contest the will and sue me for breach of contract. It's totally bogus, but the legal battle would tie up everything I have and I'd lose everything, even my truck. The legal fees would probably eat up half the estate." Until she could figure a way out and still find a way to live, her life was at the mercy of Melissa's mood and vindictiveness.

She cleared her throat. "If that's not bad enough, Annie

and Zella are always looking down their noses at me and constantly criticizing."

"I'm sorry. I had no idea. But they both work for you."

"Only because it was a codicil in my father's will. I'm supposed to give them both full-time employment, but the business can't afford that while I have to give Melissa half the profits—and Melissa knows it, which is another legal battle. Honestly I don't know what my father was thinking." Cindy sighed. "I'll be able to fight Melissa after both Annie and Zella get jobs elsewhere. For now they're working part-time and going to college, so hopefully it won't be too much longer. The lawyer says as soon as they both choose jobs elsewhere, I'm free of the codicil. Until then I'm at Melissa's whim." She turned to pick up a necklace with a pendant on it then put it down and pretended to examine the matching earrings.

"I don't know why I'm telling you this," she mumbled. The only person who knew, besides the lawyer, was Farrah. But Luke was easy to talk to and a good listener.

"You're telling me because you need to vent and that's okay." Luke smiled then picked up the necklace she'd just put down. "This would look pretty on you."

Cindy automatically raised her hand and pressed it over the gold chain around her neck that she wore under her shirt. It was the only thing of her mother's that she had, and she never took it off. Melissa had thrown out all Cindy's mother's possessions after she married Cindy's father. "I'm not really a jewelry type of person. Besides, I don't have any occasion to wear it."

He put the pendant back. "That's okay. Maybe another time."

As they turned around, Tyler picked up a necklace to match the ugly earrings and headed for the cash register with Kat trailing close behind.

Luke gritted his teeth. "What's going on? Why is he buying that for her?"

Cindy smiled, grateful for the change of subject. "They spend a lot of time together at youth group. I know Tyler likes her. He's not a bad kid. He's a good student, and he treats others right. At least from what I've seen."

They waited for Tyler to be finished at the till then continued through the market. Cindy did her best to tell them everything she knew about the market's history, including the story of Rachel the Pig, a bronze statue whose only absence from the market was for a few days of repairs and a polishing after she got hit by a taxi, which fortunately hadn't been fatal.

When they had accumulated all the vegetables they needed from Tyler's list, Luke bought a fish. They watched it fly through the air with Kat taking a video on her cell phone, including the men wrapping it to take home.

Once Luke had it in his hands, he tested the weight of it. "This is a really big fish for just the two of us. How would you both like to join us tonight, and I'll barbecue it."

Tyler shook his head. "I have to be home for supper because my grandparents are coming over. But thanks for asking."

Cindy tried to act more relaxed than she felt. She hadn't planned on doing anything more than taking them to the market, but Kat was looking at her with puppy-dog eyes and making it hard to turn Luke down. She didn't think it was a good idea, but she didn't know how to say no with Kat looking at her like that.

She pasted on a smile that she hoped didn't look as fake as it felt. "That sounds like fun. But only if I can buy dessert."

Luke smiled, and at the sight, her heart did a silly flip-flop in her chest.

"That would be great," he said. "Let's go."

Luke wrapped the salmon in tinfoil while Cindy and Kat talked in Kat's bedroom with the door closed. After a rather embarrassing trip through the women's section at the drugstore yesterday, he knew Kat was asking Cindy about girl things he knew nothing about and didn't want to know about.

And while he was in a state of not knowing, he also didn't know if what he was doing was a very good idea.

His original thought was that Kat needed a woman to talk to, but as soon as Cindy came inside his house, a million hesitations hit him.

For so long, this was exactly what he'd wanted to happen—to invite Cindy over for dinner in his home. He hadn't asked before today because he knew she'd say no. Today she'd accepted, but he knew she hadn't been very enthusiastic. She wasn't here because of him. She was here because of Kat—who would spend the evening acting as a buffer between them because, like an idiot, he'd told Kat how he felt about Cindy.

He walked outside to light the grill then returned to the kitchen to wrap the potatoes in tinfoil as well.

"I feel bad," Cindy's voice echoed behind him. "Is there anything I can do?"

He turned around. "Nope. I was going to have the salmon, some baked potatoes, and a salad. The salad's already made."

"Salad?" Her eyebrows rose. "I'm impressed."

Kat made a rude noise beside her. "Don't be. It came in a bag, already cut. Come on. Let me show you the pond in the backyard. It's got fish in it."

As suddenly as the ladies had appeared, they were gone.

Spending all the time alone in the kitchen wasn't what he'd envisioned about the day Cindy finally crossed his threshold. But neither had he envisioned suddenly having a fifteen-year-old daughter to care for. It didn't matter that she really was only his niece. With her parents gone, he didn't want to be just an uncle who happened to be her legal guardian. He loved her and wanted to be everything for her that her father now couldn't.

He put the salmon into the fridge, set the timer on his cell phone to vibrate after an hour and a half, and carried the potatoes into the backyard.

Cindy approached him and watched him position the potatoes neatly in the center of the barbecue grill.

"Your home and yard are lovely."

"Thank you," he said as he adjusted the flame and closed the lid. "My mother's only brother, who never married, made a fortune in the oil industry back in the seventies. After my parents died, my brother and I were his only living relatives, and when he died, he left me with a generous trust fund. When I gained control at twenty-five, the first thing I did was build myself this house. You can do a lot when you don't have a mortgage." As the words left his mouth, he grimaced inwardly. While he wanted Cindy to become interested in him, he didn't want his financial independence to be the reason.

"You decorated everything yourself, didn't you?"

"Yes." Luke's hand froze on the handle of the barbecue. Of all the things he thought she'd say, that wasn't on the list.

"It shows."

"Is that bad?" He didn't know quite how to take what she'd said. His home and yard were exactly the way he wanted them. Comfortable, practical, and in colors he liked. Nothing trendy or chic. His was the home of a single guy who didn't have to worry about cost, a home that didn't need a woman's touch.

Cindy smiled and rested one hand on his forearm. "I like it. It's nice. Homey and unpretentious."

He felt himself relax. "I have to do something with Kat's room, but I thought I'd let her settle in first."

"Good call. She talked to me about some ideas, but I told her she shouldn't be asking me, she should be asking you."

"She can do whatever she wants. As long as she doesn't paint the whole thing black."

Cindy grinned. "She won't. She likes pink." Cindy glanced over her shoulder. "Here she comes. We'd better change the subject. Kat wouldn't like it if she knew we were talking about her."

Luke nodded, struggling to keep a straight face. She didn't know the times that he and Kat had talked about her, and hopefully she never would.

Cindy cleared her throat, speaking louder than she had a few seconds ago. "I like your pond. But aren't you worried about cats or raccoons eating your fish?"

"Nope. They're koi. They're too big for cats but not for raccoons. When I was building the pond I did my research and built it nice and deep with steep sides and gave the koi lots of places to hide. The raccoons gave up, but the neighborhood cats still come into the yard. They'll never catch one, but it sure is annoying to watch them try."

"Maybe you should have a dog."

Kat skipped up to them. "Are we going to get a puppy? I've always wanted a puppy."

Inwardly, Cindy cringed. "No, I meant—"

"No puppy?" Kat's smile got even larger. "You mean an adult dog? From a rescue? Tyler volunteers at Homeward Pet rescue shelter in Woodinville. He says people always want a puppy, which makes it hard for mature dogs who need a good home. He says there are lots of good dogs waiting for a home. Are we going to the rescue to get a dog?"

Luke shook his head. "We can't have a dog when there's no one home for ten hours. It's not fair to lock a dog in the house all day."

Kat rocked back and forth on her feet. "Then take him to work with you. You can't get fired for bringing your dog to work. You're the boss. Or at least one of them."

"I . . . Uh. . ." He'd always liked dogs, but he'd never considered that he could actually take one to work. "I never thought of it like that. . . ." His mind whirled in circles, piecing together how he might be able to handle taking a dog to work with him all day and dealing with both a dog and Kat all evening.

Kat squealed, clapped her hands, and danced on the spot. "I'm getting a dog! I'm getting a dog!" She jumped up, spun, ran to the fish pond, and then bent down to talk to the koi. "We're getting a dog!" She dropped herself to sit on the ground beside the pond. A split second before her bottom hit the grass, she pulled her cell phone out of her pocket and started texting.

Luke sighed. "It looks like I'm getting a dog."

Cindy pressed her palms to her cheeks, and her face paled. "I'm so sorry. I didn't mean to start something."

He sucked in a deep breath, thinking of all the responsibilities he'd been handed recently. "It's okay, I guess. Besides, I've always wanted a dog. It's time to put my money where my mouth is. Do you want to help put the salad, such as it is, together while she tells the koi and everyone else about our future family member?"

Cindy followed him back to the kitchen, where he dug the bag of salad and a few extras out of the fridge and laid them on the counter.

They chatted about dogs in general until he began to think he'd be dogged out by the time he got his new dog, which he had a feeling was going to be tomorrow after church. So he changed the subject. To his delight, they were both reading the same book, a recent release by one of his favorite authors. He had a great time conjecturing with Cindy who the evil mastermind of the story's plot would be, and he knew he'd be up until well past midnight reading instead of sleeping.

He had suspected that he and Cindy had a connection since the first time they'd met, but after today he was sure.

When the timer on his cell phone set his pocket vibrating, they took the salmon to the barbecue and sat on the patio while it cooked.

When everything was ready, Kat joined them.

She pointed at his koi pond. "I don't know how you're

going to eat their cousin and live without guilt."

"You're only saying that so you can have my portion."

Kat giggled. "Busted."

Cindy giggled along with Kat. "Nice try. I wish I'd thought of that."

With Kat's return, most of the conversation changed to her interests, including a new video on YouTube that Luke knew nothing about. Instead of trying to be part of a conversation that he couldn't really contribute to, Luke sat back and let the women talk. He knew Cindy didn't do it on purpose, but he could see that she was more animated and more relaxed with Kat than she was with him. Which, despite the wonderful time he had when it was just the two of them, confirmed what he thought when he'd first issued the invitation for her to join them.

Cindy wasn't there because of him. She was there because of Kat.

He'd been falling hard and fast for Cindy, but she didn't feel the same way about him. He didn't want to admit it, but now the facts were obvious.

If he played it right, he could probably gain her interest through Kat, but that wasn't what he wanted. He wanted the woman he would eventually marry to love his niece, but it was more important that she love him first.

Cindy gasped at something Kat said, and then the two of them broke into a fit of giggles.

She liked dogs. She liked his niece. She liked his home.

She just didn't like him. At least not the same way that he liked her.

One day he would find the love of his life.

If he could get this one out of his heart.

Chapter 6

"Annie, I need you to schedule appointments as people come in for a while. I have to go across the lot to the car rental."

"I thought you weren't interested in Mr. Hottie."

Cindy sucked in a deep breath and counted to ten. "I have something I need to discuss with *Luke* that can't be done over the phone." Or rather, it was something she needed to see. "I'll be back in ten minutes."

Without waiting for Annie to reply, Cindy dashed across the parking lot. Or at least she dashed as much as her steel-toed safety boots would allow.

Sure enough when she pushed the door open, instead of a buzzer sounding to announce her arrival, she heard a bark.

Cindy couldn't help but smile at the fuzzy little dog sitting in a brand-new doggy bed in the corner of the office, looking up at her.

"What a sweet dog. Is it a boy or a girl?"

"Girl. They said she's a cross of about a hundred different

breeds. Give or take."

As Luke listed a number of possibilities, the dog stood but slowly, wobbling.

"The rescue said she's about two years old, and she—"

Cindy gasped. "—only has three legs!"

Luke stepped out from behind the counter, hunkered down, and gave the dog a gentle pat. "She was abandoned because she was in a car accident. The people who hit her took her to a vet who saved her life, but the owners didn't want to pay for the bill and neither did the people who hit her, so the vet put her up for adoption at the rescue."

The dog approached Cindy, tail wagging.

Cindy reached down to pat her and got a delicate lick of appreciation.

Luke stood. "Kat renamed her Tippy. The rescue people said she'll get more steady and balance better as time goes on."

"She doesn't seem to be unhappy."

"The vet said she'd be fine as long as we watch her weight."

"Kat's okay with this?"

Luke chortled. "The people at the rescue said the dog has been very shy and even frightened of people. Kat only said one word and the dog immediately went to her. As soon as they told her what happened, she didn't want to see any of the other dogs. It looks like Tippy's a keeper."

As Cindy looked up at Luke, her eyes started to burn. Fortunately the old Chevy she'd been expecting rumbled into the parking lot. She turned her head so Luke couldn't see her face. "That's really nice. The Chevy is early. I've got to go. See you later."

She dashed out the door before Luke could respond. As soon as she rounded the corner of the shop, where Luke couldn't see her, she swiped her sleeve across her face.

She couldn't believe she had actually started to sniffle. Over a dog. Or maybe the dog's owner.

She didn't want to like him, yet the more time she spent with him, the harder it became. But regardless of her feelings for him, it wouldn't be fair or practical to drag someone into the heat of her personal battles. Even if she could ignore the legal quagmire, if she did start a relationship with Luke, it wouldn't be long before Annie had her claws out because Annie wanted him, too.

She couldn't get involved with Luke right now, for both their sakes.

At least there was no risk of catfights if she got involved with. . .Kat.

Cindy covered her face with her hands. She almost laughed at her own joke, except it was too pathetic.

"Cindy! Are you coming?" Annie yelled from the office. "That. . .one you've been waiting for is here!"

Cindy gritted her teeth. Annie had never appreciated the beauty of a classic old car or the satisfaction of bringing one back to its former glory. At least this time she hadn't called it a wreck in front of the owner.

She pasted on a smile, took the keys from the man, and got ready to get to work.

"Kat, are you ready?" Luke checked his watch. "Cindy's going to be here any minute."

He tried not to be impatient as Kat sprinted back into her bedroom, now painted a horrible shade of girlie pink, to select a different pair of perfect shoes to wear on another shopping trip during which she didn't need to buy anything.

He couldn't believe Kat was spending another evening with Cindy. For the last month it seemed Cindy had been there nearly every evening and every weekend. Sometimes they stayed at the house, sometimes they went out, sometimes they only took Tippy for a wobble, but they seemed to spend almost all their time together.

Still, he was glad Kat had the company. Most important, last weekend, for the first time since they'd lost Andrew and Sue, Cindy had convinced Kat to go to a church service on Sunday morning. For that, he would put up with any amount of girl stuff.

Not that Cindy was very girlie. In all the times he'd seen her, including church, he'd never seen her wear a dress or even makeup. He couldn't remember her wearing anything other than jeans, and the only things she wore on her feet were sneakers, work boots, or in-line skates. When all the rest of the young ladies in the youth group went to some kind of fashion party, Cindy took Kat and the boys to a car show.

"I think you should come to the mall with us," Kat called out from inside the walk-in closet.

"I don't."

Kat gave him a long, disgruntled sigh. "You have to come. You need a new pair of sneakers. How can you possibly have only one pair of sneakers?"

"I only need one pair. These are fine."

"They're"—Kat made a gagging sound—"white."

"They're clean."

The doorbell signaled Cindy's arrival, saving him from yet another argument about his insufficient footwear.

Kat ran ahead of him to the door and yanked it open.

Cindy stepped inside and hunkered down to give Tippy a hug. "Are you ready?" she asked without looking up.

Kat ran back to her bedroom, calling over her shoulder as she ran, "Almost. I just need to change purses."

Luke sighed. The girl seemed to have a different purse to match every pair of footwear she owned, which was a lot.

Cindy stood, so Tippy wobbled back to her blanket. "Would you like to come with us? There's a sale at the shoe store. Buy one get the second item for half price."

Luke gritted his teeth. "I. . ." His voice trailed off at Cindy's expectant smile, and something went haywire inside his brain. He smiled back. "Sure. I could use a new pair of sneakers."

At the shoe store, Kat hightailed it to the purse aisle,

which was fine with Luke. That left him alone, or as alone as possible in a busy shoe store having a sale, with Cindy.

In under three minutes, he found a pair of black sneakers. With his conquest tucked under one arm, he turned to Cindy. "Since a second item is on sale for half price with one regular priced item, would you like to buy something, too? It doesn't seem right to be here and not get a bargain."

Cindy hesitated.

"It's obvious Kat's going to get a new purse with whatever footwear we came for in the first place." Luke regarded her calmly, and Cindy was reminded suddenly about his beautiful eyes.

She shook it off. "Are you okay with that?"

Luke shrugged his shoulders. "There are a lot of worse things she could be into than shoes and purses. I don't mind. Look at that, they have boots out already in the summertime. I've only seen you wearing steel-toed work boots." He grinned.

"Very funny. But you're right. I should get a pair of boots. If it snows next winter I'm going to need something warm for walking Tippy."

"I don't know if what Tippy does can actually be called walking." He gave her a wry smile.

Cindy glanced in Kat's direction. "Don't you ever say anything about the way Tippy walks. Kat will be very angry with you."

Luke snickered. "I know. Kat reminds me constantly that

54

Tippy gets around fine, she's just a little balance challenged."

"She said that she's going to train Tippy to—"

"Cindy!" a female voice called out. "What in the world are you doing here?"

Luke watched Cindy cringe. He looked at the woman who had spoken so tactlessly and recognized her immediately.

He'd only met Cindy's stepmother once before, briefly, but she was a woman he would never forget. A drop-dead gorgeous woman who knew it and used it to her advantage.

Cindy regained her composure and smiled politely. "Hello, Melissa. Are you hoping to find a good sale?"

Melissa waved one manicured hand in the air. "We're here to see if we can find just the right shade to match the dress Annie's going to wear to her graduation ceremony. I can't imagine what you're doing here. I didn't think they sold work boots."

The hairs on the back of Luke's neck bristled. To Cindy's credit, she simply looked away. Luke stepped closer to her and rested one hand on her shoulder. "Cindy and I brought Kat to see if anything catches her eye."

Melissa's eyebrows quirked, telling him she hadn't noticed he was there. On the other hand, Annie and Zella, standing behind Melissa, were smiling at him and totally ignoring Cindy.

Melissa rested one hand on Annie's shoulder. "Annie has better taste in clothes and accessories. Maybe she should go with you."

At first Annie stiffened, but then she smiled and stepped forward. "I'd like that," she said, as if Cindy weren't even there.

He could almost hear Cindy grinding her teeth. Her voice came out as sharp as a two-edged sword. "Maybe she can—"

Luke didn't let Cindy finish. He tightened his grip and eased her back away from the other ladies. "We're going to finish our shopping. Excuse us."

He didn't care where they went as long as it was far away from her stepfamily.

"Are they always so rude to you?" he asked when they were far enough that they couldn't hear.

"No. Most of the time they're worse, although a lot of the time I don't think Annie and Zella know which way to go. Melissa does her best to fill them with all sorts of poison toward me. When Melissa isn't home, Annie and Zella sometimes come to church with me, even though I think most of the time they're just trying to meet single men."

"Still, I guess that's a start."

"Enough of them. Let's go find Kat. I have the sudden urge to go to that arcade place at the end of the mall and play some serious whack-a-mole."

Luke cringed. "How about instead I'll buy you a nice chocolate milkshake?"

She gave him a shaky smile, which did something strange to his insides. "Sure. That sounds perfect."

Chapter 7

The second Luke walked in the door, he trudged over to the couch, sank down, and groaned. Usually his job was fairly stress-free, but today was the first day of a big conference at the Washington State Convention Center downtown. Through some creative marketing, he and Brent had agreed to offer attendees a discount, and they'd leased every available car. Or rather Luke had because today of all days, Brent had called in sick. Luke had spent the entire day on his feet, filling out forms or inspecting cars and checking insurance. He'd even had to help the lot boy wash a car because the man who called for it was early and impatient.

"Uncle Luke? What are you doing?"

His eyes drifted shut and his head fell back. "I'm going to have a nap. Order a pizza." Using the last of his energy, without opening his eyes, he shifted his body so he could reach into his back pocket for his wallet then sagged back as he held it up.

"What kind?"

"Whatever you want." He'd eat anything that meant he didn't have to stand. Even sushi. Maybe.

Her giggle told him that she wasn't going to order anything he liked, but he was so tired he didn't care. Kat took the wallet out of his hand and ran into the kitchen.

The couch shifted slightly, and Luke couldn't help but smile. Tippy couldn't jump onto the couch, so Kat had made a staircase out of firm pillows to allow the dog to scramble up without help. Tippy nudged his hand up with her wet nose then crawled into his lap.

He'd wanted to lie down, but he didn't have the energy or the heart to push Tippy aside.

Keeping his eyes closed, Luke listened to the sounds of drawers squeaking open and slamming closed as Kat searched for the menu from the pizza joint. Some kind of bad music drifted from Kat's bedroom. Tippy was snoring.

He didn't know a dog could fall asleep so fast.

He sighed as he started to drift into oblivion. His house used to be quiet. Not anymore. He used to be able to come and go as he pleased. He didn't have to pick up his socks.

Now there was always some kind of noise coming from somewhere, and he had learned to put his socks in the hamper right away or Tippy would get them and he'd find them in the backyard a few days later.

His mind wandered as he thought of what would make his home perfect. He had part of the equation already: a kid—even if she was kind of big—and a dog. He only needed a wife. A blond wife who came home from work wearing blue coveralls and smelled like grease. They would have fun making supper together and then get distracted as he hugged and kissed her. She'd kiss him back. They would forget about cooking and. . .

Tippy's paws pounded into his stomach.

"Luke?"

Luke groaned as the picture faded. He struggled to block out the world, but the image wouldn't come back.

"Luke? Wake up."

Tippy began to bounce in his lap.

He straightened to protect himself, winced, opened one eye, and looked up. The dream was back. Blond. No blue coveralls, but he could smell a little grease.

"Are you awake? There was a pizza guy in your driveway, so I paid him and brought it in." She held up a box.

He tried to clear his head. "Cindy? What are you doing here? No, never mind. I'm glad you're here. How much do I owe you?" He started to move his hand toward his back pocket but froze, remembering that Kat had his wallet. "I don't want you to pay, but I do want you to help us eat it." He gave Tippy a nudge, encouraging her to jump off the couch and follow Cindy into the kitchen. Then he did exactly the same.

Remnants of his dream hung in the back of his mind. It would have been so natural to step up closer to Cindy and give her a hug then a kiss. If she reciprocated his feelings. Which she didn't.

Cindy set the box on the table, leaned over it, and inhaled deeply.

"Barbecue chicken and peppers. My favorite."

The image of a perfect end to a long day faded as reality slapped him up the side of the head. "Barbecue chicken? On a pizza?" Just as he suspected, Kat had ordered something he didn't like. He couldn't imagine chicken on a pizza.

Kat appeared before he had a chance to complain and, being outnumbered, he didn't even try. The ladies put a piece of pizza on each of three plates, and they prepared themselves to say a quick grace before eating. He'd never been the touchy-feely type, but Cindy automatically rested her hand in his. Her touch, albeit light, gave him a momentary charge that zapped the fatigue out of his body, at least for the duration of their meal. It also helped that chicken on a pizza wasn't as bad as he thought it would be.

He turned to Cindy as he reached for another piece. "What brings you here today? Shopping? Homework?"

"Today we're just going to take Tippy for a wob. . .uh. . . a walk."

Kat stopped chewing for a few seconds, glared at Cindy, and then shoveled another bite into her mouth.

Luke struggled not to laugh. "Have fun. It's a full moon tonight, lots of light out there."

Kat stared at him. "Aren't you coming?"

Luke wiggled his toes and flexed his aching feet. "I hadn't thought about it."

"You don't have to come if you don't want to."

"Good." As the words left his mouth, he caught Cindy turning her head to look directly at him, so he met her gaze over the empty pizza box.

"Are you sure?" Cindy asked.

"I. . ." If he wore his comfortable black sneakers instead of the leather shoes he'd worn all day, it would probably be tolerable. As long as he didn't go far. "Okay, I'll go."

Cindy smiled. "That's wonderful. Tippy will be so happy."

It wasn't Tippy he wanted to make happy. "We might as well go now."

They rose in unison and headed for the front door, but just as Kat opened it her cell phone rang. She listened for a few seconds then flipped it shut. "It's Sasha. I forgot about a geography project we have to hand in tomorrow. I have to go. I'll see you later. I'll phone when I need a ride home."

Before Luke could say anything, Kat stepped out the door and jogged down the street in the direction of Sasha's house.

He turned and waggled his eyebrows at Cindy. "Looks like it's just you and me."

"That's okay. Lock the door and let's go."

As they walked, Cindy nodded a greeting to Luke's neighbor,

who was setting up a tripod, apparently attempting to get pictures of the full moon.

She couldn't help but wonder what Luke's neighbors thought of her at Luke's home nearly every evening. Mostly she was there to be with Kat, but yet. . .

She tried to tamp down the feelings of excitement; after all, nothing could happen. When the day came that she could fall in love, it wouldn't be with a man like Luke. It would be with a man who had no entanglements, at a time when she could finally be free of her own.

And that wasn't going to happen for a very, very long time.

She slowed her pace to let Luke catch up, after he'd stopped to allow Tippy to sniff something.

He was as good to the dog as he was to his niece; neither of them lacked for anything, especially love. Luke was a good man and smart, successful, and fun to be with.

Second thoughts ran through her mind. Maybe one day she would fall in love with a man just like Luke. But not Luke, because when that time finally came, some other lucky woman would have snapped him up.

As Tippy stopped to sniff another plant, Luke turned to her. "This is a good time to ask if you're coming to my annual customer appreciation banquet next weekend. I know Brent went over to your place yesterday with some tickets, but he didn't see you to make sure you were coming."

"Thanks for asking, but I'm not your customer. You're my customer."

"Think of it as a thank-you for giving me priority service as often as you do. We invited everyone at your place."

Cindy's breath caught. "You mean you invited Annie and Zella, too?"

"Brent gave tickets to everyone in your shop, even the guys."

"That means the one ticket under the appointment book was left there for me."

"Yup."

Cindy pictured the contents of her closet. The only things similar to a banquet she'd been to were informal lunches at the church. She didn't have a thing to wear for an evening function. She didn't own a dress or high-heeled shoes. She only owned one pair of pants that weren't jeans, and they were capris that had a grass stain on the bottom that she couldn't get off.

"Sorry. Formal banquets aren't my thing."

"It's not formal. It's just business casual."

"In my business, I wear jeans and a T-shirt with coveralls, and don't forget the steel-toed work boots." A ring of sarcasm ripped through her, remembering Melissa's comments from the shoe store.

Luke frowned. "Maybe not that casual, but I'd really like you to come."

She tried to picture what it would be like, but the more she thought about it, dressing up and going to a dinner with Luke felt and sounded an awful lot like a date. She couldn't get into the dating scene until she was out of her legal battles with Melissa, and Luke needed time without distractions to work things out with Kat

She gave him a polite smile. "I'll think about it and let you know. How's that?"

"That sounds good."

Luke pressed one fist into the small of his back. "How would you like to turn around and go home? I had a long day, and I really didn't want to go far."

"Sure, that's fine. I should go home. I think I need to get to bed early tonight." Her throat had started feeling scratchy, and she was far more tired than she should have been. "We can make it a longer walk another time."

Chapter 8

Cindy read the bottle one more time to make sure she was taking the right one for nighttime and downed the cold tablet with a glass of orange juice. She sniffled, blew her nose, and then stared at the ticket in front of her.

While part of her really wanted to go to the banquet and have fun—something she didn't do enough—the smarter part of her knew she should stay home.

Not only was she too sick to party, she saw enough of Luke as a friend in Kat's company. Spending even more time with him would become dangerous.

He tempted her enough in the shirt and slacks she saw him in every day. He was even tempting lying on his couch, fast asleep with his mouth hanging open and his dog curled up in his lap.

She didn't want to think about how tempting he would look in a suit and tie. He'd be so easy to fall in love with.

Cindy pressed one palm to her forehead. She had to have

a fever. Otherwise she wouldn't be thinking of Luke that way.

"You better not have drunk all the juice. What if someone else wants some?"

She turned her bleary eyes up to Melissa, the bane of her existence. "Don't worry. I only had one glass. It's not like it would break anyone's arm to get another can of concentrate out of the freezer. Can't you have any sympathy for me while I'm sick?"

Melissa made a noise that sounded almost like a snort. "You're an adult. You can care for yourself. Or do you want me to do that, too? I do everything else for you."

Cindy pushed herself to her feet. Her eyes burned and her head swam. "You only cook my meals and clean the house as your part of the addendum to Daddy's will so you don't have to get a job." Seething, Cindy picked up the glass and turned to leave the room, but Melissa blocked her path.

"I came here to tell you to move that ugly truck of yours. Annie and Zella are almost ready to leave for the banquet, and it's in the way."

Cindy spun around and glared at Melissa. "That's fine, because I'm going, too." She had no idea what she was going to wear, but at this moment, even if she was the only woman wearing capris, she was going to do it in defiance of her stepmother. Maybe if she zipped into Walmart on the way she could get an inexpensive skirt and some half-decent shoes. Not dressy, but she was desperate. "One day my truck will be a classic; it's a limited edition model."

Melissa made an uppity harrumphing sound and rolled her eyes. "Whatever. That truck is so like you. All noise and no class."

Cindy opened her mouth but no sound came out. She thought she'd become numb to Melissa's insults, but she wasn't.

"Annie and Zella are dressed to the nines; I'm sure one of them will attract a man tonight. I know they've set their sights on the two owners of that car rental place. A good match, I say."

Cindy's teeth clenched at the thought. Annie's words that Luke was a hottie echoed through her head. She couldn't let that happen. She stepped forward to reach for the banquet ticket on the table, but Melissa snatched it up first.

"You've been spending too much time with Luke," Melissa said, waving the ticket in the air between them. "He should be spending his time with Annie." She spun around, took two steps to the sink, turned on the water, hit the switch for the garbage disposal, and sent the ticket down.

The motor made a skip as it ground the paper into mash.

Cindy gasped then choked. "What have you done?" she sputtered.

"Mom?" A voice drifted from the kitchen doorway.

Cindy turned to see Annie and Zella staring at their mother.

Melissa flicked her fingers in the air. "Never mind that stupid truck in the way. Take my car. The keys are on the table beside the door."

Neither Annie nor Zella moved. They continued to stare at their mother.

With a sinking heart, Cindy eyed her competition.

The two of them looked good. Great, even. Today both of them had their hair in a swept-up style and wore calf-length semiformal dresses and feminine shoes. Both had on just the right amount of makeup to be eye catching.

Zella stared at the sink. "Why did—"

Melissa pointed to the front door. Her voice rose in pitch. "Go! Don't be late! Hurry!"

The two of them scuttled back then turned and hustled to the door.

The front door slammed shut.

Melissa swiped her hands down her pants. "You can't hold a candle to my daughters. Your breakfast will be ready at nine o'clock tomorrow so you can go to church, as usual." Melissa turned her nose up in the air and stomped out of the room.

Cindy sank down in the chair. Who was she kidding? She couldn't compare with Annie and Zella. Besides, it no longer mattered. Her ticket was gone.

A tear streamed down her cheek and she swiped it away.

The doorbell rang but Cindy didn't move. It wouldn't be for her. It never was. She was too ashamed and embarrassed to ever invite someone over to what was supposed to be her home.

Instead of going to the banquet, she considered clearing out the garage then moving in. All she needed to do was install a bathroom, and she could live there for free and not have to interact with her stepmother or stepsisters ever again. At least there she could have friends over. It would be a toss-up if Melissa would welcome the opportunity to get her out of the house or if she'd have a fit because it would mean putting all the garage junk into a ministorage. Or maybe if she moved into the garage, Melissa would feel she had ownership of the house, if not the business, and not contest the will.

"Yoo-hoo! Is anyone home? Cindy? Where are you?"

She turned to see Farrah, her godmother, striding toward her.

As soon as Farrah saw Cindy, she stopped. "Melissa stormed outside and left the door open, so I came in. Are you okay?"

Cindy sniffled. "I'm okay. I'm just calculating the square footage of the garage."

Farrah glanced up at the clock on the wall. "Why aren't you getting ready for Luke's banquet?"

"I'm not going. Melissa destroyed my ticket."

"What are you talking about?"

Cindy summarized Melissa's actions then stared at the sink.

Farrah gently patted Cindy's shoulder. "You can't stay here with that. . .woman. Come with me."

"What are you talking about?"

Farrah hushed her then pulled Cindy out the door, only giving her time to grab her purse before Farrah herded her into her car.

"Where are we going?"

"After a pit stop, we're going to my house. Now be quiet and trust me."

Cindy sat in silence, not daring to tell Farrah that she was speeding. When her godmother set her mind on something, there was no changing it. Ever.

Soon she noticed the route was familiar.

They were going to the shop.

Cindy opened her mouth to question Farrah, but one look silenced her.

When they pulled into the parking lot, Farrah turned to her. "Stay in the car. And duck."

Farrah got out of the car and marched over to Like a Prince Car Rentals. Cindy raised her head just high enough to peek out. Farrah spoke to Brent, showed him a piece of paper, and then left with something Brent handed her.

After they left the parking lot, Cindy sat up in the seat. "Dare I ask?"

Farrah grinned. "I just got a ticket. You, my dear, are going to the banquet."

"But I don't have a dress."

If possible, Farrah's grin widened even more. "You may not, but I do. Now hang on. We've got some miles to make."

Cindy coughed as they flew out of the business district and into the residential area where Farrah lived. "I don't know if this is such a good idea. I can barely talk. I sound like one of those raspy movie heroines from the thirties."

"That raspy sound is very sexy. Luke will love it. After all, he's a guy."

Cindy narrowed her eyes and glared at Farrah. "He's not like that. He's not just *a guy*. He's—"

Farrah snickered then broke out into a full-bellied laugh as they stopped for a red light. "So it's like that, is it? I was wondering when it would hit you. My dear, we are going to make you the belle of the ball. The best part is he'll never know it's you." She snickered and patted her purse. "You're going to knock your Prince Charming flat on his nice tight behind."

"His what?"

"Like you haven't noticed. Now be quiet and let me think."

Cindy suspected Farrah had already done too much thinking, but she was in no position to argue. She remained silent the rest of the drive. At Farrah's town house, Farrah guided her into the den to a dry cleaner's protective plastic bag draped over the arm of the love seat.

"I'm going to give you such a thorough makeover, no one will recognize you."

The thought was tempting but not realistic. But maybe, just maybe she could protect Luke from Annie's and Zella's clutches.

Cindy stood tall, sniffled, and rubbed her watery eyes. "I've never done a makeover before."

She watched in silence as Farrah lifted the plastic to reveal a silky burgundy dress. It had a fitted waist, a V-neck, and a slit up the side, and it shimmered in the light in a way that was sure to attract attention. "I think it's your size or maybe one size too big. But that's better than one size too small."

"Where did you get that?"

"Mary's daughter wore it for Brad and Tina's wedding. I was in the neighborhood so I picked it up from the dry cleaner for her." She hunkered down and picked up a bag that had been on the floor beside it and reached in, pulling out a pair of matching shoes.

"How did you get. . ." Cindy's voice trailed off as she put two and two together. And got five. "Wait. That's a bridesmaid's dress. That's why there are matching shoes."

Farrah nodded. "Yes. The dry cleaner did a lovely job on the shoes, too."

Cindy picked up the shoes and looked inside. "These are a size too big for me. They're also really high."

"It's a banquet. You'll be sitting down the whole time. Don't worry about it."

"I guess." Cindy picked up the dress. "There's a butt bow on this."

"Yes. Brittany was gorgeous in it. You'll be even more gorgeous."

"I am not wearing a dress with a butt bow."

"Why?"

Cindy waved both hands in the air above her head. "Because it has a butt bow!"

Farrah planted her fists on her hips. "For your information, this dress is very feminine and very attractive."

"I would never wear a dress like that."

"Which is exactly why you're going to wear it tonight. I also plan to do your hair and makeup. I've got some temporary hair color that would look perfect with this dress. It washes out after one use, and no one would ever know. Also, your watery eyes just gave me the perfect idea. Do you still have your old glasses in your purse?"

"Of course I do. Just in case I lose a contact."

"Take out the contacts and wear your glasses. You'll be like Superman in reverse. It's been so long since I've seen your real eye color, I barely remember what you really look like."

Cindy grinned. When she'd gotten her contacts, the optical place was running a free promo on colored lenses. With her natural light-colored eyes, they'd convinced her to get the second pair of lenses that turned her blue-gray eyes into a honey brown. Later she'd lost one of her clear ones, changed to the colored ones, and hadn't bothered to get the clear ones replaced.

She rubbed her hands with glee. She was going to the banquet, and when it was over, no one would know she'd been there.

Suddenly her joy dissolved. "But how do I get there and then home again? I don't have my truck."

"You shouldn't be driving with all that cold medication you've taken. I'll drop you off, and you just phone me when it's time to come home."

Cindy barely kept herself from dancing on the spot. "Let's do this. I can hardly wait to see the look on Luke's face when I get there."

Chapter 9

Luke wiggled the knot of his tie for the fifteenth time and looked toward the door as it opened.

His posture sagged every time a guest arrived. Cindy hadn't arrived yet.

He'd worn his best suit and his favorite tie, and Kat had helped make sure he didn't have a single dog hair on him. She'd even sent him for a haircut.

Again the door opened, and again it wasn't Cindy. First Annie walked in, then Zella.

As he contemplated asking them if they knew when Cindy was coming, Annie nudged Zella, and then they both turned to stare at him.

He didn't know if he should smile or run.

He smiled anyway. "Good evening, ladies," he said as they approached.

They nodded at each other then both stared into his eyes.

A chill ran up Luke's spine.

"Cindy's not coming," Annie started.

"And we need to tell you why," Zella finished.

Annie nodded and her voice lowered. "We thought Zella forgot her purse, so we drove back to the house and we saw Mom letting the air out of Cindy's tires."

Luke cringed. First thing in the morning he would get the compressor from work and fill them back up. "Call her on your cell. Tell her I'll pay for a cab."

Zella shook her head. "There's no point. Earlier today I saw Mom going through Cindy's closet, and then she dribbled coffee down some of Cindy's clothes."

Luke blinked, stunned that Melissa could be so devious. "I don't care what she wears. I just want her to come."

In a copycat motion, Annie shook her head. "Cindy left with Farrah; we saw them drive away. Mom said something awful to Cindy in the kitchen, but we don't know what." Annie paused then nibbled on her bottom lip. "We think Cindy was crying."

Zella turned her head and stared at a blank spot on the wall. "We talked about it on the way here. Mom's always been nasty to Cindy, and we've believed every horrible thing she said about Cindy. We even believed the lawsuit was justified, but now we're not so sure. We think Cindy deserves to keep the business and all its assets. She's worked hard with her dad for that business all her life. She's poured everything into it. She should have it. Mom doesn't want it; she just doesn't want Cindy to have it."

Annie picked up the story. "We've never seen or heard

Cindy do or say anything mean to Mom or us. She's always been nice. She's even taken us to her church a few times."

Zella laughed sadly. "Maybe she thought we'd learn something, but I think it was too little, too late. She must hate us, and I wouldn't blame her."

Luke swallowed the lump in his throat. "Cindy would never hate you. Or anyone. That's why I . . ." His voice trailed off as his words stalled. He'd almost said that was why he loved her so much. But he did love her, and he wanted to fix all the things in her life that continuously beat her down. "Why I wish she was here."

Annie and Zella nodded in unison. "We do, too. So we need to talk to her. But first we need to talk to everyone from the shop."

Without saying more, they turned and walked away in perfect unison with each other.

Luke turned and approached Brent, who was at a table with his laptop, logged into the scanner at the door, checking which guests had arrived.

"Nice crowd," Luke said, even though the crowd was missing the person he'd wanted to be there the most.

Brent grinned. "Almost everyone who RSVP'd is here, plus one ticket I didn't get logged. Some woman came in just as I was shutting down the office. I need to check if the caterers are ready."

When Brent shut down the laptop and dashed off, Luke looked up at the most gorgeous woman he'd ever seen, standing at the top of the stairs.

His breath caught.

She wore a shimmering burgundy dress that was simple yet elegant. Her hair was a mixture of brown and blond. When she stepped forward, he noticed her shoes were the exact color of the dress. Normally he wouldn't have paid attention to such a thing, but living with Kat had given him a new appreciation for women's footwear.

The woman stepped slowly down the stairs one at a time like she was having trouble. Three steps from the bottom, her ankle wobbled and her foot shot out from under her.

Luke broke into a run at the same time as the woman dropped her purse and grabbed the railing with both hands. He reached her at the same time as she righted herself. "Are you okay?" he asked, mentally saying a quick prayer of thanks that she hadn't fallen.

She steadied herself and straightened her glasses, and her cheeks turned the cutest shade of pink. She looked down at her purse. "I'm fine," she mumbled in a low, raspy voice that made Luke's heart skip a beat.

He mentally gave his head a shake and stepped closer to try to catch a whiff of alcohol on her breath. If the woman had been drinking, this was one guest who wouldn't be here long. He'd call a cab and send her back where she came from.

"Let me get that for you." Luke scooped up her purse and held it out for her, deliberately standing too close. He inhaled deeply, catching a whiff of either bad mouthwash or strong cough syrup.

"Attention, please!" Brent's voice blasted through the overhead speakers. "Dinner's ready, so if everyone would like to have a seat, I'll call one table at a time to go to the buffet. Thanks for coming, and Luke and I, on behalf of Like a Prince Car Rentals, welcome you here."

Once more, Luke looked to the closed door. Cindy really wasn't coming.

He turned to the woman, who was also obviously alone. "Would you care to sit with me for dinner?"

The woman scanned the crowd. He could have sworn for a few seconds her eyes locked on Cindy's stepsisters. "Aren't you already with someone?"

He gave a pathetic laugh. "My, uh"—he searched for the right word—"my date couldn't make it." In his mind's eye he imagined Cindy's entrance, if she had been there. She'd descend the stairs in agile hops then stand on the last one to give her some height while she looked for him. He'd walk to her and stare into her honey-brown eyes and give her a big kiss, just because he'd wanted to for so long.

He looked down into the smoky-blue eyes of the new arrival and nearly lost his breath. He'd never seen such fascinating eyes.

She smiled, making her eyes twinkle behind her glasses. "Then I certainly would like to join you for dinner. Thank you."

He started to walk toward a few of the last empty chairs

but had to slow down. Even on a flat surface, her steps were unsteady. It made Luke wonder if something was wrong; she seemed to have difficulty walking.

He pulled out the chair to seat her. While he loosened his suit jacket, the woman jerkily crossed her right leg over her left knee, uncrossed her legs, tugged her dress over her knees, crossed her left leg over her right knee, tugged the dress again, uncrossed her legs, and then crossed her ankles and tucked them under the chair.

He turned to her. "I'm sorry. I don't know your name. I'm Luke."

"My name is Ci—" The woman raised one fist to her mouth and began to cough. "Excuse me. Dee. My name is Dee."

"Dee. That's pretty. Is it short for Diedre?"

"No, it's short for something else."

He waited for her to tell him, but she didn't.

Their table was called, so they rose and walked to the end of the line, which brought them to stand near a row of plants against the wall.

Luke ran his fingers over the leaves of one of them. "So this is what these are supposed to look like." He pulled his cell phone out of his pocket and snapped a picture of it. "The one at Cindy's shop sure doesn't look like this."

Dee poked the plant. "It did a few months ago. It just doesn't get enough water."

Luke turned to Dee. "Do you know Cindy Mufford?"

Dee's hand froze on the plant. "I . . . Uh. . . Yes. I do."

He waited for her to say how long they'd known each other and how often she saw Cindy, but she didn't volunteer any more information.

A lightbulb went on in Luke's head.

"Since you know Cindy, I wonder if I might ask you a few things."

"I . . . Uh. . ." She coughed. "Sure."

After they filled their plates and sat, Luke's mind whirled as a million questions zoomed through his head.

He cleared his throat. "I'd like to give her something small but special. Something that would remind her of me just a little every day. I know she doesn't wear jewelry."

Dee's hand rose to her throat, and she ran her fingers over a thin, antique-looking gold chain. "I don't know. How about a company calendar? She'd have to look at it every day."

Luke didn't know if she was joking or not, but he figured either she didn't know or she didn't want to tell him. "I want it to be something she likes."

"She likes animals. But she can't have a pet right now."

Luke smiled. "She likes my dog, Tippy."

Dee smiled, and Luke nearly went into cardiac arrest. She had the most beautiful smile he'd ever seen. Almost like Cindy's smile.

In fact, it was very much like Cindy's smile. Except Cindy never wore that mouthwatering shade of dark, sexy lipstick.

"Yes," she said. "She does."

"Does she like any other animals?"

"Don't think of giving her a hamster or any kind of rodent."

"Fish?"

Dee laughed. "No. She'd only think of *Jaws*. A fish wouldn't be a good pet."

The more Luke talked with Dee, the better he felt he got to know Cindy, making it one of the strangest conversations he'd ever had. In addition to everything else, they talked about Cindy's favorite books, movies, and he even found out why she didn't particularly like cats.

It was a good thing that Brent enjoyed socializing with their guests all evening, because Luke couldn't pull himself away from Dee. He couldn't remember the last time he'd had so much fun, except for the last time he'd been with Cindy. In fact this encounter was almost like being with Cindy.

After Dee made a comment about the custom paint job on Cindy's truck, Luke laughed. "The next time you see Cindy, please don't tell her we spent so much time talking about her."

Dee tipped her head to one side. "Why not?"

All traces of humor left him. "Because I must look like a stalker, and what I want to be is her Prince Charming." As old-fashioned as the concept felt, that was what he wanted.

Her face turned completely serious, and she rested one hand on his forearm—a small, dainty hand with delicate fingers and long, manicured nails painted the same color as the dress and the shoes. He'd never seen such pretty hands on a woman. Not that he minded the grease under Cindy's blunt and practical nails, but the contrast between these two women was striking, yet in so many ways, they were so similar.

Dee made a slight cough and sniffled. "I'll bet she already thinks of you as her Prince Charming."

Dee's statement gave him the opening to ask the one question that had been burning in his gut—something he had to ask someone who knew her as a friend, who knew her heart, as Dee seemed to. He already thought Cindy liked him as a friend, but he wanted so much more. He wanted her not just to like him but to love him as the man who could one day be her husband. If Dee answered yes, that would give him all the courage he needed to treat Cindy the way he wanted to, but she wouldn't let him. Then he would know it was all a surface act and that one day it could really happen.

He looked up at the clock. It was nearly midnight; soon it would be time to start winding down the party and cleaning up. He didn't have much time so he had to ask now.

He cleared his throat. "Do you think—"

His words were interrupted by the ringing of Dee's cell phone. She fished it out of her purse and read the display.

She gasped. "It's my alarm company. I have to take this."

She flipped it open, listened for a few seconds, and nodded. "I'm on my way," she said then snapped it closed. "I have to go," she muttered and scrambled to her feet.

"Do you need my help?"

"No. I need to do this alone."

He remembered a few years ago when his office had been broken into. Not much had been stolen, but the place had been ransacked. More than a financial loss, he'd felt violated and it had taken months to shake the sensation. "Wait. I'll go with you."

Her eyes widened. "No. You can't."

"I can drive; that will probably be safer, especially if you need to make another phone call. Just let me tell Brent I'm going."

He turned around and spotted Brent seated a few tables away.

"Brent," he called out, "I'm going to take Dee home; she's had a break-in and might need my help."

Brent raised his head. "Who?"

"Dee. She's—" Luke turned his head to introduce Dee to Brent, but—he was alone.

He spotted her across the room headed for the stairs leading to the exit door, shoes in her hand, running in her stocking feet across the tile floor with the speed and grace of an athlete. As coordinated dodging through the crowded room as Cindy had been on her in-line skates during the hockey game.

"Dee! Wait!" Luke yelled at the same time as he broke into a run.

As he called, she turned her head, breaking her synchronization. She bumped into a portly gentleman in a bad suit, throwing her off balance. She slipped along the floor, bent at the waist, and with her shoes and purse tucked neatly under one arm, touched her fingertips to the floor. Her glasses flew off her face, but she recovered her balance and straightened. She squinted and looked right at him as he came toward her.

But before he reached her, she took off with the speed of a rocket up the stairs and disappeared through the door.

Luke skidded to a halt and picked up her glasses. One arm was badly bent but could probably be fixed. He headed up the stairs after her.

Just as he yanked open the door, he saw Dee scramble into an orange taxi, which took off with a squeal of rubber and disappeared around the corner.

He stared at the glasses in his hand. Not only did he have to return them, but he needed to ask her one more question.

She hadn't told him her last name but that didn't matter. Brent had a database of everyone they'd sent tickets to, and the scanner at the door logged everyone in by their ticket number.

He didn't know who she was, but it wouldn't take long to find out.

Chapter 10

Standing by the open door for bay two, Cindy smiled and inhaled deeply. It had been a week, but she was fully over the cold. She could finally fill her lungs to capacity without breaking into a cough, and her voice was back to normal.

Not only that, Annie and Zella had actually been pleasant to her all week. They'd even asked to come to church with her, and after the service they'd gone out for lunch and she'd had fun with her two stepsisters for the very first time, ever.

Best of all, it hadn't been hard to avoid Luke. It had almost been like he'd been avoiding her. Brent said Luke had been making calls to customers and he'd hardly been at his office for the past week. When she'd gone to his house to pick Kat up after supper, Kat said he'd been visiting clients who had been at the banquet who were unavailable during the daytime.

The banquet had been fun. It had been awkward talking about herself as a third person, but it had been worth it to spend the time with him with no pressure or consequences.

Cindy waved at Kat as she hopped off the school bus then smiled as Kat changed her path and walked toward her instead of going into her uncle's office. A quick glance at Luke's empty parking spot told her what she needed to know.

"Have you seen Uncle Luke? I need him to sign a permission slip for tomorrow morning, and I can't forget."

At Kat's question, Luke's car pulled into the parking lot. When the door opened, Cindy started to wave a greeting to him, but her hand froze in midair.

His posture was slumped and his pace was slow. He looked exhausted.

When he saw Kat, instead of going to his own office, he trudged across the lot and headed toward them.

Cindy led Kat through the building to meet Luke in the office, where he could sit down.

Annie was busy at her desk, actually doing work. She smiled briefly then returned to her spreadsheets.

"Hi, Luke, can I get you a coffee? You look. . ." The words deserted her when she saw what he held in his hand.

Her glasses.

"Maybe later. I need to talk to you." He laid the glasses on the counter. "I met a woman at the banquet who lost these. I've been to see all my corporate clients during the daytime, and then the private sector clients at night. No one knows who she is, even after I show them her glasses."

Kat nodded and groaned then pressed one hand over her

stomach. "Yeah. We've had pizza five days in a row."

Guilt roared through her. This was her fault.

Luke jerked his head toward his office. "Brent had a log of every ticket, but there was one ticket he didn't have in his database, a replacement for a lost ticket, and of course, that's the ticket of the lady I'm looking for." He sighed then looked into her eyes. "I made her promise she wouldn't tell you that she was talking to me because we talked a lot about you. Good stuff, but I thought you'd be embarrassed if you found out. It's been a week, and I haven't been able to find her. I really want to give her back her glasses, so I've given up on finding her on my own. As a matter of a fact, she knows you quite well. Dee. How can I contact her?"

"I, uh. . ." Cindy stared down at her old glasses. The day after the banquet she'd called the banquet hall's office, and they hadn't been turned in. She'd assumed the janitorial staff threw them out, and that would have been okay. With her contacts, she only needed them for a backup. Which now she'd never do, since Luke had seen her wearing them.

Luke held the glasses up. "When she dropped them they got bent, but I had them fixed. They're good as new."

She couldn't believe he'd spent money on her old glasses. Or that he'd spent a week, day and night, looking for her.

Luke put them back down. "She knows you. Quite well, as a matter of a fact."

The phone rang and Annie answered it. She listened for a few seconds then put the caller on hold, stood, and joined

Cindy at the counter. "Joe Fitzgerald is on the phone. He's wondering about the warranty and wants to know. . ." Annie stared down at the counter then picked up the glasses. "Hey. I thought you said you'd lost these." She turned to Luke. "Where did you find them?"

"They're yours?"

Cindy felt like she could melt from the intensity of Luke's stare. He looked at all the parts of her she'd changed, thanks to Farrah, that were back to normal. The hair color had taken three washes, but it had eventually come out. She'd put her contacts back in during the taxi ride. Her nails had felt a little funny after she'd taken off the fake ones, making her wonder why women did things like that. It had taken two days for her ankles to stop hurting after trying to balance in Brittany's shoes, but she'd liked the shoes so much she'd gone to the same store and bought the same pair, in the right size, for the day that she might actually need to wear them. Of course that meant buying a dress first.

"Dee?" Luke's voice came out an octave lower than usual. "Cindy. Why?"

Beside her, Annie pressed her hands over her mouth as she studied Luke's intense stare. "Oh no. Did I say something I shouldn't have?" She cleared her throat. "Come on, Kat. Let's go get a Coke."

Luke continued to stare while Annie and Kat made a quick exit, leaving them alone in the foyer. "You said had a break-in that night. Was that real? Is any of this real?"

Her voice came out in a little squeak. "It was real—but a false alarm. One of the guys must have left a door unlocked and someone tried to open it. When the alarm went off, whoever it was got scared and took off."

"You looked so different that night. How did you do that to your eyes?"

"I'm wearing colored contacts. I lost the clear ones before we met."

"Then I guess you know how I feel about you."

Her heart pounded. "Yes."

Luke stepped closer. "You still haven't answered my first question. Be honest. Why didn't you want me to know it was you?"

Cindy held her breath. If she was going to be honest, she'd have to tell him that she'd fallen in love with him, especially after he'd had no hesitation about making it known that he loved her, too. Being with him felt so right, but the timing was all wrong. She was about to jump off a cliff to battle with Melissa in court, and she wouldn't come out unscathed.

She doubted she would win the house, but she refused to lose the business. Her mother had thought it cute that daddy's little girl loved to pretend she was fixing cars with him. Even as a child she spent more time with her father, playing with his tools at the shop, than playing dolls with her friends.

Then when her mother died, she hadn't just played with the tools—instead of going to daycare her father had taken her to the shop, and when she got old enough, she'd learned to actually use them. Together they'd built a successful business, Cindy working at her father's side when all her friends got other jobs, which earned them money. She'd even forgone her dream of going to business college to keep the business running when he married Melissa and needed to cut back on his hours. When he died, she'd completely taken over.

Mufford Brake and Muffler was her father's legacy and now it was hers—or at least it would be after the court battle. The situation was ugly enough, but if Luke got involved, knowing Luke had money would only give Melissa more ammunition and motivation.

She couldn't do that to Luke. Or Kat.

Cindy gulped and looked up into Luke's eyes. "Because I can't let this happen, this thing between us. I can't drag you and Kat into the middle of my family's battle zone. I have to do this alone."

Luke stepped closer, resting his hands on her shoulders. "Is that what you really want?"

Cindy rested one hand on his chest, feeling his heart pound beneath her palm.

What did she really want? Until now, all she'd wanted was to carry on her father's legacy—the business was all she had left of him. But was that what her father would have wanted for her? Of course she needed the income, but she had skills. She could always work for someone else.

What her father wanted for her was for her to be happy.

If she was happy fixing cars that was fine, but there was more to life than work. What would really make her happy was beneath her palm: Luke and the love he offered.

Was fighting Melissa for total ownership of Mufford Brake and Muffler worth letting go of Luke?

She nibbled her lower lip while he smiled and looked down at her, his question still hanging with one quirked eyebrow.

"No," Cindy said on a sigh. "It's not what I really want. If I have to push you away to get control of the business, then it's not worth it. I'd rather have you. I love you, Luke."

Luke groaned and pulled her closer. "I've wanted to do this for a very, very long time." He tilted his head, closed his eyes, and kissed her. He tangled the fingers of one hand in her hair, the other hand drifted to the small of her back to pull her closer.

And Cindy kissed him back with all the love in her heart.

A bang from the shop reminded Cindy where they were. With the deepest regret, she nudged him away. He didn't fight her, but she could tell he didn't want to stop.

When she could see his face, he opened his eyes, glanced over her shoulder, and then focused on her eyes and grinned. "We have an audience."

"Oh, no. Kat. . ." Cindy's cheeks burned, and she increased the distance between them.

As soon as they were separated, the door from the shop creaked open. Kat skipped through. "When's the wedding?"

she squealed. "Do I get to be a bridesmaid? Can I put a bow on Tippy?"

Cindy squeezed her eyes shut.

Luke stepped forward once more and grasped Cindy's hands with his. "What about an answer to Kat's question?"

Cindy groaned. "Sure. As long as it's not a butt bow."

Luke froze. "A what?" He shook his head. "Not that question. The other one. About the wedding."

"Wedding? What wedding?"

"Ours." He raised one hand to cup her cheek. "Cindy, will you marry me?"

"I, uh. . ." Her brain stalled and her head swam. She could be Luke's wife, but she hadn't given any thought to being a stepmother for Kat. A stepmother. . .like Melissa. Luke picked up her hands. "I know what you're thinking. You're nothing like Melissa. Kat already loves you; she told me so the night of the banquet, and you already love her. Everything will be good. Great. We can work out all the details. We'll be fine."

She stared into his face. He was right. When they all loved each other, everything could be worked out.

She took a deep breath. The expression in his eyes told her she was doing the right thing. "Yes, I'll marry you."

Behind them, Annie gasped. "This is so wonderful! I have to tell Zella." She ran to the desk to retrieve her cell phone but picked up a piece of paper instead. "I forgot to tell you. The lawyer called. He said he needed to talk to you right away, that it's important."

Cindy pressed her fingers into her temples. "I know what he wants," she muttered. "I had some questions about making the garage into a suite and living there. I should probably call him back and tell him it's no longer necessary." She opened her eyes and looked at Luke. "Please tell me you don't believe in long engagements."

Luke's eyes widened. "Short. Really short. How about next week?"

Cindy didn't say anything; she only hoped he wasn't joking as she picked up the paper with the lawyer's number.

Luke pressed a quick kiss to her cheek. "I'll leave you to your phone call. Tonight when we're finished with work I want to take you out for supper to celebrate." He turned to Kat. "Without you."

"Then I'm going to give Tippy more chicken pizza."

"You go right ahead, as long as I don't have to eat it." He grinned. "I'll be back at closing."

Before he could turn around, the phone rang. Annie ran to pick it up then started waving one hand in the air. "It's the lawyer! Don't go!"

Cindy's stomach dropped into the bottom of her steel-toed work boots as Annie pressed the button to put the call on speaker.

"Cindy? I have some bad news for you," the lawyer's voice droned then paused.

Cindy sucked in a deep breath. "If it's about the garage,

don't worry about it. I don't need it anymore because I'm getting married soon." Her mind swirled. She was happy about getting married, but at the same time she felt the magnitude of what she was giving up. "I also need to tell you that I'm not going to fight Melissa contesting the will." She tried to tell herself that it really was a no-win situation anyway. Even if she fought Melissa and won, the legal fees would use up most of the equity of the business. She wondered if Melissa was so vindictive that it had been her plan all along.

"Married, you say? That changes everything." She heard the shuffling of paper echo through the phone. "Here it is. Effective on the date of the wedding, the terms of the will of David Mufford changes the conditions of his assets left behind to, 100 percent of the business of Mufford Brake and Muffler reverts to Cindy Mufford, and 100 percent of the house reverts to Melissa Mufford. I have a list of which contents of the house go with Cindy and what stays with Melissa. There is no contesting this." He paused, and the tone of his voice lightened. "Cindy, your father did this because after you're married you won't need the house, and Melissa never wanted the business. He didn't want you to know about this until after you were engaged, so you wouldn't choose the wrong man. I assume you've chosen the right one, so congratulations, and I hope you live happily ever after with him."

She could barely believe it, but she'd just heard it. Emotion tightened her throat, and a tear rolled down her cheek as she looked up at Luke.

He smiled down and squeezed her hand.

"Yes," she choked out. "I met my Prince Charming, and we certainly will."

LOVE BY
THE BOOKS

Dedication

Dedicated to my writing buddies in Scribes211—
in alphabetical order—Bob Kaku, Donna Mumma,
Ginny Hamlin, Jennifer Uhlark, Linda Truesdell,
Ruth Reid, and Sarah Hamaker.
I couldn't have done this without you guys/gals.

Chapter 1

Annie Wilson's hands froze over the keyboard as someone yanked open the door of Mufford Brake and Muffler. She tried not to cringe. She was having a bad day already, and she had a bad feeling it was about to get worse.

Brent from Like a Prince Car Rentals strode to the counter and looked up at the clock on the wall. "Is the red Ford finished yet? You said it would be ready half an hour ago."

She stood and approached him, glad for the barrier of the counter between them. "I'm sorry, no. As you know, we're short a mechanic this week, and we're running a bit behind."

Brent ran his fingers through his hair. "I don't mean to be snappy, but I'm short someone, too. I don't have a minute to spare with Luke gone."

Annie swept one hand in the air toward the shop. "The guys are working as hard as they can with Cindy gone. We took your Ford without an appointment, and we're doing our best." She turned her head to the west, in the direction of the ocean and ultimately Hawaii, where Luke and Cindy were. "Do you think they're thinking of us and what's going on while they're gone?"

"I doubt it. At least they shouldn't be. I sure wouldn't be thinking of work on my honeymoon." He turned his head toward Hawaii, too, and his expression softened. "I still can't believe how quickly this happened. It took him so long to get her attention, and then it felt like the next day they were married."

Annie sighed. "I can't believe that story Luke told Cindy about getting a great deal on the plane tickets, but only if they used them right away."

Brent nodded. "I know. But it worked."

Annie didn't believe anyone really fell for that line, yet somehow they'd managed to make a wedding happen in two short weeks. Although with the way her mother had treated Cindy, Annie couldn't blame Cindy for wanting to get out of the house as fast as possible.

Ever since the night of Brent and Luke's banquet, Annie's eyes had been opened to her mother's behavior toward Cindy, which had shown her the real Cindy. She'd believed all her mother's lies and wrongly acted just as awfully as her mother. Even though her mother had no remorse, Annie couldn't shake the guilt. In an attempt to make things right between them, Annie had done her best to pull every string she could to make the wedding happen.

And in order for Cindy to actually go on a honeymoon, Annie had volunteered to run things at the brake and muffler shop. Now that she was a college graduate, she'd be looking for a job at a public accounting firm, but those plans were put temporarily on hold.

She knew she would be in over her head, but she hadn't counted on Luke's partner and his bad attitude.

Brent checked his watch, as if he didn't trust the clock he'd just looked at only minutes ago. "How much longer will it be? The people who reserved it will be here soon, and I haven't given it an inspection yet."

"I'll have to ask Oscar. I'll be right back."

As she turned to walk into the shop, the hair on the back of her neck bristled. She couldn't believe Brent had the nerve to follow her.

She spun around, holding up one hand to stop him. "Customers aren't allowed beyond the yellow line."

He pointed down at the line they were both about to cross. "Neither are you if you're not wearing safety boots." He stared down at her feet. "Unless those are steel-toed sandals."

Annie couldn't help but wiggle her exposed toes. She hadn't thought about going into the shop before; she'd never needed to. "Never mind the sarcasm. Wait here."

She shuffled across the floor, being careful not to trip on any loose nuts or debris. "Oscar, how much longer?"

"Five minutes. Or more if he's being a pain."

Annie bit back a grin. "Just get it done," she muttered and

walked back to the yellow line.

At her return, Brent turned and walked back to where he should have been in the first place.

"Five minutes and it's all yours."

He checked his watch again. "I'll be back in four, which should be enough time to start filling out the form." He turned and left the second he finished his sentence.

Annie didn't know whether to be angry with him or feel sorry for him. Even though she didn't like his manners, or lack thereof, she could understand his situation. She felt the same without Cindy running things. Luke and Cindy had only been gone four days, and already everything was nearing a disaster. She'd never appreciated Cindy's organizational skills. Instead of learning from Cindy's instructions, for the past year she'd listened to her mother and only answered the phones and done a minimal amount of actual work. Most of the time she'd been there, she'd done her homework for college. Now she was trying to run the place, and she was totally unprepared.

Annie watched as Oscar lowered Brent's fleet car down on the hoist, mentally counting the seconds until his return. She'd been so unfair to Cindy. No matter what it took, for the two weeks Cindy was away on her honeymoon, Annie vowed to do everything she could to make up for her past sins. Even if that meant dealing with Luke's partner.

Brent Wallace gripped the pencil so hard he didn't know

how it didn't snap.

During the time that Luke had been pursuing Cindy, it had been their unspoken agreement that Luke would be the one to go over to the brake and muffler shop when they needed something. Or even when they didn't. Brent had found Luke's besotted behavior amusing. But what hadn't been amusing were the times when Luke came back frustrated over Cindy's sisters'—or rather, her stepsisters'—behavior. He'd often grumbled about Annie being the worst slacker he'd ever seen, in addition to being downright disrespectful to Cindy, who, despite the family relationship, was the boss and should have been treated accordingly.

Even without Cindy there, Annie didn't follow the rules. He could understand her not wearing regulation safety footwear, but sandals with her toes showing. . .

Cute little toes with bright-red nail polish. . .

Brent shook his head to clear the image from his mind.

Luke had asked him to make sure Annie could manage the place on short notice in Cindy's absence, but Brent understood what Luke meant. Luke had meant for him to keep an eye on Annie to make sure she actually worked.

It was going to be a long two weeks.

Chapter 2

Annie flexed her fingers and rubbed her aching wrist. It had been the fastest and busiest two weeks of her life, and she'd never been so sore.

Halfway through the first week, Jack called in sick, and then the next week Oscar caught the same bug. Instead of turning customers away, Annie had put down her accounting pencil, borrowed Cindy's coveralls, and with Brent's words echoing through her head, she'd bought a pair of safety boots.

The mechanics had given her the lackey jobs, calling them easy, but they hadn't been easy for her. While it didn't take much skill to change a tire, the tools were big and heavy, and the jarring from the impact wrench had surely loosened her teeth. She'd also never known that tires were so heavy.

She forced herself to keep her eyes open as she locked the front door and flipped the sign to CLOSED. Now that the staff had gone home, it was time to do the bank deposit, e-mail orders for all the parts they'd used, and double-check they had everything they needed for the next day's appointments.

Every night she hadn't gotten home until nearly eleven o'clock, and then she had to be back at 6:30 a.m. to open up. By the end of the first week, she'd considered bringing a sleeping bag, except there was no couch and that would have meant sleeping on the dirty floor. Tonight she felt like she could do exactly that, maybe even without a sleeping bag.

Tomorrow was Saturday, their busiest day, but at least Zella would be there to answer the phone and handle the walk-ins.

Annie sank into her comfortable office chair, leaned back, and stretched her throbbing feet, wincing when the tops of her toes rubbed against the steel in the front of the boot. The boots were murder on her toenail polish, but she hadn't had time or the energy to fix the damage.

Cindy often worked six days a week. Now Annie knew why.

Cindy was coming back on Monday, but Annie still wouldn't be able to slow down. It would take at least a week, but she wasn't going to leave the computer until all the bank-statement reconciliations and fiscal month-end financials were done.

Before she started with the day's paperwork, she gave herself a minute to let her head fall back on the top of the chair. Her eyes drifted closed of their own accord, and she didn't care. For a couple of minutes, she could take a break. . . .

The rattling of the door handle jolted her back to the

present. Fear snatched her breath away.

Someone was trying to get in. . . It was dark out. With the lights on inside, she couldn't see who was out there, but whoever it was could see that she was alone.

If she called 911 on a Friday night she could be dead by the time the police got there.

The door rattled again. "Annie? It's Brent. Let me in."

Gasping for a breath, she jumped to her feet. As annoying as Brent was, he was harmless. Automatically she raised her hand to smooth out any wrinkles in her clothing then froze.

The coveralls were smeared with grease and oil and something else black and slimy she couldn't identify. A few wrinkles were the least of her problems.

Annie sucked in a deep breath, walked to the door, clicked off the dead bolts, and pushed it open.

Brent walked in then pulled the door closed behind him and flicked the lock. "Are you okay? I saw you all sprawled out and the deposit book lying on the floor."

She rubbed her eyes with the back of her hand. "I'm fine. I must have knocked it down when I dozed off. It's been a rough week."

"You shouldn't have the money out like that when you're alone in the building. You've been doing the same thing every day. Cindy stands over there when she's doing the deposit so no one sees what she's doing." He pointed to the corner where the counter met the wall, the only place in the front office sheltered from prying eyes.

"At the end of the day I just can't stay on my feet that long." She looked up at Brent as he looked down at her. "Wait a minute. How do you know what I've been doing every night?"

"It's not hard to see you. I've been working late every night, too."

"I didn't know you were there. I thought you left the lights on for security."

"We have a burglar alarm for security. The lights were on because I was working. I was in Luke's office, so you probably didn't see me."

All this time, she'd been nervous because she thought she'd been alone. He'd been across the parking lot all along. Not that he would have been able to do anything besides call the police if an armed robber had come, but it still made her feel a bit better.

She ran her fingers through her hair, not caring about the additional grease she was adding to what was already there. She'd be washing her hair when she got home anyway. "Thank you for keeping an eye on me. But I think it's time for both of us to get back to work. How long are you staying tonight?"

"As long as it takes," he muttered then turned and walked toward the door. After opening the door, he paused and called back over his shoulder, "Don't forget to lock it behind me."

As if she would forget. She was terrified to be alone

so late. Her only consolation was that she was wearing steel-toed boots, and a kick would hurt a potential intruder more than if she were wearing her leather pumps. But still, it was a comfort to know that Brent and his surly attitude were close by.

Monday Cindy would be back, and life could get back to normal.

Brent gritted his teeth as he stared at his partner. "What do you mean, you want to bring Annie in to help? We don't need help. We especially don't need *her* help."

Luke shrugged his shoulders. "When Walter calls in sick we've always just waited for him to get better, but this time we can't."

Brent stared at Walter's empty desk. "Maybe he'll come in tomorrow?"

"No, not the way he sounded. We have to do the deposit today because we have to pay the rent on Monday. Normally I don't have a problem, but it won't balance. I don't know what I'm doing wrong."

"Maybe I can figure it out."

Without waiting for Luke's approval, Brent sat at Walter's desk and thumbed through the pile of balance sheets. "This is a lot of stuff that didn't get done. I know he only wants to work two days a week, but do you think we should see if he wants to increase his hours?"

"He won't. I already asked last month end."

Doing the mental math at what they needed to do to get the deposit done, Brent cringed. "This is going to take hours. What's not adding up?"

"The whole thing."

Brent clicked on the icon to reactivate the computer screen. At a surface skim, it looked like Luke had done everything right. It was actually hard to do something wrong because it was such a user-friendly accounting program. Until now.

Luke pointed to the total on the screen then the total on the adding machine, which was short by hundreds of dollars. "While she's not a CPA like Walter, Annie is an accountant. I'm pretty sure it won't take her as long as it would take us to figure this out. Besides, I was thinking of hiring her on to help Walter with our month-end work. I know Walter wants to do it himself, but he's getting a little more behind every month." He glanced toward the muffler shop then back to Brent. "Besides, Annie needs the work. Cindy told me that Annie is still looking for a job. She's lost a lot of time helping plan our wedding and taking care of Cindy's shop while we were gone. Now she's got a couple of weeks to catch up on Cindy's bookkeeping."

Brent's hand froze over the adding machine. "I can't believe you'd consider hiring her after the way she treated Cindy."

"Cindy says she's changed."

"I wouldn't be so sure of that." Every night he'd stayed late to watch what she did after the shop closed. The first thing she did after everyone left was spend nearly an hour on the computer, when Cindy only took ten minutes, which made him think that Annie was catching up on her personal e-mail instead of working. She never did the bank deposit the way Cindy did, and the last night he'd watched, instead of doing the bank deposit, she had a nap.

The only thing Annie had changed was her footwear.

However, for now they had a problem that needed fixing, and if Luke couldn't figure it out, Brent knew he wouldn't be able to either—after the last two weeks of mayhem, his brain wasn't working on all cylinders yet. He had to trust Luke and give Annie the benefit of the doubt. With caution.

"Fine," he mumbled. "But just for today."

Instead of phoning, Luke jogged across the parking lot, where the first thing he did was kiss Cindy.

Brent shouldn't have watched but he did.

At first it was a little peck on the cheek, and then they snuggled closer and wrapped their arms around each other. Luke turned his head and said something to Annie then kissed Cindy again. Only this time it wasn't just a little peck. It was the fully charged kiss of a man who'd come back from his honeymoon sooner than he wanted to. Annie got up and walked away, but Brent couldn't stop watching his friend and Cindy.

It was like watching the closing kiss of the leading actor

and actress from a movie, except this was real life.

One day he hoped God would find him a woman like that. She would appear out of nowhere and the moment he saw her, he'd be a goner, just like Luke.

"Brent? Did you want to see me?"

Brent tried not to flinch. "Annie. I didn't see you come in. Luke and I have a problem with our deposit. We can't balance, and it's out by a lot. Our regular accountant phoned in sick, so we were wondering if you could figure it out."

She checked her watch and sat in Walter's chair. "Of course." With a swipe of the mouse she reactivated the screen and began clicking through the menu.

"Do you need any help with the program?"

"No, I've used this one before. I'm okay."

He returned to the lease agreements he had to finish, but as he worked he kept an eye on Annie.

He counted every one of twenty minutes; Luke hadn't returned, and Annie hadn't left.

"I think I found your problem. You have some invoices that the tax portion is wrong, plus it's adding wrong, which is strange because it's supposed to auto-calculate. I'll do a manual override to fix it."

Within minutes she had it fixed, just as Luke said.

Brent ran his fingers through his hair. "Thanks. How much do we owe you?"

"Nothing. It didn't take long. Consider it returning a favor."

When he'd watched her at night and stayed until she closed up and drove away, it hadn't been a favor for Annie. It had been a favor for Luke.

Just as she stood, Luke walked in the door, his ear to his cell phone.

"Thanks, Walter, I hope you feel better soon." He returned his phone to his pocket. "I told Walter we had a problem but not to worry, we had it fixed. He said he would be in Friday, like usual."

Brent turned to Annie. "If you wouldn't mind, can I hire you for a few hours on Friday to go over what you found with Walter? He'll need to see what was wrong, and what you had to do to fix it."

Annie nodded. "Sure. But it's—"

Brent held up one hand to interrupt her. "I want to pay you for your time. No more favors."

She opened her mouth then shook her head. "Okay. See you Friday."

Chapter 3

Brent watched every step Annie made as she walked in. She went straight to Walter's desk but didn't sit down. She plunked a coffee mug on the corner then looked around, almost like she was nervous.

Brent sighed and walked toward her. "Walter's not coming. He called in and said he was still feeling sick and didn't want to spread his germs."

Her eyes widened, and she looked straight at him.

All he could do was stare back. Something was different about her, but he couldn't place it. Or maybe it was because for the past few days, whenever they didn't have a customer, Luke had been singing Annie's praises, repeating what Cindy had said about Annie doing a great job while they were gone. Adding to that, apparently now one of the mechanics had developed a crush on her.

In a way, he could see that happening. If he hadn't known about the way Annie had treated Cindy, she could be a very likable woman.

Annie reached for her cup. "I guess I should go then."

Brent shook his head. "Luke thinks we should hire you to help with our month-end financials."

"I thought your regular accountant did that."

"He does, but Walter's been falling behind. Cindy said you might be open to try freelancing, so Luke wants to hire you for two days a month. Would that work for you?"

She smiled so brightly she almost beamed. "Yes, it would. I've been thinking that instead of getting a job and going all the way downtown every day, I would work from home and start my own business."

"That's kind of what Walter does. We don't need someone full-time."

"Luke told me Walter works for a bigger company that contracts out smaller jobs."

"Exactly," Brent said. "Now I've already logged in. We need you to check all these orders from the past week then do the deposit."

He showed Annie how they entered their invoicing then left her alone. But still, he was going to keep an eye on her.

Annie didn't know whether to jump for joy or run for the hills in terror.

Brent and Luke's company was small, so their project should have been easy, but because their company owned an entire fleet of cars, there were many liabilities, especially the insurance. From what she'd seen, they operated smoothly and ran at a profit.

Once she became accustomed to their procedure, checking the invoices and entering their expenses wasn't difficult. However, when she started to enter the deposit, the same thing that happened to Luke happened to her. Everything she'd entered that had been paid for reconciled, but a couple of older invoices didn't balance with the credits when she entered them into the general ledger.

She didn't want to accuse their accountant, but she had to make Brent and Luke aware that he'd made the same mistake a number of times. Perhaps a reminder for Walter to be more careful wasn't out of line.

Or maybe it was out of line. She knew Brent and Luke had been using the same accountant since they'd started their business. She'd only graduated from college a couple of months ago, and while she had a degree in accounting now, Walter was a CPA.

No, that didn't make her bad or inaccurate. She was just inexperienced. The bottom line was that the ledgers balanced or they didn't. If she was going to do the job they were paying her to do, she had to make them aware.

Just not today. For today, she would fix the errors and go forward.

Before she knew it, Brent flipped the sign on the door to Closed.

He turned to her. "How did you do?"

She looked down at the piles of paper and sighed. "I've finished most of it and balanced your bank deposit, but I haven't started closing off your month end."

His brows furrowed. "Why not?"

Since it was her first day, she didn't want to tell him about the errors or that correcting them had taken time she hadn't expected.

Unless it was a test. She didn't know how much Brent or Luke knew about general accounting or bookkeeping, but since it was inconsistent with the programming that there were errors, she wondered if they had duplicated the same thing Luke had found earlier and wondered if she would find it or be able to fix it.

Above all, she couldn't lie or mislead him. In the pastor's sermon last Sunday he'd shown how omission of the truth was as much a lie as telling one.

Annie cleared her throat. "I found another error that was the same as the other day, and it took me a while to fix it."

It was almost like the gears were whirring in his head. He cleared his throat. "Show me."

Butterflies warred inside her stomach as Brent dragged a chair to sit beside her. She pulled up the corrected entry and did her best to explain.

Brent straightened in the chair and stared at the monitor. "How did this happen?"

"I don't know."

His look said she should have known, but she didn't.

She hoped he wasn't having second thoughts about hiring her. She hadn't graduated at the top of her class, but she'd still graduated with honors. If she had just fixed the problem and said nothing, he wouldn't have doubted her—he would just have thought she was slow. Annie needed this job to build her reputation.

She studied his face. Not only would he make a very good business reference, he would also make a very good friend. Cindy and Luke thought the world of him. Of course, they never talked about how handsome Brent was. It was almost funny that his hair color was nearly the same nondescript shade of brown as hers, but his eyes were mesmerizing. Dark brown as rich chocolate, and he had lashes any woman would kill for.

As if he could tell what she was thinking, he jumped to his feet.

"It's time to go. I need to check all the doors and lock up."

He strode to the back door and walked out. From her chair, Annie watched him as he walked through the lot and checked every car, making sure every door was locked and every trunk was closed. Every car was just a quick check, but when he got to a green car he stopped. After checking that it was locked up tight, he bent and pressed his hands to the window as he looked inside, and she thought he smiled.

Annie's breath caught. All she could do was stare. A Mustang convertible. Her dream car.

She couldn't afford to buy one, but as soon as she got her

first paycheck, for one day, she could rent this one. It didn't matter that so far she only had one customer. One day there would be more.

On second thought, she hadn't done anything to celebrate her graduation from college, so she could justify the expense of taking a day and driving to experience the sights and sounds of Seattle on a hot day with the top down.

After she drove through the city she would go to Alki Beach and cruise along the beach road. Maybe she'd stop for a burger and go run to the shore and wiggle her toes in the water. Then she'd keep going east to Redmond and idle through Marymoor Park and wave at everyone who was out for a breath of fresh air. She'd be getting fresh air, too. Or she could boot it up the I5 and journey north to Canada and go to Vancouver's Stanley Park. She sighed. No, she'd never make it back home in time to return the car for the one-day rental deadline.

The second Brent opened the door to come back into the office, the questions burst out: "How much to rent the Mustang? Is it available next weekend? What's your deadline to have it back?"

He smiled and sighed. "It's not a lease car. Sorry."

Her whole body sagged. "Then what's it doing here?"

"We're hiding it. The best place to hide a car is with other cars."

"Why would you hide such a magnificent car?"

"Luke bought it for Cindy's birthday."

All she could do was stare at the car. She'd bought Cindy a sweater and matching scarf.

Brent grinned ear to ear. "Luke said Cindy's truck is sometimes hard to park when she goes downtown, so he bought her something smaller. I can hardly wait to see her face."

"I guess this means you're coming to the birthday party."

"Wouldn't miss it. See you Wednesday."

Chapter 4

B rent looked up as the bell tinkled. "Walter, it's good to see you. Are you feeling better?"

Walter pressed his fist against his chest as he walked to his desk. "Almost, but it still hurts right here." He gave a feeble cough then sank into his chair. He flicked through the small stack of papers in his basket. "Where's everything that piled up while I was gone?"

Brent smiled. "It's done. Luke's sister-in-law did it for us." His smile faltered. Annie wasn't really a sister-in-law; was there any such thing as a stepsister-in-law? He shook his head. "Sorry. I got distracted. Annie just graduated with a degree in accounting, so we've hired her to help you since we've been getting busier." He glanced through the glass door to see Annie step outside Cindy's shop. "Here she comes."

Instead of the relief Brent expected, Walter scowled. "I don't want any help. I have everything all set up and it's under control."

"Actually, Annie found a few mistakes. Luke and I needed

to do a deposit, and we couldn't get it to balance with the invoices. I've asked Annie to show you what happened. She said there was some kind of programming miscalculation."

Fortunately Annie walked in the door, sparing him from having to try to explain something he knew nothing about.

"Oh good," Brent said, his relief evident. "Walter, this is Annie. I'd like you to show her everything she'll need to close off the fiscal month end, generate the profit-and-loss reports, and show her where everything is filed." He wheeled a chair for Annie to sit with Walter then went back to work.

While he worked he kept an eye on the two of them, watching Annie point out what had happened and Walter explaining as he fixed it. He didn't understand what Walter said, but he felt certain Annie should have. Yet judging from her expression, it didn't look like she did either.

He wasn't as sure as Luke that hiring her was a good idea. As a recent graduate she would know the current accounting programs, but theirs was no longer current. It was the same program they'd bought when they started their business. Since not much changed in the way they did business, Walter saved them money by using the older version, and everything had been running fine. Until now.

When Luke walked in from a sales call, Brent laid his pen down. "How did it go?"

Luke slid the folder into the pending slot. "They still have to run it past their board, but it looks good."

Brent glanced outside to the green Mustang, parked

where Cindy's truck used to be. He smiled, thinking of Cindy's face and squeal of glee at the birthday party. "You just gave her that car yesterday—I can't believe you took her car instead of yours for a sales call."

Luke tossed his key ring on the counter. "I promised her I'd put gas in it, so she was happy to let me have it." He ran his fingers through his messy hair, a sure sign he'd been driving with the top down. "Gotta take it when I can get it."

At Luke's words, Brent saw Annie gazing at Cindy's new car with stars in her eyes, while Walter grumbled and typed furiously.

Luke turned to Annie. "Has she let you take it for a spin yet?"

Annie sighed. "Yes, but only around the block. It was magnificent." She sighed again then closed her eyes.

Brent imagined the wind blowing through her hair. He could picture her in Cindy's car. It would suit her.

Luke cleared his throat. "Cindy told me she needed to ask you something about a back order that was supposed to come in today."

Walter waved one hand in the air. "Go. I have to fix this anyway."

Annie stood. "I'll be back in about twenty minutes."

It should have felt normal for the three men to be alone in the building, but for some reason it didn't. Brent stared at Annie's purse and coffee mug sitting on the corner of Walter's desk. He couldn't believe it, but he'd begun to enjoy her presence.

Evan, the lot boy, came in through the back door. "I'm glad you're back. I have to show both of you a dent in the silver Maxima."

Brent pulled the file for the car out of the cabinet then followed Evan and Luke to the lot. He made a mental note to use this car to show Annie how to do the insurance claim in case Walter was out sick again. Although, he was very happy to remind himself, this was the first time Walter had taken sick time in five years.

When Brent and Luke returned to the office, it was vacant. Walter had left a note stuck to the computer that he'd gone out to pick up his prescription and would be back in ten minutes.

"What do you think? How's it going?" Luke asked.

Brent looked absently at the computer, recalling Walter's scowling face and Annie's nervous expression. He didn't understand why Walter and Annie didn't seem to get along. Every time Brent had talked to Annie about their accounting issues she seemed very intelligent. And she wasn't afraid to ask questions. But clearly Walter didn't like her. It didn't make sense.

Before he could come to any conclusions, Walter returned.

"Hey, Walter, how's it going with Annie?" Luke asked, sparing Brent the need to be subtle.

"Not good. She's making a lot of mistakes."

Brent's stomach clenched. That was the same thing Annie had said about Walter. If accountants had turf wars, he didn't want to be in the middle of one.

Luke frowned. "Then it's up to you to teach her how to do it right."

"I could get everything done faster if I did it myself."

Luke crossed his arms. "I want you to give her a fair chance; that's all I ask."

When Walter stormed back to his desk, Brent motioned with his head for Luke to join him outside.

Once the door closed behind them, Brent could no longer hold back. "I didn't want to say this, but—if Annie isn't good at what she does, why are you so intent on hiring her? I don't want her if she can't do the job." He shook his head. What was he saying? He still wanted to see her. He wanted to get to know what made her smile, to know that *he* could make her smile. He couldn't help it; he wanted to get to know her better.

Just not on the job.

Luke narrowed his eyes. "Cindy says she's been doing an outstanding job. And without Annie's mother in the middle, they're starting to become friends. Annie promised to make up for all the miserable things she did, and Cindy said she seems very sincere." Luke lowered his voice to barely above a whisper. "As a new Christian sister, family or not, I think she deserves a chance."

A cloud of guilt pressed heavily on Brent's chest. He'd resolved to give her the benefit of the doubt and he would. "Fine," he grumbled. "But if she can't work with Walter, she's gone." Or, if she did something absolutely fantastic, he would feel better, Walter would feel better, and everything would be fine.

"That's fair. Let's go back inside; here she comes."

Brent smiled at Annie. "Ready to get back to work?"

Strangely, Annie wouldn't look at him. She simply nodded and returned to the chair beside Walter. She only stopped working briefly to greet Kat when she got off the school bus. Then Kat went to the lot to help Evan wash cars, and Annie went back to the computer.

The sounds of splashing water drifted in through the air vents.

Brent hadn't minded when Luke hired Kat. It was good for a teenager to learn responsibility. Not to mention that Evan worked harder and faster, either to impress Kat or to compete with her. It didn't matter which one. It only mattered that their cars were cleaner than they'd ever been. But hiring a kid to wash cars was different than hiring an accountant. Anyone could wash cars. And Evan and Kat got along. Walter and Annie didn't.

At the usual time, Luke and Kat left. Not long after that, Evan left, then Walter, and then Annie picked up her purse and coffee mug and returned to Cindy's shop, leaving Brent alone.

The quiet in the office was a dramatic change from the tension of the day. Brent replayed the sound of Walter grumbling and bickering about Annie not knowing what she was doing in his head.

After the last car due was checked in, inspected, and parked, Brent locked up.

He hoped things would go better tomorrow.

Seated at her desk, Annie looked up at Brent, hovering above her, waiting for her reply. She looked through the window, across the parking to Like a Prince Car Rentals, where Luke sat at Walter's desk staring at the computer screen. "I suppose I could go help him. Is it the same problem?"

"He's not sure."

She waited for Brent to say more, but he didn't.

She turned back to watch Luke, hoping that he would jump up and do a little Snoopy dance to show he'd figured out what was wrong.

He didn't.

Annie walked to the shop door and called to Cindy that she was going to Luke and Brent's for a few minutes, hoping that Cindy would say she needed her to stay and watch for new customers coming in.

She didn't.

Slowly, Annie turned. "I guess I can go."

She wanted to keep working on Cindy's bookkeeping. She'd enjoyed coming back to a system that worked and data that made sense.

Instead she followed Brent and began the same battle

with his accounting program as the last time, trying to find out why the credits didn't balance against the debits.

It took hours, but she finally found the problem, which puzzled her even more than the data itself. The best she could do was create a general journal entry to make everything balance then wait for Walter to fix it, because she couldn't figure out what he'd done.

The arrival of the school bus and Kat told her she'd spent far too much time fixing someone else's problem. Even though it had taken so long and she would have been perfectly justified to charge by the hour, she chose to let it go because she wanted Luke and Brent to hire her permanently.

As she reached for the deposit book, Cindy walked in.

"Hey, Kat," Cindy said. "I guess I'll be taking you home today."

Luke stepped out of his office. "Why?"

Cindy blinked at the sight of him. "What are you doing here? I thought you left."

"Why would you think that?"

"Because my car isn't here."

Luke turned to Cindy's usual parking spot, where her freshly washed pickup truck shone in the sunlight. "Why did you bring the truck? You were just complaining about the gas mileage."

"I brought it because you took the Mustang."

Luke swept his hand in the air toward his parking spot, where his blue Caliber sat. "I didn't bring the Mustang. I brought my own car."

Cindy's face paled. "I brought my truck because the Mustang was gone."

"When I left this morning, it was in the driveway."

Kat gasped and covered her mouth with her hands. "It was there when I left for school this morning."

The silence that hung in the air was deafening.

Cindy's voice came out in a squeak. "I think we had better call the police."

Chapter 5

Brent should have been accustomed to being alone, but suddenly he felt abandoned.

Cindy, Luke, and Kat had all dashed off to meet the police at their house. Annie took off to take care of the brake and muffler shop. And Evan wasn't coming in because they'd let him have the day off to study for a test.

He couldn't believe the car had been stolen right out of Luke's driveway between the times Luke and Cindy had left for work. This thief was very daring. Luke lived in an affluent neighborhood. Not only did all the houses have security systems, but the neighbors watched out for each other, although Luke said it was simply an excuse for being nosy. Maybe the police would find a neighbor who saw something.

As he did every evening, Brent watched the three mechanics as they left Cindy's shop then stood at the door and watched Annie lock up and leave. Then, as he did every night, he checked the perimeter, locked the gate, and reentered the office to tidy up. He shook his head at Luke's messy desk and closed the office door so he wouldn't have to look at it. His own desk was always neat, so he continued to Walter's desk, where he began stacking the papers into an orderly pile, since Annie had left things in a mess when she'd gone back to the muffler shop.

On the desk beside Annie's half-full coffee mug was her watch.

He picked it up to put it in the safe, but the rough surface of the back made him flip it over.

It was engraved: *School behind you, the world before you. Love, Dad.*

A lump formed in his throat. He didn't know anything about Annie's side of the family except that her mother had married Cindy's father and they'd all lived together in the same house after Cindy's father died. Yet the watch seemed a recent gift, since Annie had just earned her bachelor's degree a month ago.

He didn't know the next time she was due to work at Cindy's shop, but if it wasn't for a few days, he didn't want to just put the watch in the safe. It was obviously special, so Brent slipped it into his pocket. He knew she lived only a few minutes out of his way.

Besides that, seeing her away from the office would be a good place for a nonconfrontational discussion about her ability, or inability, to handle their accounting program.

Maybe that would be a good topic to bring up over dinner. Or maybe they would end up talking and not discussing work at all.

LOVE BY THE BOOKS

Annie sat alone at the kitchen table, poking at her supper, unable to eat. She couldn't believe Cindy's car was gone.

The police had talked to a few of Cindy and Luke's neighbors. One person had seen the car as it turned the corner, remarking that Cindy had apparently left for work a bit early, as if he already knew her timetable.

The ring of the doorbell made her drop the fork.

Thinking of police chases and stolen car rings, Annie held her breath and tiptoed to the door.

Brent stood on the landing, his hands in his pockets, checking out the neighborhood.

Part of her was glad to see him, but she wasn't in the mood for company. She was less in the mood to discuss another problem with his bookkeeping.

Annie sighed and opened the door. "Hi, Brent. What brings you here?"

He pulled her watch out of her pocket. "I came to give you this."

Immediately she wrapped her fingers around her naked wrist. If she weren't so annoyed with him for his lack of confidence in her accounting skills, she could almost think he was a nice man. "Thank you," she mumbled as she took it from him and fastened it to her wrist.

"It looked like it was special, so I thought I'd deliver it instead of waiting until I saw you next."

"I appreciate it. It's very special." She waited to see if he would turn and leave, but he remained still, like he was waiting for an invitation.

"Would you like to come in?" she asked, hoping his answer would be negative.

"Yes, I would."

She stepped aside as he entered.

He looked around the mess. "Is someone moving?"

Annie's cheeks heated up as Brent looked around at the boxes piled everywhere. "This is so embarrassing. We reorganized after Cindy moved out. We're going to have a garage sale next month."

"Then why aren't these boxes in the garage?"

"We can't seem to find the time for all three of us to get together to move them. I've been putting in extra time at Cindy's shop, and Zella's been working the late shift all week. Then yesterday Zella went to Portland for a seminar, and Gramma hurt herself a few days ago, so my mom went to stay with her. I can't carry some of these boxes by myself, so they'll have to sit here until we're all home at the same time."

Brent grimaced as he scanned the boxes piled haphazardly through the living room. Cindy knew Brent's office was always meticulous, and she suspected he was a neat freak at home, too.

He turned back to her. "I read the inscription on the back of your watch. Graduation gift?"

Annie's throat tightened. "Yes. After my parents split

up, my father moved to Europe. When I started college he mailed me this watch and told me to keep it on the corner of my desk, not to put it on until I graduated. He told me to look at it when I got discouraged and to remember that a few hours studying would mean years of success after graduation."

"That's really something. I think—" The ringing phone cut off Brent's words.

"Excuse me. It might be my mom. She'll be calling about Gramma." Annie dashed off to take the call. Her grandmother hadn't broken anything, but the ankle was badly sprained and bruised—which was serious enough at her age, so her mother would be staying for at least a week. Annie didn't want to be rude to Brent, but she needed to hear the doctor's report, so she listened for longer than she wanted to.

When she returned to the living room, Brent was gone. And so were all the boxes. The front door was wide open.

She dashed outside to see Brent placing the last box in front of the closed garage door.

He wiped his palms down the sides of his pants and blew out a deep breath. "If you'll open the door, I'll slide them in."

Mentally, Annie cringed. The main reason the boxes were in the living room for so long wasn't only that they were too heavy for her or her mother or sister to carry. The garage was so messy that they would have to reorganize it before the boxes would fit inside. She wasn't prepared to do that by herself, but she didn't know how to ask him to carry the boxes back inside the house.

"Thanks for doing this, but—"

He raised his palms in the air to silence her. "My pleasure. I know how a mess like that would drive me nuts. I don't mind."

Maybe he didn't, but she did. "I'm sorry, but we can't do this now. The light in the garage is burned out and we won't be able to see."

Brent glanced over his shoulder. "Then you had better hurry and open the garage door before it gets completely dark. We can always use the headlights from my car, but for now I think we're okay."

From her previous experiences with Brent, she suspected that it would take more time arguing with him than moving around the contents of the garage. She sighed and ran into the house and pressed the button to open the garage door.

To her horror, the garage was even messier than she remembered. She couldn't even squeeze around the clutter to get through to the front of the garage.

She ran back through the house to Brent, who stood at the front of the garage, not moving, his hands on his hips while he sized up the jumble of clutter, old furniture, and a freezer that had seen better days. "When was the last time you had a car in here?"

"Years," Annie muttered.

"Where did you think you were going to put these boxes?"

"I don't know. I don't remember it being this bad." Obviously neither had her mother or Zella because the three of them had agreed to put these boxes in the garage.

Instead of picking up a box, Brent inched his way into the garage. "I'll think I'll just move some stuff and pile them up here." He lifted a few boxes and placed them on top of some others to make space for the new ones.

"No, it's okay. You don't have to do that." Even more than embarrassing, she didn't want him hurting his back lifting the heavy boxes as high as they needed to be to make room for more.

"I think I can clear out a space over here." Without waiting for her response, Brent started clearing a space until he came to an old sleeping bag carelessly tossed over more boxes. On top of the sleeping bag were dozens of empty boxes, strewn helter-skelter. "This should be easy to tidy up," Brent muttered as he reached for the closest box. When his foot reached the edge of the sleeping bag, instead of hitting a solid mass beneath it, the blanket fluttered.

Brent lifted the corner of the sleeping bag. "This isn't boxes under here, it's. . ." He lifted the blanket higher.

Annie's heart stopped. It definitely wasn't boxes. It was. . .

Brent cleared his throat. "It's Cindy's car."

Chapter 6

B rent blinked then said a mental prayer that God
would wake him up, because surely this was a bad
dream.

He reached forward and touched the shiny green surface.
It was cold. This was real.

Now he knew why Annie hadn't wanted him in the
garage.

Brent stared open-mouthed at Cindy's car, still half-
covered and buried in boxes.

He didn't know what he felt like doing more—to hit
something or to vomit.

When Annie first saw the Mustang, he'd thought the
stars in her eyes were adorable. She'd looked happy for
Cindy, even knowing it would be many years before she
could have a car like it, between her lack of a job and a
student loan to pay back. He'd liked that about her. She'd
handled her sister getting her own dream car with grace.

Or so he'd thought. Now. . .he didn't know how to deal

with this. No one he'd ever known had stolen anything more than a chocolate bar from the corner store as a child. He'd been raised in a good home, in a good church, to trust people, and to live worthy of being trusted.

He didn't want to believe it, but his eyes didn't lie. He'd wanted to get to know Annie better, but this was something he wished he hadn't learned.

"Why?" he finally managed to choke out when he could find his voice again.

She didn't reply. Not that he'd expected her to. He didn't know what he saw more in her wide eyes and pale face—guilt or fear.

His brain raced as he battled whom to call first—Luke or the police.

On autopilot, he pulled his cell phone out of his pocket and flipped it open, but his finger hovered over the keypad. He still couldn't believe Annie had done this. He'd thought he could like her; something about her drew him. Like a moth to a flame, apparently. He usually was a good judge of character. He stared at Cindy's missing Mustang, hidden in Annie's garage. He didn't want to believe Annie had stolen it. But with the evidence in front of him, he couldn't say she hadn't.

He aimed for the button to call Luke.

Annie's fingers wrapped around his wrist. "Wait. It's not what it looks like."

"How can this not be exactly what it looks like?" He had

to force himself to say it out loud. "You stole Cindy's car."

"I didn't. I don't know how it got here." Her voice lowered. "You have to believe me."

"I want to believe you, I really do, but you have to give me a good reason why I should."

She gulped and tears filled her eyes.

Tears. He wasn't falling for that. It was the oldest trick in the book.

His eyes lost focus, so he turned and looked outside, away from Annie into the fading light of nightfall.

"I would never do something so horrible. Especially to Cindy. She's been so nice to me, when for so long I was so rotten to her. I didn't take her car."

"Then who did? Don't tell me your mother, because I know she's out of town."

She gulped again. "So is Zella."

At least she was being honest about that. "Then how did it get here?"

Annie let go of his wrist and stared up at him through watery eyes. "I don't know."

He hit the button on his phone.

Luke answered on the first ring.

"I found Cindy's car." Brent turned his back to Annie. He couldn't look at her while he talked to Luke.

"That's fantastic!" The scrape of Luke's hand covering the receiver echoed in his ear then Luke's muffled voice as he told Cindy. "Where? Is it okay?"

Brent's stomach clenched. He'd only seen the front right fender, but he knew Annie wouldn't have damaged it. Unless she'd borrowed it without permission then had an accident and was hiding it.

With one hand he pushed aside as many of the empty boxes on top of the sleeping bag as he could reach then lifted up the sleeping bag as high as he could. "Yes, it looks okay."

Luke repeated his reply to Cindy. "You didn't say where you found it."

Brent sucked in a deep breath. "It's. . ." He paused, trying to think of the best way to say it, but there was none. "It's in Annie's garage."

A silence hung on the line. He could imagine that the same string of thoughts were coursing through Luke's mind that haunted his own.

Luke's voice came out sounding choked and very quiet. "How did it get there?"

"She says she didn't steal it, but—" He let his words hang. "Luke, I don't know what to do." He didn't want to call the police and have Annie arrested, but this wasn't a chocolate bar, and Annie's mother wasn't going to march her down to Luke and Cindy's house and demand that Annie apologize and pay for it.

"Cindy and I will be there in ten minutes."

Brent turned back to Annie. He had a feeling this was going to be the longest ten minutes of his life.

Annie stared up at Brent. Even in her most frightening and

disconcerting nightmares, she'd never had a worse feeling of apprehension.

This wasn't just a movie or DVD that was easy to steal. Someone had hot-wired Cindy's car then broken into her garage to hide it. She'd never heard of a thief breaking into a house to *leave* something. That made it so much worse. The only reason the car was here was to hide it in a place no one would ever look.

Her mind raced, thinking of how the thief had gotten in. There was no visible damage to the lock or anywhere on the front door. She'd recently opened the patio door at the back to let in some fresh air, so she knew both the glass and the locks were intact. The garage door couldn't be opened without a remote or from the inside.

Either someone had come in through a window or had a key. Except the only people who had keys to the house were herself, her mother, her sister, and Cindy.

"I have to check the windows," she said to Brent. She ran into the house, running from window to window to check the locks.

Every lock was fastened and every pin was in place.

She froze, her heart stopped, and she couldn't breathe.

Someone had a key to her house.

And if that someone had come into the house once, he could come in again. He could come in while she slept and murder her in her own bed. She was alone in the house for a few days, and apparently someone knew it.

Her stomach roiled. "I'm not safe here," she said, her voice quivering. "I'll go stay at a friend's house, but I can't stay away forever. In the morning I'll call a locksmith and get all the locks changed."

"That sounds like a good idea." Brent stuck out his hand, palm upward, and his eyes locked on hers. "By the way, where's the car key?"

All she did was stare up at him. "I. . ." Her brain stalled. She had no idea where the keys were. "I don't know. Probably in Cindy's purse."

As if she'd conjured them up by thinking about them, Luke's car appeared down the block. As Luke pulled into the driveway, Brent walked into the garage, pushed a path to the car door, and looked in the car. "There's a key in the ignition."

Cindy got out of Luke's car before it had even come to a full stop and ran to the Mustang. While Cindy stood there, looking at her car, Luke approached Annie. "We're not going to call the police, but we want an explanation."

"I don't know how it got here." Tears burned her eyes. She turned to Cindy. "You've got to believe me. Why would I steal your car? It's not like I could drive it anywhere."

Cindy looked at her with an expression she couldn't read. "I don't know. I need time to think."

Luke and Brent cleared everything away from the car, and then Luke opened the door as much as he could and inched the car out of the garage.

Cindy's eyes turned red and became glassy. "We have

to go to the police station now and report that it's been recovered. We're going to apologize and tell them a family member borrowed it without permission. We've also got to contact the insurance people." Luke slid out of the Mustang and got back behind the wheel of his own car, while Cindy got into her car, adjusted the seat, and then put it into gear and started moving forward.

Annie bit her tongue and watched as both cars disappeared down the block.

Then she looked up at Brent.

She hadn't been able to read Cindy's expression, and she couldn't read Brent's either.

"Please tell me you believe me. I didn't steal it."

He wouldn't look at her. "I'll wait here while you pack a suitcase and call someone you can stay with."

All she could do was go inside and throw her pajamas and her toothbrush in a bag. She called the first person she could think of who would let her camp out on her couch, and then she got in her car and drove away with Brent standing in the driveway watching her.

Not that she thought she would sleep. She probably wouldn't sleep again until she found out who did this. And why.

Chapter 7

Brent stared at the computer monitor and ran his fingers through his hair for what felt like the tenth time. "I don't know what I'm doing wrong, but I can't find this invoice," he muttered to Luke, who hovered over him. "I know I entered it. We should call Annie over."

In unison, both Brent and Luke turned to look out the window, across the parking lot to Cindy's shop, where Annie sat working at her desk.

Luke frowned. "No. I'll call Walter."

Brent's heart sank as Luke picked up the phone.

He'd done a lot of thinking overnight—he'd hardly slept, with his brain firing in a million directions at once.

And he had come to the conclusion that Annie couldn't have stolen Cindy's car. First of all, stealing it would be stupid, as she'd said. It wasn't like she could drive it anywhere—everyone she knew would recognize it. She had no means to sell it—she didn't have those kind of connections, praise the Lord. Most of all, the look in her eyes when he'd asked for the keys told him she really didn't know where they were. Besides, she wouldn't have let him into the garage if she'd known it was there. Nor could she have lifted the heavy boxes that surrounded the car.

What really frightened him was that someone who was strong enough to lift those heavy boxes had had access to her house and garage. At least the locks had been changed. And the thief no longer had the key for the car. Brent had taken the key from the ignition when he saw Luke ready with his own keys, and then before he could offer the key to Cindy, she'd used a key on her keychain to start the car and go home. That meant both keys were accounted for, and a third key had been used to steal it—a key that Brent now had in his pocket.

Finding the origin of the third key would solve the mystery of who had driven the car into the garage, and the relation between that person and Annie would reveal why Annie was being set up.

He stared at the prompt box on the screen of the accounting program, stating that the information he was seeking could not be found. Whatever Annie had done to Walter's system was another mystery; they'd never had any trouble finding an invoice or lease agreement until Annie started working with the program.

Brent turned to Luke, who appeared to be listening to voice mail. Until now Brent had been the one hesitant about Annie, but now Luke showed a reluctance to trust her. It stung in a way Brent couldn't explain.

Luke hung up the phone. "Walter's not there. We'll have to call Annie."

Brent stood. "No. I'll talk to her first." He left without waiting for Luke's rebuttal.

Annie flinched when the bell tinkled.

The first thing he noticed were the dark circles under her eyes, similar to the ones he'd seen under his own that morning.

He cleared his throat. "We need to talk."

She glanced around, but Brent knew Cindy was in the shop with the mechanics.

"Sure."

"I'd like to contract your services today. It shouldn't take more than an hour, but of course I'll pay you for the required four. I'd prefer to talk to you in private, not here. Can you take a break? We're so close to the Space Needle, we can go to Seattle Center and have a coffee and a hot dog at the fountain."

Annie looked up at the clock then pressed one hand to her stomach. He suspected that, like him, she hadn't been in the mood for breakfast and was now feeling it.

"I don't really want a hot dog."

He forced himself to smile. "Breakfast burrito? We can pick up a couple on the way."

"I guess so. Let me tell Cindy I'm going out."

Annie walked into the shop, stopping at the yellow line.

He didn't hear what she said with the door between the office and the shop closed, but Cindy nodded.

"I need to be back to let Cindy go for lunch," she said as she retrieved her purse. On her way out the door, she rummaged through her pocket then popped a couple of what looked like antacid tabs into her mouth.

For the entire drive to the Seattle Center area, she kept her head turned toward the window, including when he picked up a couple of breakfast burritos at a drive-through. Likewise, she didn't say anything when he pulled into the parking lot, nor did she say anything as they headed toward the seating area around the International Fountain.

Brent cleared his throat. "I guess the first thing we should talk about is the car."

Her whole body stiffened and she missed a step. "I didn't steal it. I don't know how it got in my garage."

Clutching her purse to her chest like a shield, Annie came to a sudden halt. Her voice dropped to nearly a whisper. "Are you bringing me here away from everyone so you can tell me Luke and Cindy are going to have me arrested?"

"Luke never said anything about pressing charges." Although it had hit him hard when Luke suddenly preferred that Annie not do their accounting.

"If he does, I'll be thrown in jail. My fingerprints are all over the steering wheel and the dash and the glove box and everywhere. I even looked in the trunk and under the hood when I took it out for a drive the day before yesterday."

"But yours won't be the only prints on it." He hoped. At a minimum, Cindy's and Luke's prints would be on it. Come to think of it, his own prints would be on it, too.

Annie shook her head and clutched her purse tighter. "Don't you watch *CSI*? The crook probably wore gloves. This wasn't just taking a newspaper from someone's doorstep. This is grand theft auto."

This time Brent's smile was genuine. "I do watch *CSI*. All of them. It's shown me that no matter what precautions someone takes, there's always something to be found."

Annie blinked and her eyes welled up. "But they're not going to look that close. The car was found the next day, there's no damage, and no one was hurt. Without a dead body, there's no reason to call the FBI and have them take days to go through it and pick and test every hair or grain of dust. It was in my garage; I'm the only suspect." She swiped her arm across her eyes then clutched her purse again. "What if the only reason Cindy's not having me arrested is that I'm her stepsister?" She sniffled then swiped at her eyes again. "I'm sorry. Maybe we should go back."

He ran his hand over his pocket where he had the key, doubly glad he'd kept it. He hadn't thought about fingerprints until Annie mentioned it, but perhaps something could be proven. He'd learned from *CSI* that fingerprints on a stolen item didn't prove a person had stolen it, only that he'd touched it. But certainly it would mean something if Annie's prints weren't on the third key. That would mean she never used it, and that should point toward her innocence, even if just by omission.

"You should eat," he said. "We're almost there." With a gentle nudge he prompted her to continue walking toward the fountain.

They got a seat close enough to get misted by the water, which cooled him enough to help clear his thoughts. He'd never been involved in something so serious before, and he didn't know what to do. He only knew that he was holding a key piece of evidence. No pun intended.

He reached into the bag and gave her one of the burritos then opened his own and took a bite. He pressed his hand over his pocket. "I have the key that was used to steal the car."

Annie choked, coughed, gasped, and pressed one hand to her throat. "Why don't you turn it in to the police?"

"This isn't television; I don't know what they would do. Officially the car is no longer considered stolen because Cindy reported it returned. I don't know if they'd even want it now. To be honest, I'm not really sure what to do with it."

"It doesn't make sense to me why a thief wouldn't have taken the key with him."

"Probably because he didn't want to take the chance of being caught with the evidence. As well, leaving the key in the ignition makes it ready to go when he gets back." As the words came out of his mouth, Brent's stomach clenched. When the thief came back, he would get the car out the same way he got it in—by going first through Annie's house in order to get into the garage. Locks could be picked, and if not, then windows could be broken. He'd once seen a movie where a thief cut through a window and got in without actually breaking the glass, so there had been no sound.

Key or not, the thief could make a silent entry in the middle of the night when no one would be watching.

For at least the rest of the week, Annie was alone, unprotected.

"You can't stay at the house. The thief is going to come back for the car."

Annie shook her head. "I already thought of that. After I had all the locks changed, I put signs on all the doors and windows and the garage saying the police found the car and it's gone."

He pinched the bridge of his nose. "And you think he'll just go away?"

"He has to. There's no more reason for him to be there. Whoever did this will see the signs and leave."

Brent couldn't see the thief disappearing quietly in the night. His mind bounced to the skewed thinking of the villain in the last book he'd read, a mystery by T. J. Zereth. All he could see was Annie being the victim of the thief's anger for foiling what could have been a perfect crime. "I don't think so."

Annie stood. "I do. I also think it's time for me to get back to work."

Brent stood as well. This hadn't helped him feel better

about things—everything felt worse. "This wasn't the real reason I wanted to talk. I wanted to talk about why you've been having such trouble with our accounting program."

"I don't know why. I know that software, but it's not working how I was taught."

He waited for her to say more but she didn't. Instead she gathered the wrappers, walked to the nearest garbage container, stuffed them in, and returned to the parking lot.

Brent hurried to catch up to her. "I guess that discussion is over."

"I guess it is."

They made it back to his office in what he considered record time, and Annie seated herself at Walter's desk.

Standing behind her, he watched in silence while Annie struggled to find his missing invoice but couldn't.

She pushed the chair back and looked up at him. "I really have to get back so Cindy can have her lunch. Just reenter your invoice, and I'll try to figure it out tomorrow."

He experienced some degree of relief that she promised to come back tomorrow, but that didn't help his fears for tonight. He pictured Annie alone and stalked by an enraged thief.

Brent rammed his hands into his pockets. "I don't like you being alone at the house tonight. I think you should have someone stay with you."

"None of my friends can stay the night, and I won't ask them to. Everyone has to go to work in the morning."

He sucked in a deep breath as she opened the door to leave. "Then what about me?"

She froze in her tracks and spun around. "You? Stay at my house?"

"Yeah. With Cindy gone, you have an extra room."

"Absolutely not."

Before he could respond, she was gone.

Being reasonably intelligent, he didn't approach her again for the rest of the day, but he watched her as much as he could through the window, across the parking lot. After she left he finished his tasks, went home, and packed what he would need.

By his usual bedtime, he was where he wanted to be—on Annie's front lawn.

He had just tucked the flexible support poles into their slots when Annie's front door opened.

She stood in the doorway wearing a ratty T-shirt and baggy sweatpants that had seen better days. She stared at his tent, firmly set in the corner of her yard behind the bushes then back to him. "What is that?"

He shrugged his shoulders. "It's a one-man tent. Can't you tell?"

"I can tell. What I should have asked is, what is it doing here?"

"I'm spending the night. So I can keep an eye on things." As he spoke he strolled to her garage and straightened the sign she'd taped to the door, advising the thief that the car was already gone.

"Are you crazy? What will the neighbors think?"

He pressed his hands over his heart and dropped to one knee. "That I'm a scorned lover, pining for a glimpse of you at the golden first light of morning."

Annie lowered her head and pinched the bridge of her nose. "Or a demented homeless person. Brent, go home. I give up. I'll call someone who can spend the night with me."

Brent pointed to his wristwatch. "Too late. Your friends are probably in bed by now." Even though he'd wanted someone to spend the night with her, the more he'd thought about it, if the thief was good at picking locks in silence, Annie and her friend would sleep through it. Both women would be mugged in the middle of the night, helpless against an armed robber. It was better for Brent to be where he could catch the thief before the break-in happened. He was a light sleeper, especially on the thin sleeping bag versus his comfortable bed. Also, here he would have the element of surprise.

So he didn't have to shout, he approached Annie to talk to her on the porch. "This will be just like camping, except I don't have to pay for a site and there won't be any raccoons."

Her mouth opened but no words came out.

He smiled. She was weakening.

"So it's settled. Sweet dreams." He jogged to his tent, crawled inside, and pulled up the zipper before she could protest.

The sleeping bag was almost unrolled when he heard tapping on the tent.

He unzipped the door just wide enough for a peek.

Annie's hand, holding a key, poked through. "If you insist on doing this, here's my house key so you can use the bathroom and the shower after I leave in the morning. Lock up before you leave. Good night."

Chapter 8

Annie cringed, feeling his pain, as behind her Brent pressed his fist into the small of his back and groaned softly.

She squeezed her eyes shut, blanking out Walter's computer and the mess of the accounting program, replacing it with the image of Brent's tent hidden behind the bushes in her front yard.

Brent's presence in her yard all night had made her realize the potential for danger was real. At first she'd simply double-checked all the locks in the windows accessible from the ground. Since Brent was so concerned, she'd put a board in every window, including the second floor and the patio door. Then she'd tucked a fishhook next to every lock that could be reached through a broken window and attached a Christmas bell to every window so if the window was moved, the bell would ring and wake her up. She'd even scattered marbles on the floor beneath each window, in case a thief did manage to get in.

The only possible entrance she'd been unable to booby-trap was the front door. And that hadn't mattered because Brent wasn't far away.

She'd slept like a baby, comfortable and secure in her soft, warm bed, while Brent had slept outside on the cold, hard ground.

Before she left for work she'd made coffee and muffins for Brent's stomach, but there was nothing she could do for his back.

Brent stepped forward and rested one hand on top of the monitor. "Have you found my missing invoice yet?"

Annie shook her head. "No. I also can't find a few adjustments that I made for journal entries either."

Luke appeared behind Brent. "Walter's done our accounting since we started our business. He's never had trouble."

She gritted her teeth. She was starting to question Walter's methods, but she couldn't find anything specific that was wrong. All she could do was open a different customer file and continue her search for the invoice that she knew was there but couldn't find. Then her cell phone beeped with a text message.

As soon as Luke and Brent were occupied elsewhere, she grabbed her phone to read the message. Zella's reply confirmed what she already knew. Zella had never given a house key to anyone. The only extra house key was one their mother had made and left with their neighbor in case of an emergency.

This evening she would visit their neighbor, but for now her priority was finding Brent's missing invoice.

After painstakingly searching every customer file, she found nothing.

Brent returned from dealing with his customer. "Did you find it?"

Rubbing her tired eyes, she sighed. "No. The only thing that could have happened is that you accidentally deleted it."

"That's not possible. There are no numbers missing in the sequence."

Luke tapped his fingers on the back of the chair. "We'll just wait for Walter to come back. Thanks for your time, Annie. We'll call if we need you again."

Annie had never felt so dismissed. She left quickly and returned to finish up her work for Cindy.

She hoped Cindy still wanted her around.

Brent started to count to ten but only made it to seven.

He turned to Luke, reminding himself that Luke had been his best friend since high school. "How could you do that? You pretty much just fired her."

Luke waved one hand in the air. "You saw it for yourself. She can't do it. Not only is she not able to balance, she can't work the program."

"Neither can either of us."

"Neither of us are accountants."

Brent pointed toward the computer. "You don't have to be an accountant to do basic data entry on a system like this. It's designed to be user friendly for idiots like us."

Luke frowned. "Us *idiots* never had any trouble with it until Annie came along to help. Since then, nothing has worked right. I hope it doesn't take Walter too long to fix whatever Annie has done."

Mentally, Brent began a list of the things that had gone wrong. While what Luke had said was true, some of the things that had gone wrong hadn't been touched by Annie until after he or Luke discovered they didn't work. "What if this is a software issue? We haven't gotten an upgrade since we bought the program. If the problem is caused by an incompatibility with old software and a new operating system, then you've accused Annie for nothing. What if Walter has been having the same trouble?"

"Walter would have told us."

Somehow Brent wasn't as sure as Luke. "I don't think so. I'm going to go talk to Annie."

Brent dug in the bottom drawer until he found the CD of the program disc. As he walked toward the door, Annie's car drove out of the parking lot.

Instead of going to Cindy's shop, he called Cindy on his cell. "Why did Annie leave?" he asked, raising his voice over the background noise of power tools.

"I don't know. She said she had something to do at home. I don't know when she's coming back, or even if she is coming back."

Brent sucked in a deep breath. He didn't want Annie to go home alone. He'd planned on accompanying her to check out the house before she went in. Just because it was daylight didn't mean her house was safe. The way he figured it, the thief had put the car in the garage during the daytime while she was at work none the wiser. So he could be there right now—angry that the car was gone.

"Thanks." He snapped his phone shut and turned to Luke. "There's something I have to do. I don't know when I'll be back."

Because of the rising panic, it felt like he caught every light red on his way to Annie's house. When he arrived he found her car parked in the driveway, but the tightness in his gut intensified when she didn't answer the door. The sign still taped to the garage door that the Mustang was no longer there didn't calm him.

He was ready to kick the door down when he heard Annie's voice in the distance. Following the sound, he saw her next door, talking to her neighbor.

Knowing she was safe, he sank down on the porch step to wait for her.

She started walking home, and as soon as she saw him, her pace quickened.

He didn't want to admit how worried he was, so he pushed himself up and stood slowly, trying to appear casual as she approached. "What were you doing next door?"

She held up a key. "I asked Nadine for our house key back.

I told her I changed the locks. She usually has it hanging on a hook by the door, but it had fallen down under the table. We found it, but it was covered in dust and obviously hadn't been used for years. This is the only spare key there is, so I'm right back to square one."

Instead of making him feel better, the confirmation that the only known spare key hadn't been used made him feel worse. "The reason I came is because I wanted to talk to you about something."

"You couldn't have phoned?"

"No, I have to show it to you. I need to ask you some computer-related stuff."

"I'm no expert. I really don't know much about computers."

He waited behind her as she unlocked the door then followed her in.

"I was wondering if part of the reason we've been having trouble is because of our old program and our new computer." He held up the program disc. "I wondered if you know someone who knows more about it."

"I might. Let me put the disc into my computer so I can get the dates and version number." As she accepted it, a smile broke out across her face. "Wait. I have a better idea. My mother has a really old computer. She says it works fine and has no need to upgrade it. Let's install it there and see if it works any differently. I even have all your data with me."

Brent sucked in a deep breath. "What do you mean?"

"I do a backup every week out of habit. I did one from

your system a few days ago, so it's even fairly current. Let's see if this works."

Patience was not a virtue of Brent's; it seemed like forever while they waited first for the ancient computer to boot up and then through the grueling amount of time it took to install the program. Finally when everything was loaded, Annie called up the file. "Here we go. Let's see the most recent invoices entered." She hit the button and recalled the last number used.

"That's my missing invoice."

Annie hit a few more keys, and a stream of numbers appeared. "Here's my missing journal entry." She sighed. "That means this is good news and bad news. It appears that the problems have been compatibility issues all along. So that's good news. But the bad news is that you have to buy the upgrade and hope that no data has been compromised. That doesn't really make sense to me, but we have the proof right here."

Brent tried to be happy, but all he could see was a lot of extra work, and expense, to get all the data fixed.

Annie stood. "If you don't mind, I have to get back to the office. There's still a few things I need to do."

Brent followed her out, then waited in his car while she locked up. He followed her back to the parking lot, but when she went back inside the muffler shop, instead of going back to check on Luke, Brent followed Annie.

Cindy stood at the counter, writing in the appointment

book. "Annie, what are you doing back? I didn't really expect you."

"I have a couple of things I wanted to finish up." She headed back to her desk, but didn't sit down. "My computer's turned off."

Cindy nodded. "I needed to put in a special order, so I shut down what you were doing and used your computer since it was already on, then I guess I automatically turned it off. I don't mind if you go home and finish what you were doing tomorrow." Without waiting for a response, Cindy turned and went into the shop.

When the door closed behind her, Brent saw it as an opportunity. "I think we have a lot to do tomorrow to re-enter the missing data, so let's take advantage of this as a break before the grueling work begins. Let me take you out for dinner."

"Dinner? But—"

"No buts. Let's reward ourselves for solving the problem." Brent held his breath.

Annie sighed. "Okay. Let's go."

He turned and stared walking toward the door with his back to her, so she wouldn't see him smile. "We'll take my car."

Chapter 9

Annie fiddled with her napkin, folded it neatly beside the water glass, straightened the cutlery, and then picked up the water glass, shaking it a little to see if she could get the ice cubes to settle.

Anything to have something to do with her hands.

She listened woodenly when the waiter came to announce the special of the day and give them the menus.

She held hers up between them like a shield. Although she didn't know why. Since Cindy and Luke's wedding, she'd seen Brent nearly every day. Today was no different than any other day.

Except for the romantic music strumming in the background. And the flickering candles in the muted light. And the aroma of sizzling steaks and good food that could never be duplicated by a toss-in-the-oven lasagna. And the fact that someone else was going to do the dishes.

Not to mention that she was sitting across the table from a tall, dark, handsome man.

Annie shook her head behind the menu. That wasn't a thought she wanted to have about Brent. She wanted to work for him, not have his children.

She thunked her head to the table.

"Annie? Are you okay?"

No, she wasn't. She bolted upright. "Sure. Fine. I'm fine. Very fine. Couldn't be finer."

Long fingers wrapped over the top of her menu and gently lowered it down until all she could see were Brent's deep-brown eyes melting into her soul.

"Are you sure?"

She cleared her throat. "No, I'm not sure. I don't know why you'd want to celebrate that you have to spend hundreds of dollars for an update to your accounting program, or that you'll probably have to reenter the last week's worth of data. Or..."

His voice deepened. "Or?"

She gulped. "Or why you'd want to celebrate in a place like this." At her words, she ducked her head then jerked it a little to the right, pointing his attention to the couple in the booth beside them who were doing more smooching than eating.

"Because this place was highly recommended."

She didn't want to ask if whoever had recommended it happened to mention it wasn't a place to eat and run. This was a romantic hideaway.

Although, from the look of Brent sitting back in his

chair, casually sipping his coffee and reading the description of every item on the menu, he didn't appear to be in much of a hurry.

"Don't you have to get back to work?"

"I texted Luke. I told him we were having a meeting and to cover for me. I'll do extra hours for him next time he wants some time off."

Annie scanned the area. It was rather early for suppertime, and while there were enough people there, none of the other couples were conducting business. At least not the corporate kind.

"Relax." Brent smiled. "I just thought we could talk and get to know each other better."

The waiter returned to take their orders, sparing her an immediate need to reply.

But when he left, Brent leaned forward, clasped his hands together, and rested them on the table. "So tell me about yourself. Something I don't already know. Who's your favorite author?"

She let out the breath she hadn't realized she'd been holding. This one was easy. She smiled. "T. J. Zereth."

His smile faltered. "Really? I would never have pegged you for a murder mystery reader."

Annie's smile widened. "But he's so great. There's always a mini-mystery within the big mystery, and it just keeps you hooked until the last page. Zella and I always fight over his new releases, about who gets to read it first. The last one, neither of us could wait, so we both bought a copy."

"Yeah, I enjoyed the last one, too. Any idea when his next one comes out?"

She didn't know, but they found plenty to discuss about the last book, barely pausing when the waiter arrived with their meals. While they ate, Annie learned as much about Brent as he learned about her, and she found it very interesting that they enjoyed many of the same movies and television shows.

She wanted the evening to last forever, except the staff was starting to give them not-so-subtle hints that they wanted to seat others at their table.

Brent's cheeks darkened when he glanced at his watch. It wasn't often she'd seen a man blush, and Annie found the trait quite endearing. Despite the fact that the night hadn't been a date, she couldn't remember the last time she'd enjoyed herself so much in a man's company.

What made the evening even less like a date was when instead of driving her home, he drove her back to Mufford Brake and Muffler so she could pick up her car and drive herself home. To her surprise, when she got out of his car, he turned it off and stood beside her while she fished in her purse for her keys in the otherwise empty lot.

"You don't need to watch me get in the car. I do this every night," she said as she flicked through her key ring for her car key and inserted it in the lock. "I hope you're not going to follow me home and spend another night sleeping in my front yard. I'll be fine. I've booby-trapped every window, including the patio door, with a board, fishhooks, and marbles. I also have my cell phone fully charged and I'm going to sleep with it in the pocket of my pajamas, besides having the house phone beside the bed in easy reach. You don't have to follow me home. I'll be fine."

He broke out into a wide grin. "Fishhooks and marbles? That's pretty creative. I'm impressed. However, that's not the reason I'm walking you to the car and waiting for you to get in safely. What I'm really doing is waiting to ask if you would like to accompany me to church on Sunday."

She pulled the door open but didn't get in. "Church?" If he'd asked her for a real date, she didn't know what she would have done. Church she could handle. Annie flicked her hand in the air in her best imitation of a Southern belle, even though she'd never been farther east than Arizona. "Why, sir,"—she attempted to mimic a sweet Southern drawl—"are y'all askin' me for a date?"

Brent shuffled closer. Almost in slow motion, his hands raised until he rested them on her shoulders. "No. This was a date. And now it's over, so I'm going to say good night."

Annie's heart pounded. This hadn't been a date. This had been. . . What had it been? They'd talked, they'd had fun, they'd shared some laughs, and she'd had a good time. He'd even insisted on paying for her meal.

She didn't know what to think. Unlike Luke, Brent trusted her accounting skills, and he was the only one who truly believed she didn't steal Cindy's car. Setting up his tent for the night to watch for her safety had been valiant, even if it was over the top.

Still, she appreciated his concerns for her safety. Brent was a nice man, and she couldn't help but like him.

All thoughts disintegrated as she felt either Brent's thumb or a finger under her chin, nudging it up. "Good night, Annie," he muttered, and his lips covered hers. Not a peck. A real kiss. Like the kind that ended a real date. Tender, gentle, but insistent. Like he meant it.

His hands drifted down to her back, pressing her closer. Her brain turned to mush as she slid her hands around his waist and kissed him back, sinking into the heat of his kiss and the warmth of his embrace.

The blare of a horn from a car driving by jolted them apart, making her realize what they'd been doing—in the middle of the parking lot, no less.

Before he could say anything, she got into her car and yanked the door shut. She didn't look up at him as she inserted the key in the ignition and drove off without giving the engine any time to warm up.

She didn't want to think about what had just happened.

But she knew she was going to anyway.

Chapter 10

Brent picked up the wastebasket under Luke's desk and dumped the contents into the green garbage bag then walked to his own desk to do the same.

He didn't mind working every second Saturday; he loved his job. But as a co-owner, regardless of the number of employees, his joy didn't extend to cleaning the office. He didn't mind wearing his jeans to work and washing cars, but he drew the line at washing the floor.

Although, one day when he became a parent, he knew he would appreciate it if his son's boss gave him a day off to be with his family for a special day.

Brent had made a joint decision with Luke to cancel the contract with the janitorial service and give Evan the job of cleaning the office on Saturdays for extra money. It had been a good financial decision as well, because paying Evan by the hour was cheaper than paying a flat fee to the cleaning service. It was even cheaper on days Evan wasn't working, because both he and Luke had to do it for free. Like today.

While he was taking out the garbage, he wondered what Annie was doing.

Thinking of her, he looked into the parking lot, empty except for his own car.

He couldn't believe he'd kissed her in the parking lot. Yet at the same time, he couldn't have *not* kissed her.

His eyes drifted shut as he emptied Walter's wastebasket. She was a good kisser. He felt the warm fuzzies wash over him as if he were a teenager, making him want to kiss her again. He would see her again tomorrow, only this time he wouldn't kiss her in the church parking lot. He'd wait until he took her home. After he took her out for lunch.

The rustle of papers made him look at the floor. If he hadn't been holding the garbage bag in one hand and a wastebasket in the other, he would have smacked himself in the head. He'd been so lost daydreaming, he'd missed the garbage bag and dumped Walter's trash on the floor.

He hunkered down to gather the strewn papers, frowning that most of the things in Walter's wastebasket should have been put through the shredder.

He picked up a couple of second pages of invoices that were blank except for the customer's name and address and the total invoice amount. For this, he would have to speak to Walter. He shook his head as he picked up a receipt. After scanning receipts, the originals were supposed to go into a box to be stored for whatever length of time the IRS required. Brent stood and laid the paper on the desk to smooth it out then froze.

This was a receipt from the hardware store—for two keys.

He sank down into the chair to press it flat with his fingers to make out the date.

It was the last day that Walter had been in. The day before Cindy's car had gone missing.

Events of the morning flashed through his mind. It was the day he'd first introduced Annie to Walter. Walter had not been very pleased that they'd gotten him help. Then later in the morning, Walter had left to pick up a prescription. Brent only remembered because he'd been annoyed that Walter had stuck a sticky note on the monitor, and Brent had thought it wouldn't be good for the screen.

Sure enough, the crumpled sticky note was also in the pile of paper on the floor.

Brent didn't remember the time, only that it was later in the morning. The time on the receipt for the key appeared to be in that time frame.

His temples throbbed as he tried to recall everything that happened. Luke had been out on a sales call, and Brent had teased Luke about taking Cindy's new car. Then Evan had called both him and Luke into the lot to check a dented car, and Annie had gone back to help Cindy with something.

Walter had been alone in the office, giving him access to both Annie's and Luke's keys.

But there was no reason for Walter to steal a car. Walter

wasn't a thief. He was a CPA and made a good income. Brent didn't know how many other businesses besides theirs Walter handled, but he knew Walter's schedule was very busy.

It also made no sense that he would hide a stolen car in Annie's garage. Walter didn't know Annie. Although, since they used Annie's services, her address was listed in their account files as a vendor.

Brent flopped back in the chair and pressed his hands over his eyes. He was only letting his mind play tricks on him because he was desperate to prove that the thief wasn't Annie. It wasn't possible or likely that Walter would steal Luke's wife's car. He wouldn't call Walter a friend, but he was certainly more than an acquaintance. He'd been with them, and well paid by them, since they started the business when Luke and Brent graduated together from business college.

But among the many things he'd learned over the years was never to assume and to be careful to whom he gave his trust.

He scooped the rest of the papers from the floor and sorted them like Walter should have, either into the shredder, the receipt box, or what was really trash, but he put the receipt for the keys in his pocket.

Before he saw Walter again on Tuesday, he needed some answers.

Even though he took the later shift, Brent arrived at the

office at opening time, the same time as Luke.

He stood behind Luke while Luke unlocked the building and punched in the alarm code. "I've called Annie in this morning. I don't care if you fired her. I unfired her."

Luke spun around. "You, of all people, should know the reasons for that. Even if she didn't steal Cindy's car, which in my opinion is still not resolved, she's messing up our accounting. Walter only has limited time to fix it, and it's time to wrap up the fiscal year and submit everything for taxes."

Brent's stomach clenched as he pulled the receipt for the keys out of his pocket and handed it to Luke. "One issue at a time. I found this in Walter's garbage. It's a receipt for two keys. Annie and I went to the key kiosk yesterday after church. I showed the man Walter's picture and the receipt, and he remembered the keys because he had a hard time with the Mustang key, and Walter was in a hurry."

"Are you saying that Walter stole Cindy's car and then hid it in Annie's garage?"

"That's what it looks like."

Brent could see Luke's confusion as he tried to make sense of what he'd just been told. He didn't want to believe it either, but the facts were there. And as horrible as it was, it was what he wanted to be true, to prove Annie's innocence.

"I know it doesn't make any sense, but I have proof he copied both keys, and he was back with the originals before anyone noticed they were missing." Now more than ever, he was glad he had the key. If it had Walter's fingerprints on it, it wouldn't necessarily prove Walter's guilt in the eyes of the law, but it would in Luke's and Cindy's eyes, and right now that was what mattered the most.

At the sound of a car entering the parking lot, both men turned to watch Annie's car back into the parking spot nearest the door.

"I asked her to give me ten minutes to talk to you before she got here."

Luke swiped his fingers through his hair. "With Annie being Cindy's stepsister, I'm trying to be gracious. But I still don't feel good about having Annie come back. Everything is messed up enough without making it even worse."

Brent steeled himself. "The mess isn't Annie's fault. We've figured out that the reason for the computer problems is a software issue. She made a backup file, I had the backup program disc, and we opened it on her mother's computer. Everything worked so I've asked her to check it against the current file on our office computer. If we find our missing data, then the simple solution is to buy a program upgrade."

Luke shook his head. "It can't possibly be that simple."

Brent could only hope that what worked in theory would work in fact. "It can. She's bringing her mother's computer in with her today because we know it works."

"You're sure about this?"

Annie cut the engine and opened her door. "As sure as I can be. Help me carry in the old computer and we'll know for sure."

Luke's face tightened. "Be warned. I intend to watch everything she does. Like a hawk."

Brent had to agree. If the situations were reversed, he would have felt the same way. He sent up a prayer that he was right and pushed the door open. "I wouldn't have it any other way. The sooner we get started, the better."

Chapter 11

Annie had never felt the burn from someone's glare like she did from Luke as the men exited the building. The lack of trust stabbed into her heart, yet she could understand it. Until a few months ago, she hadn't been a good person in his eyes. She had a lot of wrongs to right, and she was doing her best, but it was going to take time.

Still, she felt like a puppy dog abandoned in the rain—and it must have shown because Luke's expression softened, and he dragged one hand down his face.

"I'm sorry," he muttered from behind his hand. "Brent just showed me some evidence that links Walter to stealing Cindy's car." He reached into her backseat for her mother's huge old monitor, while Brent opened the other door to get the tower. "The reason we hired Walter is because he's my uncle's friend, and my uncle recommended him. I can't believe he'd do such a thing. Not that I want to believe you would have done it either. It's been tough for everyone."

She wanted to feel better about Luke's apology, but she couldn't help but notice the omission of the mention of her struggles with their accounting work.

With his head stuck into the car, Brent hadn't been able to hear a word his friend had said, nor could he say anything in her defense. Annie hadn't realized until that moment how much knowing that Brent was on her side meant; Luke was not only Brent's business partner but his best friend.

Letting Luke go inside first with the big monitor, Brent followed carrying the tower, and she went inside last with the keyboard and mouse.

Even the fragrant aroma of fresh coffee as she walked inside didn't defrost the cold in her heart. She wondered if she'd ever make Luke believe in her again.

Behind her the coffee machine beeped to signal the end of the brewing cycle as they started setting up her mother's computer.

"Coffee. . . ," Luke and Brent mumbled in unison.

Annie nodded. Maybe a cup of coffee would give her brain a kick start. She couldn't remember the last time she'd had a good night's sleep.

Brent stopped to attend to a customer who came in for a prebooked rental, so Luke crawled under the desk to finish plugging in the computer cables. Annie poured three cups of coffee, needing to do something with her hands before the nervousness made her crazy. By the time Brent was done, both computers were booted up and ready to go. She pulled her flash drive out of her purse and was ready to insert it into the USB slot when her mother's monitor went purple then black.

Brent raised one hand to the back of his neck, and Luke leaned his forehead against the wall.

"Wait," Annie said. "It's nothing. It's just a loose connection. I only have to wiggle it, and it will be fine."

She leaned over the back and around her mother's monitor but couldn't reach properly because of its size and the awkward angle. Squeezing her lips together, she stuck her tongue out of the corner of her mouth and reached a little farther. She'd almost wiggled it into place when she felt her feet start to slip on the tile floor. A flash of stars blinked across the back of her eyes when her hip banged down into the corner of the desk. To prevent herself from knocking herself out on the desk, she dropped her flash drive and grabbed the desk with both hands.

Brent ran to her, wrapping his hands around her waist to steady her as she righted herself and stood. "Are you okay?"

As she gazed up into his eyes, the pain flitted to the back of her mind. She should have been thinking about the computer, but all she wanted to do was kiss Brent. With all the lights on.

Behind them Luke cleared his throat.

Brent's hands fell to his sides, so she turned and reached to the desktop for her flash drive, but it was gone. Her breath caught at the sight of coffee splashes on the desk beside her cup.

"No. . . ," she muttered. Her stomach dropped into her shoes as she picked up a pen and poked into the coffee. Sure enough, she felt the lump of her now-ruined flash drive at the bottom.

"Have you got anything on there that doesn't have another backup?"

She shook her head. "No, but this was brand new."

Brent checked his wristwatch. "The office supply store at the mall won't open for two more hours."

She reached for her purse. "It's okay, I still have my old flash drive. It doesn't have as much memory, but it's fine for what we need."

His head tilted to one side. "You need two flash drives?"

"I have lots of photos," she mumbled then inserted her old flash drive into Walter's computer. "I'll recopy the file I need and we'll be fine. I just have to find what folder it's in. When I saved it a few days ago I did it as I shut the program down and saved it to the E drive, but there has to be a folder for backups here somewhere. I'll just do a search on the same document type."

The results netted a few obvious backups with varying dates, but a large file caught her attention. "I think I found it, but there's another one named with a number that has a file creation date of just a few days ago. The file is huge. I'm going to see if this is better."

After copying and transferring both files, she opened the larger one and immediately found Brent's invoice. "Here it is. Everything is fine."

"No, that's the wrong amount." Brent leaned closer. "It's the right date and customer, but the amount is wrong."

"Let me check the other file." She closed the numbered file, opened the properly named one, and pulled up the invoice in question. "Here it is. The amount is different."

Luke stepped closer and also leaned down for a better look. "How can that be?"

Her mind ran a million miles an hour in circles, as she hoped what she thought wasn't true.

She opened the main file on Walter's computer then opened a summary from a few months ago from the numbered backup. "The two profit-and-loss summaries for the same month are different in these versions. The difference is over a thousand dollars." After pointing to the differences, she opened the previous month on both versions and found the same discrepancies.

Her stomach began to churn. "I need to do some more checking."

While both men watched, she pulled up files from the previous tax year. As she saw more discrepancies, the tension in the room grew palpable. As if he were reading her mind, Brent laid his hands on her shoulders and pressed his thumbs into the knots in her back.

Whenever a customer came in, Brent left to look after them, leaving Luke to watch her.

After more checking, when Brent had once again

returned, she sucked in a deep breath to say what she had to say. She didn't want to, but she had no choice. "It's the same thing. The profits are lower in the numbered file. In both versions the money going in is the same, but in the file that was hidden, more came out."

Brent pulled his chair closer and sank into it. "If you're saying what I think you're saying, then this is. . ." His voice trailed off.

Behind them Luke remained silent.

"Embezzlement," Annie choked out. "The version here"— she pointed to the backup she'd opened on her mother's computer—"is the working version that everyone would see. The one with the number, the hidden one"—she pointed to Walter's computer—"looks like this is the one submitted to the government." She hit a few more buttons. "This one shows a lot of money being paid to a holding company." She didn't have to look hard to confirm that the holding company had a fictitious address and contact information and was paid in cash. "It's all untraceable, but the debits and credits are all done so it looks legitimate on the surface."

"How much money is gone?"

"From what I've seen, it's approximately the same every month, which would make it look like a recurring expense. It looks like twelve to fifteen thousand dollars a year."

Luke shook his head. "Embezzlement means jail. While that's a tidy sum, it doesn't seem enough to justify taking the risk of being caught."

"Maybe it is," Brent said. "What if he's doing the same to every place he works at? He's here only half a day, twice a week. He does work for over a dozen businesses regularly, plus he wraps monthly for more. If he's getting away with the same thing everywhere, that's potentially"—he paused while he did the mental math—"a quarter of a million dollars a year that he could be skimming. Plus the car. But that doesn't make sense. The car is so traceable, and the police look for a stolen car."

Annie straightened in her chair. "I think that's exactly why he stole it. Neither of you suspected anything was wrong. But an outsider who's an accountant would look at things differently and see inconsistencies. What happened until now when things didn't balance?"

Luke sighed. "Walter always fixed it."

"Yeah," Brent muttered. "Did he ever fix it. We trusted him. Every time, he kept right on without missing a beat, and we were none the wiser."

Annie glanced at the monitor as the screen saver came on. "But when I started making corrections and adjustments, he knew it wouldn't be long before I figured it out. I think he stole the car and put it in my garage to get me out of the way."

One corner of Brent's mouth twisted. "But it was found the same day, and we didn't have you arrested. That's got to be hitting the panic button for him right now."

Both men stood then nodded at each other.

Annie stood as well. "What are you going to do?"

Brent rested one hand on her arm. "We have to call the police and go talk to him." He turned to Luke. "Who's going to stay to take care of things here? We've got a business to run."

Luke ran his fingers through his already messy hair. "I'll go. He was a friend of my uncle before he died. I'm the one who should confront him."

Using the business line, Luke called the police. At the same time Brent used his cell phone to call the bank to freeze their account, even though Annie suspected that Walter probably had never forged a check. It was cleaner to dip into the cash and change invoices and expenses to make everything balance.

Before Luke left, he approached her. He rammed his hands into his pockets and made direct eye contact while he spoke. "I don't know what to say. I'm really sorry. I should have believed Cindy and trusted you. I have to go. The police are going to meet me at Walter's office in ten minutes."

She could tell his regret was sincere—there was no question about forgiving him. As he left, Annie wondered if Cindy's trust had slipped a bit as well. Annie wouldn't blame her if it had.

The only one who had trusted her while her life was turning upside down was Brent, who clearly had a thing for her, but she couldn't return his affections because to do so would have cast doubt on him as well. But now she could.

She turned to face him.

He smiled down at her with stars in his eyes.

It made her feel like a giddy teenager.

She raised her arms and slid her hands around his back. "Thanks for being the only one who supported me."

Brent's smile grew, and he rested his hands on her hips. "I knew you didn't do anything wrong."

Her heart fluttered, knowing he was going to kiss her.

His eyes closed and his head began to lower.

The buzzer signaled a customer walking in.

Brent released her, stepped back, and cleared his throat. "Hold that thought. I'll be right back."

She did indeed hold that thought, trying not to grow impatient while Brent dealt with his customer.

The second the man left Brent returned, wasting no time putting his arms around her.

"Where were we?" he asked, grinning.

She shuffled closer to him. "I think you were going to—"

The phone rang.

Brent raised one finger in the air and ran to answer it. After his initial greeting, he only listened and nodded a few times then hung up.

"That was Luke. When he got to Walter's office with the police, his boss said Walter had e-mailed this morning to say he was sick and wouldn't be in. They're on their way to Walter's house. Now where were we?"

Annie smiled. "We were—"

The buzzer signaled another person coming in the door.

Brent literally groaned. "I'll be quick. I promise."

This time Annie made a fresh pot of coffee and poured herself a cup since she'd only had one sip of the first one.

She'd drunk half before Brent's customer left with his rental car.

Again, Brent wasted no time in putting his arms around her, only this time he pulled her close, pressing them together from nose to knees. "I think—"

Brent's cell phone buzzed inside his pocket.

It was odd feeling someone else's phone.

She backed up so Brent could pull the phone out of his pocket. Again he listened, nodding to a one-sided conversation, then flipped his phone closed.

"That was Luke. Walter's gone. Looking through the windows, it appears he left in a hurry. The police say he probably left the country. They're getting a warrant now to search the house, and Luke said they're going to check Walter's bank records. If he's left the country, there's nothing we can do but count our losses and go forward."

All thoughts of romance dissolved. "I'm so sorry. I don't know what to say."

"There's nothing to say. Even though this is going to be a mess, at least we've put a stop to it. Now, where were we?"

He extended his hands forward, but Annie raised her palms and backed up a step. "Forget it. I see someone coming."

Sure enough, the buzzer sounded, and this time two people walked in.

"Let's take a rain check until later," she said.

Brent grumbled, and he certainly wasn't his cheery self until Luke returned.

"Excuse us," he said to Luke as he wrapped one arm around her, "we're taking a rain check." Not giving her time to protest, he led her into the private office and shut the door.

Before she could say anything, Brent wrapped his arms around her and kissed her so hard and fast she was sure her toes curled. His lips left hers only long enough to whisper "I love you," and he kissed her again.

"I love you, too," she whispered back with all the love in her heart.

"Will you marry me?"

Annie froze. "What did you—"

A knock echoed through the door. "Sorry to interrupt, Brent," Luke called through the door, "but you've got to come out. The police are here. We've also got a lineup of people waiting." In addition to muffled voices came the echo of the ringing phone.

Brent sighed. "I don't believe this."

"Don't worry. I know you're busy." Without giving him a chance to respond, Annie dashed out the door and ran to Cindy's shop.

Numbly, she turned on her computer and got to work, but she couldn't concentrate on the numbers. Only Brent.

She loved him from the depths of her soul, but in the short time she'd known him, she didn't know if it was enough.

It had taken her three years to decide on her career—was it possible to decide on the lifelong relationship of marriage in a few weeks?

Instead of working, she walked to the window and stood to watch him. She ran through a mental list of all his qualities, and even though she was sure he had a few bad ones, she loved him anyway.

Which gave her the answer she needed.

When the police had gone and there were no more customers in their office, at least for the next few minutes, Annie jogged across the parking lot to Brent and Luke's office.

Luke pointed to the back lot, where she found Brent inspecting a scratch on a returned car.

She approached him and tapped him on the shoulder. "Now where were we?" she asked.

He spun around so fast one of the papers flew off his clipboard.

She grinned. "Because I was about to say yes, I'll marry you."

He embraced her, holding her snugly to his chest. "I'm glad you said that, because I was ready to pitch my tent in your front yard again."

Annie squeezed him and sighed. "Please don't do that. My neighbors already think you're crazy."

"But I am crazy. Crazy about you."

She sighed. Annie always thought happily-ever-afters

were only for fairy tales, but for her, it had really happened.

Even though Brent only had a tent and not a castle, he was her prince, and he always would be.

TILL DEATH
DO US PART

Dedication

Dedicated to my son Justin, who may or
may not be related to the "real" T. J. Zereth.

Chapter 1

Zella, dear, now that your sister and stepsister are married, when can I start planning your wedding?"

Zella Wilson gritted her teeth at her mother's question. Between her height—she was always the tallest girl in every class—and a name that began with Z, she'd always been chosen last for everything except the basketball team. She'd always resented that, but she was more than happy to be the last to get married.

"You can start when I set a date."

"But you can't set a date until you're engaged."

"And I can't be engaged until I have a boyfriend."

Her mother raised one finger in the air. "Exactly! Which is why I've arranged for you to meet Judy's son Ryan at the Seattle Aquarium on Friday."

Zella spun to face her mother. "For your information, I already have plans for Friday night."

Her mother crossed her arms. "What plans?"

"Uh. . ." Her thoughts stalled along with her voice. She

didn't have any plans except to relax after a busy week, but she sure didn't want to get fixed up with the dorky son of her mother's best friend.

Ever since Annie's wedding, her mother had also been hounding Zella to find a man and get married. But not because she wished for her daughter's eternal joy and happiness.

No.

Melissa and Judy had so much fun doing Annie's wedding, they'd decided to start their own business as wedding planners. Zella overheard them plotting a showcase wedding for her. It was a marketing extravaganza to attract the attention of all the upscale couples in the city. The fact that Zella didn't have a fiancé didn't seem to matter.

Zella refused to be a part of such a sham, and if Judy's son was willing, then that was even more reason that she didn't want to meet him, much less spend an evening with him. When she finally did find her Mr. Right, she would not rush to the altar. She refused to have her marriage end in divorce as her mother's first marriage had, a result of getting married too fast for the sake of getting married.

Her mother didn't care if Zella was divorced a year later, as long as she made the wedding an elaborate social media blitz. But Zella cared. Now that Zella had been going to church with Cindy and Luke, she'd learned so much about the right kind of love between both people and God. She now had a different viewpoint on what she wanted her marriage to be—and she intended to take her time finding it.

Zella stiffened, taking full advantage of being four inches taller than her mother. Even if she didn't have plans, she would not go out with Judy's son or on any blind date her mother set up. The last time she'd weakened she'd gone to Folklife with some guy her mother had recommended— where they'd enjoyed some Thai takeout from a food vendor then found out the hard way that he had a seafood allergy. Zella had spent all night with him at the hospital, trying to explain to the guy's overbearing mother why she'd allowed her son to eat something that was made by someone they didn't know without asking for an ingredient list.

Melissa glared at her, her arms crossed. "If you have plans, where are you going?"

Zella glared down at her mother. The last thing she wanted was another confrontation. Ever since the night of Luke and Brent's company banquet when she'd discovered her mother's true colors, these confrontations had been flaring up with increasing frequency. "I'm going to..." Her mind raced as she scrambled to think of something on short notice. Glancing around the room, she spotted the community newspaper on the kitchen table, open to a page for local clubs and events she'd just been reading. She blurted out the only thing she could remember. "My book club meeting."

"Book club? What book club?"

"This book club." She stepped to the table and put her finger on it and read the first sentence. "At the library. We meet...every Friday night."

"Don't you have anything better to do on Friday night than sit with a bunch of people and read? How boring."

"I like to read. And we do more than just read at the book club. We also. . ." She tried to imagine what a book club would be like. When she bought books she often checked out reviews online, and many times people commented on the reviews. "We discuss the books we're reading. Now if you'll excuse me, I have some reading to do to get ready for our meeting."

As Zella walked into the library, a bad case of the jitters poked at her.

After her mother had left the kitchen a few nights ago she'd gone back to read the article on the book club for more information, but the newspaper was gone. She'd checked the library's website, but all they had on the book club was the time and name of the meeting room.

She didn't know what book they were reading, the size of the group, what genre the group focused on, or if they focused on any genre.

She read a lot, but with the number of books available, the chances that she'd already read the book they would be discussing were slim.

Still, it really didn't matter. The existence of the book club provided her with an excuse to leave the house every Friday night without being pestered to go on any more blind

TILL DEATH DO US PART

dates. At least on Friday nights. The idea was actually next to genius. It couldn't have worked better if she'd planned it.

Since she didn't know what they were reading, she'd brought her largest purse and tucked inside a few recent releases from her favorite authors.

Zella sucked in a deep breath to give herself some bravado and opened the door.

As she stepped inside the meeting room, the fragrant aroma of fresh coffee wafted up to greet her. Which was a good start.

Everyone seated at the large table turned toward her and smiled to greet her.

Three men and six women. A good-sized group. All adults, ranging from early twenties to an older lady with a bad dye job who appeared to be well into retirement.

"Welcome," the elderly lady said. "My name is Sheila. Help yourself to the coffee and have a seat."

Zella smiled back. So far so good.

While she poured a cup of coffee, the conversation nearest her centered around a book she hadn't read. However, it sounded interesting, and the woman speaking was very excited about the story line. This was one book that Zella would ask for the author and title and buy it.

Coffee in hand, she took an empty seat and tucked her purse under the table.

Sheila folded her hands on top of a stack of printed pages, still smiling brightly. "It's nice to see a new person here.

How did you find out about us?"

"From the community newspaper."

About half the people seated around the table expressed surprise in silence, while the oldest of the three men smirked, looking rather smug.

"Let me introduce everyone," Sheila said. "Beside me is Terri, next is Jorg, then Sasha, Jessica, Jon, Patty, Michelle, and beside you is Trevor. What's your name?"

"My name is Zella, and I'm pleased to meet you all."

Her name came back, repeated en masse by most of the people in the group. "Zella?" Everyone raised their eyebrows and stared.

A couple of them wowed.

Beside her, Trevor, who looked to be about the same age as her, quirked one brow, leaned back in his chair, crossed his arms over his chest, and blatantly studied her. "Interesting. Is it real?"

Zella felt her cheeks heat up. "Um. Yes."

This time a few people gasped. Now everyone was staring at her intently, waiting.

"Yes, it's my real name. It's kind of odd, but there's a story behind it." She knew she was starting to blabber out of nervousness. "It was my grandmother's dying wish that I be named Drizella after her own grandmother. My mother thought it was a horrible name, but my father had promised his mother under duress, so my mother agreed if it was shortened to Zella." She laughed weakly. "I've never met anyone with the same name, and I don't expect I ever will."

Sheila straightened the pile of papers in front of her. "That's a nice story, dear. Now we should get started or we're going to run out of time." She pulled a bundle of papers from beneath the stack. "We're mixed genres here. When Patty and I started this group, we thought it would be best to offer different viewpoints, depending on what we've chosen as the group's focus for each week."

Zella nodded. "I like that idea." While she loved to read romance novels, she had a few murder-mystery series authors she always followed, and she liked to vary her reading. She'd even read some speculative fiction, although she sometimes found the complicated fantasy settings hard to follow.

"We're sorry that you didn't contact us in advance because now you'll have to follow along what we're doing today without having read it first. But if you have any comments, don't be shy. We always welcome comments and suggestions."

Instead of handing her a book, Sheila slid the bundle of printed pages to her. It was labeled the third chapter of a book by an author she'd never heard of.

While she waited for everyone else to shuffle through various totes and folders, Zella scanned the pages. Even though she didn't have time to read much, she recognized it as the book the two ladies had been talking about while she was pouring her coffee.

One of the ladies, who she thought might have been Patty, continued digging through a tote bag while everyone else waited for her, providing Zella with an opportunity to ask a question. After all, Sheila had told her not to be shy.

"Excuse me, but I see you've given me chapter three. If this is the book I heard Sasha and Michelle discussing, I'd love to read the whole thing. Do you have an extra copy for me?"

Sasha froze and her mouth dropped open. "Really? Are you serious?" She turned and grasped Michelle's hands and gave them a squeeze while looking at Zella. "Are you sure? I'd love to send you the whole thing, but I'm not done yet. I need a better complication to get my protagonist to the final battle. What I had was coming out too contrived." She looked around the table at everyone seated. "I was hoping we'd have time to do a little brainstorming before we go home tonight."

Zella tried not to let her mouth hang open. The book wasn't finished? Complication? Protagonist? Brainstorming?

Afraid to move, she kept her head still while she tried to subtly glance around the table.

No one had a book in front of her or him. Most had printed pages, the same chapter 3 that she had been given, but everyone else's was filled with red notes and scribbles. Instead of paper three of the people there, including Trevor, the man beside her, had laptops.

Trevor turned to her and smiled. "It's okay if you didn't bring anything of your own; after all, it's your first time here. If you think the group is a good fit for you, you can e-mail a chapter to Sheila, and she'll send it to everyone else so we can read it for next week."

Zella gulped. This wasn't a book club that read books. This was a book club that *wrote* books.

Trevor's smile widened. "Don't worry. You look like you're about to be drawn and quartered. I'm going to guess that you're not published? If you're not ready to share your work yet, that's fine. You can submit to the group when you're ready."

Zella struggled to breathe. She could barely write a grocery list, never mind a whole chapter. She certainly couldn't write enough chapters to make a whole book. Back in high school she'd excelled in math but done abysmally in English.

She didn't belong here. But if she left, she had no place to go except home, where her mother was waiting for her with a list of eligible men desperate enough to fall into their planning clutches.

For tonight she didn't have to do anything here but read. That's what they'd told her.

Tonight she would do her best to go with the flow, and by next Friday she would figure out something else to do.

Maybe she could make a few significant comments, and then she'd never have to see these people again.

She cleared her throat and dug a pen out of her purse. "It's okay, I'm ready. Let's begin."

Chapter 2

Trevor Jones leaned back in his chair and watched the newbie fidget in the chair. She didn't look completely terrified to the core of her soul, but close.

Of the people he knew who were writers, many were shy and didn't do well in groups or social settings. The saying that writing was a solitary profession was very true. It took a long time to write a book, and most of that time had to be spent alone in order to concentrate. Very few people could do it. But of those who could, often it was because that person preferred to be alone than in a social setting. He wondered if Zella was one of those people who didn't interact well with others.

Watching Zella almost cower as Sheila offered her extra copies of Sasha's first and second chapters, he thought that might be true. Unlike himself. While he was far from the life of the party, he enjoyed going out and doing things with friends—when he had time, which often was nonexistent between deadlines and the day job.

The hard facts of the writing life were that until a writer had a few bestsellers under his belt, he needed another income to keep a roof over his head and food on the table. Which meant rich parents, a supportive spouse, or a day job to pay the bills until the next royalty check. Or all of the above.

Trevor didn't have rich parents or a wife to help support him as he made his uphill climb, but according to his agent, he was almost at the point he could quit his day job—or at least take a few years off—to write full-time. Not yet, but he was close.

Unless he didn't make his next deadline. Then it would all be over. The day job wouldn't be a choice, it would be a necessity.

"Okay," Sheila said as she straightened her pile of paper. "Let's get started. Patty, do you want to go first?"

Instead of paying as much attention as he should have to comments the group made on Sasha's latest project, Trevor focused on Zella.

As the only one who hadn't previously read the chapter, Zella was at a distinct disadvantage, yet she managed to chime in once or twice. He found it intriguing that the more she read and the more the discussion intensified, the less nervous she became and the more she participated.

The same happened when they pulled out three other members' chapters they'd been working on. By the time they turned the last page of Jorg's chapter, all traces of Zella's nervousness had disappeared.

He couldn't help but smile, even though he was the only one. He loved brainstorming, and he saw that Zella had a vivid imagination and jumped right in, digging into plot configuration and red herrings. She was a great fit for their group.

Too bad this wasn't the week to do one of his chapters. He was curious to see what she would think.

Sheila noisily slurped the last of her coffee then thunked her mug down on the table. "We're done, people. Unfortunately we're late again—the librarians are going to come in here any minute and kick us out. We can't disrupt their scheduled closing or we won't be allowed to come back. Everyone's got to help clean up."

Trevor could now see that Zella wasn't shy at all. She pitched in to clean up the scattered papers and coffee supplies without hesitation.

He liked that. Since most writers were voracious readers, at least when they weren't on a deadline, she probably was, too. He liked that as well. Also as a writer, you had to be an effective time manager to balance making an income, writing, family, and still having friends and a social life. He really liked that in a person, too.

He realized he was assuming a lot, so he wanted to get to know her better to find out if all these things he wanted to be true about her actually were.

Having young children at home, Patty and Sasha grabbed the envelopes Sheila had prepared for them and scampered out of the room. The other ladies and Jon weren't far behind, leaving himself, Jorg, Sheila, and Zella to finish up. Like he did every week, after he'd finished stacking the chairs and knocking down the table with Jorg, Trevor was now ready to put the box of coffee supplies on the top shelf for Sheila.

He froze before he took his first step.

Zella had already lifted the box and was effortlessly sliding it into its place on the top shelf.

The woman stood about nine inches taller than Sheila. He looked down to Zella's feet. Sneakers. She wasn't even on her tiptoes.

She had to be nearly six feet tall.

At six foot four, he towered above most women.

He wouldn't tower over Zella Wilson. With her long legs and sensible shoes, she would keep pace with him when they walked together.

He wondered if she liked to go hiking. Or if she did rock climbing. She could with legs like that. Looking at her from the back, she was slim, but rather than being vainly model skinny, she was adequately filled out and looked physically fit. Maybe she'd even give him a run for his money on the track.

If he wasn't sure then, he was sure now. He definitely wanted to get to know her better.

Trevor approached her. "If you don't have any plans, I was wondering if you'd like to join me for a cup of coffee at the place down the street."

As he waited, he could barely believe the way his heart was pounding—he was actually nervous. It had obviously been too long since he'd asked a woman for a date. Not that this was a date, but it was the closest he'd come since his last deadline.

Sheila reached up and rested her hand on his forearm. "That's a great idea. I'd like that." Sheila turned to Zella. "Would you like to come, too, dear? What about you, Jorg?"

Jorg shrugged his shoulders. "Sure. I've got nothing better to do."

Zella glanced between all of them, checked her watch, and then smiled nervously. "I'd like that. Lead the way."

Trevor gritted his teeth. A group outing wasn't what he'd had in mind, but if it was this or nothing, he'd take it. "See you all there in five."

As she carried her coffee cup and muffin to the table to join everyone else, Zella reminded herself to keep quiet and just listen. She had the same bad habit as her sister Annie, which was to talk too much when she got nervous.

She couldn't try to bluff her way into having these people think she was trying to be a writer. The best thing would be to sit quietly and let them assume. Then she had a week to actually try to write something, so even if she wrote really badly, which she was sure she would, at least she could have a small taste of what it was like. She hadn't been sure what they were talking about when they groaned about sagging middles, but she didn't think it had anything to do with anyone's waistline. Except maybe for Jon.

Zella shook the wayward thought out of her head as she sank into the chair and clamped her lips shut.

Sheila turned to her. "What did you think of our group, Zella?"

So much for being quiet.

Zella maintained her smile, trying not to let her nervousness show. "I learned a lot. How long has the group been together?" It was kind of answering a question with a question, but she needed to change the subject and get everyone else talking.

Sheila grinned ear to ear. "Six years. We started out in my basement, but it got too small when more members joined, so we moved to the library. How long have you been writing?"

Zella gulped. "I. . ." She couldn't lie to these people. "Not long." Approximately three hours. Not that she'd actually written anything, but she had started thinking about it.

Beside her, Trevor shook his head. "Can't you see she's nervous? Give the woman a chance to get used to us." He turned to Zella. "I thought we could talk about something else. Like the last Mariners game when the roof on Safeco Field got stuck. Or if you're going to Bumbershoot this year." He paused, making a lopsided grin. "I wonder how they came up with a bizarre name like that."

Zella bit back a giggle. "I know the answer. The word

bumbershoot is an old slang for umbrella, and it refers to the festival being a figurative umbrella for all the acts and performers. But I think it really refers to the fact that because it's here in Seattle, everyone had better have an umbrella because it will probably rain."

Sheila waved one hand in the air. "That's so crowded and too noisy. I plan to spend the long weekend catching up on my reading. I have a stack of books, and I'm so behind."

Trevor took a sip of his coffee. "You're retired. How could you get behind on anything?"

Sheila snorted. "For your information I have a stack of books from the Romancing America series to read, among others. What about you, Zella? What do you like to read?"

Zella thought of the five books she had in her purse. "A variety, I guess. Mostly romance, but I also like mysteries. Right now I'm reading the latest T. J. Zereth. He's my favorite author. His website says he lives right here in Seattle. I've been waiting for a book tour so I can meet him and get his autograph. Or maybe get my picture taken with him. Wouldn't that be exciting?"

Trevor's eyes widened, and he slapped his napkin over his nose and mouth and started to cough violently. With his napkin pressed to his nose, he thunked his cup down on the table so hard that some coffee sloshed out, while it sounded like he was almost gagging. Sheila jumped out of her chair to avoid the splash, while Jorg ignored both of them, staring at Zella with eyes so wide she thought they might pop out of his head.

"A picture with the enigmatic T. J. Zereth, huh?" Sheila handed the sputtering Trevor a handful of napkins out of the holder, patted him on the back, and then grabbed Jorg's napkin to wipe the spill before returning to her chair. "Yes, that would be exciting."

Jorg leaned back in his chair and crossed his arms over his chest. "I read his latest one awhile back. What do you think of Mrs. Rubenstein?"

All three of them stared at her, waiting, and Zella wondered if this was some kind of test that she would pass or fail for admission into their club. So far she hadn't read anything in the book that had been off-kilter or questionable, nor had she read far enough to make a judgment call on the character—a short, eccentric, elderly lady with a sharp tongue and a quick wit who was constantly changing her hair color. Who, if she had to personalize, probably looked a lot like Sheila, which now that she thought about it, was very funny. Perhaps the group had teased Sheila about the resemblance, but Zella didn't know Sheila well enough to comment or if Sheila would think such a thing was amusing.

"I can't say," she said, trying not to laugh with the picture in her head, comparing Sheila to the character. "I haven't finished the book yet. Please don't give away the ending."

They talked a bit about a few other books, some of which she'd read, most she hadn't. When they were done, everyone stacked their empty cups and used napkins on Trevor's tray.

He sighed. "You might as well give me your garbage, too. Everyone always does. Will you be joining us next week?"

When they all rose at the same time, Zella automatically looked down at Trevor as she started to reply. But when he stood to his full height, she found herself looking at his collar instead of his eyes.

She looked up. Sometimes she was at eye level with a man, but she seldom had to look up, never if she wore fancy dress shoes instead of her nice flat sneakers.

Standing beside Trevor, for the first time, for one of the rare times in her life, she actually had to look up into a man's eyes.

He had lovely, sky-blue eyes that contrasted strikingly with his thick brown hair and a slightly larger than average nose that made him even more masculine. Just like it went in fiction, he truly was tall, dark, and handsome.

Really tall. Really, really tall.

Since she was now going to be a writer, for her first project she could create a fictional Trevor as her perfect boyfriend, writing about him so her mother would think it was real. Her mother wouldn't have to know that the relationship she was going to allude to was made up. It would even be plausible— plausible, she was already thinking of writerly words—if she saw him every Friday.

As soon as she worked up a story, she'd let him read it, and then "accidentally" let her mother see it.

Zella grinned. "Wouldn't miss it. See you then."

Chapter 3

Because he was the first to arrive, Trevor unpacked the book club's boxes and started making the coffee.

Coffee.

He nearly groaned out loud as he automatically raised his hand and swiped at his nose.

As a teen he'd done it with pop, but he'd never had coffee come out his nose.

Unconsciously, he shuddered at the memory. His nose had burned for the longest time, and an hour later he thought he'd coughed up some coffee. Quite frankly, it was the most disgusting thing that had ever happened to him. At least it had been only lukewarm. If not, it would have done some serious damage.

He wasn't sure he was ready to drink coffee again, but everyone else would want it. Maybe except for Sheila, who had actually seen the coffee come out his nose. Then, bless her heart, she'd given him a handful of napkins and helped wipe up the mess.

Just as he plugged in the coffee urn, a shuffle echoed behind him.

He turned and looked down. Way down. The woman was more than a foot shorter than he was, yet somehow she still ruled the roost. Even in the back room at the library.

Sheila stood before him, her arms crossed, foot tapping, echoing in sharp raps on the tile floor. "You're not going to tell her, are you?" Her accusation rang with censure.

Trevor spun around and strode toward the folded tables leaning against the wall and dragged one out so he didn't have to look at her as he replied. "How can I?" He yanked the table legs down and snapped the locking mechanisms into place, probably a little harder than necessary. "I'm her favorite author and she's got stars in her eyes, thinking it would be exciting to get her picture taken with me. But that's not what I want. This is the guy I want her to see." He thumped his fist to his chest. "Trevor Jones, windshield repair technician and ordinary guy."

"Tell her. You'll still be just as ordinary. Trust me."

He sighed and pulled the table up to stand on its four legs. Only Sheila could be so blunt to the point of painful and get away with it. He never had to worry about his ego getting too big with her around. Some days he wondered about her husband. Often he contemplated sending the man flowers. "I can't. My agent has done a lot of work and marketing in building the persona of T. J. Zereth. But he's not real. I'm nothing like that guy." The picture of himself as the elusive mystery author flashed through his brain. Between the trademark black fedora, large dark sunglasses, and creative lighting used in the photo shoot, even his own mother hadn't recognized him when she saw his photo all glitzed up on the website, or the smaller version in the back of his books. No one but his best friends, his family, his pastor, his agent, and his writing group knew his secret, and he intended to keep it that way. Until the time was right. Which wasn't today.

Before he could tell Sheila that he wanted to make an announcement to the group that his identity was to be kept confidential, Zella walked into the room.

He gulped at the sight of her. As an author, he knew love at first sight was only fiction, but something in his brain had obviously misfired. Besides, technically this wasn't the first time he'd seen her. It was the second. Third if he counted going to the coffee shop separately. "You're early," he muttered, barely able to find his voice.

She nodded. "Yes. I need to talk to you. I wrote something, and I need your permission to use your name."

He almost asked her which name but bit his lip instead, hoping he wasn't going to draw blood.

"My mother wants to set me up with the son of a friend of hers, so my plan is to show her that I have a boyfriend so they'll leave me alone. Can I use your name for my fictitious boyfriend? I need someone I'll see often."

Trevor tipped his head to study Zella. She didn't look like a woman who would be desperate for a boyfriend, which made him wonder why her mother would be so pushy. At the same time, that probably meant she didn't want to be in a relationship with him either, so in that case, a fake relationship was better than no relationship, and he really liked the part about seeing him often. "Sure. I can do that for you."

She pulled a notepad out of her pocket. "Great. What do you do for a living?"

Before he could respond, Sheila raised a finger in the air. "He's a—"

"—a windshield repair technician," Trevor finished. "I work for a local auto glass shop. I repair and replace broken windshields mostly."

Zella's brows crinkled as he interrupted Sheila, but he couldn't take the chance that she'd say too much. One day soon he would tell Zella the whole story, but not today.

Sheila rested her fists on her hips. "Unfortunately he sometimes inhales a little too much of that glue."

Trevor smiled sweetly. "Ignore her. She sometimes inhales too much correction fluid. Look, everyone's starting to arrive. Let's sit down."

While everyone came in and caught up on chitchat, Trevor answered a myriad of other personal questions—what kind of car he drove, where he lived, and added which church he went to. He held his breath and waited for a response, nearly sagging in relief when she smiled and told him what church she went to and that she was a relatively new believer. It was important to him that any girlfriend—or more if things progressed—be a woman of faith.

Before he could ask if she wanted to join him at church on Sunday, everyone sat down and they were ready to start.

Zella pulled a larger pile of papers out of her tote and looked at Sasha. "I read the chapters you gave me, and I want to tell you how much I enjoyed them. This is a really great story."

Sasha beamed. "Thank you. Did you bring something for us? I'll gladly critique a chapter or two for you."

Zella shook her head. "I'm still working on it. I didn't get a whole chapter done. Hopefully next week."

"What genre is it?"

She glanced at Trevor then turned back to Sasha. "It's a romance. The G-rated kind." She looked around the table, making eye contact with everyone there. "I know we went over four chapters last week, but I really didn't have a chance to read them in detail or connect what belonged to who. What does everyone here write?"

Trevor's stomach clenched tighter and tighter as everyone in the circle gave a short description of what genre they wrote and a few details, until it was his turn.

"I write mysteries. Any gory parts and deaths are all offstage, and the plot and subplots are the main characters trying to figure out who done it. That's about it."

A silence hung in the air. He knew everyone was waiting for him to tell Zella his pen name. Especially Jorg, who was leaning forward in his chair.

Sheila cleared her throat. "It's always a challenge to try to figure out who the villain is in every story Mr. Jones writes. Isn't that true, everyone?"

At the formal rendition of his real name, everyone glanced around at each other and a few nodded.

He wanted to mouth a thank-you to Sheila, but he couldn't with Zella watching him.

There was a pause as everyone began shuffling through their pages. This time, Trevor was in no hurry. This time, one of the chapters they were going to discuss was his. He didn't want Zella to recognize his style and associate him with his pen name.

Sheila tapped her pencil to the top of her stack. "Let's get to it, everyone. We'll start with Trevor's chapter. It's from his latest project, titled *Till Death*."

He froze in his chair, waiting for Zella's comments when it became her turn to speak. She answered the questions the group had set up as their guidelines for critiquing chapters then straightened the papers and handed the pile to him. "This was really good; there wasn't much I could say. Except that the death of your victim should have been more subtle. I think he should have been poisoned. You need him to die with no physical injury and without evidence."

He frowned. "I think you're right. But how?"

Zella broke out into a grin and rubbed her hands together. "I can help you. I'm a pharmacy technician. I can ask my boss, and he can help me look up all sorts of things that could kill someone and leave no trace."

Trevor pressed his palm over his heart. "I think I might be falling in love. Will you have lunch with me tomorrow? Then we can discuss it further without boring the rest of the group."

Shiela and Jorg turned and stared at him, so he waggled his eyebrows in response.

Zella's eyes widened. "I. . .I guess so."

He smiled. He hadn't been kidding that he might be falling in love. This was going to be the beginning of a beautiful friendship.

Or, he hoped, more.

Chapter 4

Zella slid the piece of paper with her notes across the table toward Trevor. "I started making a list, but then I realized that you'd have to have a prescription for those things. Either that or your character would have to break into the pharmacy. So that wouldn't work. Then I thought of arsenic, but a person would get very sick before he died, so it's not subtle enough for what you need. I thought antifreeze would be better, but it can take up to twenty-four hours to die from that, too. The fastest way to poison someone legally would be good old-fashioned carbon monoxide."

He broke out into a grin. "Legally? Isn't that an oxymoron?"

"You know what I mean."

He had the nerve to laugh. While he did, Zella reached forward to grab the last grape out of the plastic bowl between them on the picnic table. "You snooze, you lose," she said as she popped it into her mouth.

Trevor sighed and covered his stomach with his hands. "That's fine with me. I ate way too much. I meant to make just a light picnic lunch, but I couldn't decide what to bring and ended up packing more than we needed."

Yet, judging from all the empty bowls and containers, they'd managed to eat almost everything. She thought that having a picnic lunch at Cougar Mountain Regional Wildland Park was a great idea, although it certainly hadn't been what she'd expected. She'd expected to do takeout.

Trevor stood. "I'm sorry, but I just can't sit any longer. Would you like to take a walk on one of the trails instead of going back? Unless you have other plans."

The only thing she had to do was go home and face more questions from her mother about the new man she'd been seeing and when she was planning on marrying him. While it warmed her heart to see both Cindy and Annie happily married, she still wasn't sure she believed in happily-ever-afters. Not only did she live with the example of her mother's first failed marriage looming in front of her every day, two of her workmates at the pharmacy were on the brink of divorce.

She truly hoped for the best for both Cindy and Annie and that they really had found true love at first sight, as unrealistic and impractical as that may be. For herself, she wasn't going to take the chance of following in her mother's footsteps with falling in love too fast and then falling out of love just as fast. When she met the man of her dreams, first they would be friends. Then if they were still together they could get engaged after three or more years, and then they'd stay engaged for a year before they got married, ensuring they weren't rushing into a lifelong commitment they would both later regret.

Zella looked up at Trevor, waiting patiently for her while she stood there staring at the trees, lost in her own little world.

He smiled, bringing out the most adorable little crinkles in the corners of his eyes. "Welcome back. You looked lost in thought for a while."

The heat she felt in her cheeks had nothing to do with the warm Indian summer day. "Sorry. I'd love to go for a walk. A nice long walk." Maybe until midnight, when she could sneak into bed without having to talk her mother.

She helped Trevor scoop the empty containers into the cooler and load everything into his car, and then they headed for the entrance to the Coal Creek Trail. As they entered the path, Zella removed her sunglasses and hung them on the neckline of her T-shirt. Despite the bright sunshine, Trevor wasn't wearing sunglasses, even though most people had been.

He turned to her. "This isn't a five-minute walk in the park. Are you sure you want to go for a hike? I shouldn't have sprung it on you without warning."

Zella nodded. "I love this kind of stuff. I haven't been on a good hike for a long time. This actually reminds me of the last time I was out this way on my mountain bike."

Trevor's eyes widened. "Mountain bike? I've always wanted to do the Snoqualmie Valley Trail, but my friends thought I was crazy."

"It is kind of a crazy trail. It's about thirty miles. It's not a casual ride."

"You've done it?"

Zella shook her head. "No. I'd like to one day, though."

She almost thought he was going to ask if she wanted to partner with him to do the ride, but he'd stopped talking. Not that she minded. In fact, as much as she enjoyed the quiet sounds of nature as they walked, Zella also appreciated the comfortable silence of being with someone who didn't need to fill every second of airtime with talking.

After about a mile, Trevor broke out into a grin.

Zella looked around them but didn't see anything out of the ordinary. "Is something funny? Am I missing something?"

He stopped walking and shook his head. "No, nothing like that. I hadn't thought about it before we got here, but I've got a scene coming up where my antagonist chases my primary female character through the woods. As I'm walking, I'm getting a mental picture what it would be like."

Zella couldn't help it. She rolled her eyes. "That's so B-movie. You wouldn't really do that, would you?"

"I wouldn't have her trip or anything. Besides, she escapes. I haven't figured out how yet, but she escapes without being hurt. No close calls. She's just scared but smart about it. She doesn't look back; she doesn't trip; she just hightails it out safely. But since she's so fast, she doesn't see the guy who was chasing her." He rested his fists on his hips and looked around them. "I have an idea. How about if I chase you through here, and then I can get a better idea of what I'm writing about. Kinda like research. If this were a movie, they'd call it method acting."

Zella waved one finger in the air in front of his face. "Not a chance. I have a better idea. If you're having your character fleeing for her life, then I should chase you."

She waited, expecting to be chastised, but instead his face lit up. "That's a great idea. Think you could catch me if you really tried?" He looked down her legs then down to her sneakers.

"Maybe. I'll count to five to give you a head start, but you'd better run for your life." Zella pulled a pen out of her back pocket and held it up like a knife, ready to stab him. " 'Cause I'm gonna kill you, missy."

A rush of power surged through her. Of all the men she'd dated, she'd always been a bit taller, a bit leggier, and on the track, for those who had the ego to race her, a bit faster. She had a feeling that of the women Trevor dated, he probably didn't come across many who nearly equaled him in height, and therefore, probably speed. It had been a few years since she'd played on the basketball team in school, but back then, she'd been the fastest on the girls' team and a worthy opponent for the boys.

Trevor opened his eyes as wide as saucers and covered his mouth with his hands. "Eek!" he screamed like a girlie-girl, which, at his size, was utterly ridiculous. He raised his hands in the air. "Don't hurt me!" he squeaked, in what was probably his best imitation of a distressed heroine, spun around, and bolted off.

Zella counted quickly to five and took off after him.

For an alleged damsel in distress, he ran pretty fast.

The air burned in her lungs, but she pushed herself hard and was actually catching up on him.

She wondered if he heard her because he lowered his shoulders and increased his speed marginally.

Then, just like a dumb blond in a cheap movie, he ran off the path, into the trees.

Like the classic evil villain, Zella called out, "You cannot escape!" and followed.

With the change in terrain from the well-traveled path, she lost a little momentum, but so did he. Trevor now had to crash and push through the overhanging branches, which, at his height, greatly impeded his speed. He raised both his arms to shield his face as he ran. And with Trevor clearing the path before her, Zella started to catch up.

She wondered if he heard her closing in because he turned back toward the cleared path. If she were a real bad guy, she supposed this should have made her even angrier, so she roared her anger and tried to run faster.

A few yards ahead of her, Trevor almost made it to the clearing, but his foot caught in a root, his arms flew up in the air, and down he went.

Unlike the movies, there was no slow motion. He covered

his face with his arms a split second before he hit the ground with a resounding thump so hard she could hear the air expel from his lungs.

Once he hit the ground, he didn't move.

He hadn't done it on purpose.

"Trevor! Are you hurt? Can you speak?" Zella dropped to her knees and pressed her hands to the center of his back. She could see and feel the fast expansion of his chest with his heavy breathing from the exertion of the run. When he didn't reply, she grabbed his shoulders and tried to roll him over. She could barely move him.

In a flash of movement, his arms came free. He grabbed her shoulders, and before she knew what happened, she was on her back. Above her, Trevor pinned her to the ground with her wrists pressed into the dirt above her shoulders.

A scratch, smeared with dripping blood, marred his cheek.

"Are you okay?" she asked.

He blinked then shook his head. "The stars are starting to clear. I'll be fine. You make a really bad villain. You were supposed to stab me, not check to see if I was breathing."

"But you're hurt." Even though he had her pinned to the ground, if she really were a bad guy, she should probably be considering how to get him off and regain her advantage. He was probably still unsteady enough that if she tried, she could knock him off, or if she used what she learned in her self-defense class, do some serious injury to him with her knee.

His expression softened, his gaze dropped to her mouth, and he froze.

Zella thought her heart stopped beating then picked up even faster.

Just as his head started to lower, he stiffened, sucked in a deep breath, rolled off her, and stood. She didn't think it was her imagination that his hand shook just a little bit as he extended it to her to pull her to her feet.

She accepted his help and stood.

He wiped the blood off his cheek with the corner of his T-shirt and stuffed the hem back into his waistline. "That was a little embarrassing, but I think I learned something. I probably have a little more empathy for all those women being chased through the woods by the evil zombie. It's actually harder than I thought, and it was pretty stupid to go off the path."

Zella reached up to brush the scratch on his cheek. "I hope you don't get a scar. We'd better find someplace to wash that up."

"Yeah. It probably doesn't look too good either. This might sound like a stretch, but once we finish the trail, we're about twenty-five minutes away from the aquarium. I'm sure they have a nice washroom with good antibacterial soap, and we can take a break and see all the exhibits."

Zella nibbled her bottom lip. It hadn't been long ago that her mother had tried to send her to the aquarium with a blind date, and she'd narrowly escaped. Yet now with Trevor, she actually wanted to go.

She smiled. "Sure. That sounds like fun. I even have my camera in my purse. I'll try to catch your good side, but no promises."

He grinned, reached forward, gripped her hand, and twined his fingers with hers.

As they walked, he kept her hand wrapped in his. She tried to tug her hand out, but he tightened his grip then patted their joined hands with his free one.

"What are you doing?" she asked.

"Practicing holding hands with my girlfriend. You gave me some help with my story, so now I'm going to help with yours. Once we get to the aquarium, we can call it a date."

"A date? But—"

He smiled, making him so handsome her breath caught. "No buts. Call it research. Now let's go be romantic."

Chapter 5

Zella closed the door with a distinct *bang*, loud enough to make sure her mother heard her coming in. She kicked off her shoes—her three-inch heels, which for the first time, she'd worn in the presence of a man and still had to look up at him—and sauntered in the door.

Her mother sat on the couch, pretending to read a book that Zella knew she'd already read. She was wearing her favorite bright-pink sweater. And it was clear she was very curious.

Immediately her mother stood. "You must have had a very exciting weekend with Trevor. You didn't get home until midnight last night, you're late again tonight, and you have to get up for work in the morning. Did you have a nice time?"

Zella bit back a grin. Actually she hadn't come home last night until after 1:00 a.m. because after the aquarium closed they'd gone out for supper, then to a late movie, and then to an all-night coffee shop. For the first time, she'd had to set the alarm Sunday morning so she would get up on time.

Especially since she'd gone to Trevor's church, not her own.

Today, since they'd been dressed in their church clothes, he'd taken her to a nice restaurant for lunch, then they'd gone to the Museum of Flight, then for dinner, and then to the Seattle Repertory Theatre, where he'd somehow scored tickets to what turned out to be a delightful performance.

Even though she'd concocted the pretend relationship to stop her mother's incessant matchmaking, she'd enjoyed every minute of her time spent with Trevor. They'd even had fun when they pulled off the road on their way home and she'd put her cell phone on speaker to have a three-way conversation with Jeremy, the head pharmacist at the drug store where she worked, about possible fatal side effects from some new pharmaceuticals. "Yes, I've had a lovely weekend. Now if you'll excuse me, as you reminded me, it's past my bedtime and I—"

The electronic tune of her cell phone sang out from her purse. "Excuse me," she muttered as she dug through her purse.

The display showed that it was Jeremy. "I need to take this. Good night, Mom." Zella turned around and flipped it open. "Hi, what's up?" she asked as she walked into her bedroom and shut the door.

She listened intently as Jeremy gave her a list of side effects for one of the medications she'd asked him about.

"That sounds exactly like what he needs to know. Are you sure a person would just get sleepy and not realize he was going to pass out and never wake up?"

"Positive. I looked up all the side effects and risks in the manufacturer's file."

She couldn't help but smile. "Are you sure it's possible to be fatal?"

"Yes. An overdose would be enough to kill the average adult."

She nodded, even though he couldn't see her. "Then that's perfect. Do you think mixing it in with something spicy, like chili or curry, would mask the taste and a person wouldn't notice their food had been laced?"

Instead of a reply, Jeremy laughed. He'd been quite amused when she'd told him she was starting to write a book and fascinated when she'd explained that she needed to help another friend who was writing a book find a way to murder someone—on paper, anyway.

"Stop it," Zella snickered, barely able to keep from laughing herself. She could hardly believe she was doing this, but she was. "I need to find paper to write this down."

As she pulled the bedroom door open, she caught a flash of pink disappearing around the corner.

Zella nearly groaned. If her mother had thought she was going to hear her exchanging words of love with Trevor after they'd just parted, her mother had another think coming.

She found paper in a drawer and carefully spelled out the name as Jeremy repeated it. "Thanks. I'll see you at work tomorrow. 'Bye."

Before she changed into her pajamas, Zella texted Trevor the name of the drug Jeremy had researched, smiling as she imagined his reaction.

Just as she hit SEND, she wished she could take back her message. Now that Trevor had the information he needed, he would probably be up half the night writing, working the new details into his story. He'd be a wreck all day at work, but he'd be a smiling wreck.

Zella crawled into bed thinking of Trevor's smile and the adorable crinkles at the sides of his beautiful blue eyes. She wished she'd known that killing someone could be such fun.

Once again, Trevor checked the time.

He couldn't call Zella at work because it certainly wasn't an emergency. It wasn't even important. All he wanted was to hear her voice. He didn't have a single thing he needed to say. She'd be working until six o'clock. And if he calculated in the typical Seattle rush-hour traffic, she wouldn't get home until seven.

He didn't want to wait that long to talk to her.

He had it bad.

At 7:01, he hit the speed dial button on his cell phone.

"Hi. It's me." He mentally kicked himself. He was already sounding lame.

She giggled. He froze. Giggled? He held the phone away for a second to be sure he'd called the right person. Not that he knew anyone who would giggle at him.

"Hi, Trevor. I'm soooo glad you called."

"You are?"

"Aw, that was so sweet. Thank you."

It was sweet that he called when he didn't have anything to say? Maybe Sheila was right, maybe he did inhale too much glue and he'd missed part of the conversation. "You're welcome. I guess."

"That's a great idea. I'd like that."

"Uh. . . Okay. . ."

"That sounds like fun, too. Saturday sounds great."

He shook his head to clear his thoughts, and then the lightbulb went on. "Your mother is listening, isn't she?"

"Of course." Her voice lowered, and she sighed. "That sounds so romantic."

His heart picked up speed. He'd give her romantic. He lowered his voice, giving himself a husky edge. "Yeah. And when we get to wherever you think I'm taking you, I'm going to pull you close and hold you tight and kiss you like. . ." His mind raced. Kiss her like what? He wrote murder mysteries, where people died or lived the length of the story in fear. He didn't write romantic stuff, and he'd never had a serious relationship where he wanted to be romantic. All he'd wanted with previous dates was to have some fun.

But whatever was happening with Zella—even though it hadn't been long since they'd met—was different.

"I'd kiss you like. . ." He paused. He'd kiss her like a lover.

Hard and deep, so she thought about him at night and until the next time they saw each other, so he could kiss her like that again, hidden, away from prying eyes. But he couldn't say that out loud. He cleared his throat. ". . .like I've wanted to for a long time. Because that's what I want. Romance. Flowers. Flickering candlelight and stolen kisses."

He heard her gasp on the other end of the phone. "Stop that," she whispered.

His palms started to sweat. He hoped that wouldn't compromise the electronic circuits on his cell phone. For the first time in his life, that was what he really wanted. Romance. And he was going to make it happen. Especially the stolen kisses part.

"I'm going to be at your house in twenty minutes for the first one." He made a quick smoochy noise over the phone and flicked it shut.

He ran into the bathroom, brushed his teeth, touched up his deodorant, rammed a pack of spearmint gum in his pocket, and dashed out the door.

He'd promised her romance and stolen kisses, and that was exactly what she was going to get.

Chapter 6

Numbly, Zella poked at the pile of mashed potatoes on her plate.

"What's the matter?" her mother asked from the other side of the kitchen table. "Did I use too much salt? You'd better hurry and finish your supper if your young man is going to be here soon."

If she hadn't already lost her appetite enough, her stomach lurched, threatening to give up the little she'd managed to eat.

She had no idea what he'd meant by stolen kisses, but she had a bad feeling that he really was on his way, right now, to come and get one.

All she'd wanted to do was make her mother think she was going on another date with him. She'd planned to tell him, with her mother listening, to meet her somewhere. Then the second she got in the car she would have phoned him back to tell him to stay home and do his own thing, and she was going to go to the library. Except he'd completely sidetracked the conversation, and now he was on his way.

For stolen kisses.

"You're going to change, aren't you? You're not going to wear the same thing you wore to work, are you?"

"Actually, I was just going to change into my jeans and a T-shirt."

Her mother tsked and pushed her empty plate away. "Regardless of what you're going to wear, it's nice that I'm finally going to meet Trevor. I'd never heard you mention him, and now suddenly you're seeing him almost every day. He must be very special."

She almost told her mother that Trevor was special but then realized where the conversation was headed. If she said Trevor was special, then it wouldn't be long before her mother would start pressing for engagement details. If she said there was nothing special between them, then it would be back to fending off attempts at more blind dates. This was a path she had to tread lightly.

"I'm not sure yet. So far I'm quite fond of him." As the words left her mouth, she realized how very true they were. She might not be falling in love with the man, but she certainly was developing a good friendship. As all the clichés went, they enjoyed most of the same things and peacefully agreed to disagree on those they didn't.

She pushed her plate away. "I really shouldn't eat anything more. Trevor always likes to grab something when we're out, so I don't need two suppers in one day."

Her mother's eyebrows rose. "How much does he eat?"

"Quite a bit. He's a big man."

"Oh dear. I can give him a good diet for men."

Zella sighed. She hadn't realized before how much her mother was hung up on appearances. "Don't worry, Mom, he's not fat; he's just tall and he eats a lot to maintain himself."

"That's good to hear. How about his relatives? Are they healthy? Is anyone on any expensive medication?"

Zella stood to put her plate in the dishwasher, about to ask why her mother would ask such a thing, when the doorbell rang.

"That would be Trevor. I'll get it."

Without looking, she knew her mother was right behind her.

She opened the door to Trevor holding a single pink rose toward her. "This is for you."

"Oh my," her mother gasped from behind her.

Zella forced herself to smile, accepted the flower, and stepped back.

"Mom, this is Trevor."

Trevor looked down at her mother and nodded a greeting. "Good evening, Mrs. Wilson."

Her mother's cheeks darkened, and she straightened and stretched in an unconscious effort to be as tall as possible. Then she made a futile effort to fluff up her hair. "It's actually Mrs. Mufford. Zella and Annie kept their father's name when I remarried. But Annie's married now, so her last name is different than either of us." She waved one hand in the air in front of her face. "I'm talking too much. Please, just call me Melissa."

He nodded again. "Good evening, Melissa. It's a pleasure to meet you."

Zella was torn between feeling swept off her feet and annoyed that he was overdoing it with the charm. "Let me put this in some water. I'll be right back."

Instead of searching for a vase, she put the rose in water in a tall glass and dashed back to the door, where now her mother stood talking to Trevor, standing too close and twirling one finger through a lock of her hair.

"I'm ready," she said as she picked up her purse. "Let's go."

Instead of getting into the car, he walked around to the passenger side, clicked the remote lock, and opened the door for her.

Zella planted her fists on her hips and turned to him. "What are you doing?"

He stood with his hand still on the handle, waiting. "I'm opening the door for a lady."

"Oh brother. And what was with the flower?"

"I thought you liked flowers. You told me on Sunday that if you'd been wearing more comfortable shoes, you'd have wanted to go to the University of Washington Botanical Gardens."

"I did. I mean, I do. But I didn't mean for you to go buy me a flower."

One corner of his mouth quirked up. "I didn't buy it. On

my way out the door, my neighbor asked me to help her get something she couldn't reach. I told her I couldn't stay for tea because I was on my way here, so she cut a flower from her garden for you and sent me on my way. Did you like it?"

Her heart softened, not because he didn't waste his money on the flower, but that he'd helped his neighbor. "Of course I liked it." She slid into the car, letting him gently close the door for her then watched him jog around to the driver's side to get in.

He turned the key to start the engine, but before he put it into gear, he raised one hand and brushed her cheek with his fingers, making her automatically turn her head toward him.

Before she could ask what he wanted, he lowered his head and brushed a soft kiss to her lips then turned to hold the steering wheel with both hands.

Without thinking about what she was doing, she raised her fingers to her lips. Not that she'd been kissed by many men, but he was a good kisser. Gentle, soft, and just enough to make her wish that it had lasted longer. "What was that for?" she asked with her fingers still in front of her mouth.

He grinned. "That was the first stolen kiss."

Zella gulped. "First?"

Trevor put the car into gear. "Yup. Buckle up. We're on our way."

"Where are we going?"

"To a little coffee shop by my place. A few friends of mine have a small jazz ensemble, and they're playing there for the week."

Good. A public setting. Where she could be safe from more stolen kisses.

Except when they got there, he led her to a small table in a dimly lit corner with a RESERVED sign on it. He moved the two chairs so they were side by side instead of across from each other, facing the band, and held the chair for her to sit.

"How did you arrange this?"

"I know the owner. Let me go get you a coffee."

Of course he brought back her favorite, a caramel latte with chocolate sprinkles.

He didn't say anything as the band stepped onto the small stage, but when the music started he twined his fingers with hers and held her hand under the table. At the end of every song he released her hand just long enough for a short applause.

They barely said more than a dozen sentences for the duration of the evening, but like their time on the trail—except when she was running after him trying to kill him—the silence was comfortable.

They were just two friends enjoying a relaxing evening together.

Except that friends probably didn't hold hands.

The leader announced their last song, a ballad, and the music began again.

Zella found herself wishing the evening could last longer, even though she had to get up early for work the next morning.

Halfway through the song, Trevor's hand slid out of hers.

She turned to him and opened her mouth to ask why he'd pulled away, when his fingers rested on her cheek.

"This is kind of a romantic song, so. . ." His words trailed off, and he closed his eyes, lowered his head, and kissed her.

This time, it was no quick brush of his lips. He settled in, gently and tenderly and sweetly.

Slowly, he broke contact, returned to a sitting position in his chair, and laced his fingers between hers. He'd said he was going to be romantic, and he was. She hadn't seen this coming, and she wasn't sure how she felt about the change.

Instead of watching the band, she watched Trevor, who didn't seem to notice where she was looking.

She wished she knew what he was thinking. All she'd wanted was to be friends, but friends didn't act this way. A friend wouldn't have kissed like that, leaving her heart pounding and her head swimming.

And if she were just a friend, she wouldn't be wanting another one just like it.

She applauded politely after the last song ended, and like all the patrons, they left the building while the band packed up.

During the ride home she chattered endlessly about the band, barely letting him get a word in edgewise, until they arrived at her house and he stopped in the driveway.

She quickly scrambled out of the car, but like a gentleman, he also exited the car and escorted her to the front door.

"I've been wanting to do this for a long time," he said in a low, husky voice, exactly like he'd sounded earlier over the phone.

Knowing what was going to happen, she let him grip her waist and gently pull her toward him, and he kissed her again. Only this time, his arms slowly slid until they were wrapped around her and he embraced her fully. She slid her arms around his back, clutching him like she was drowning as he kissed her with passion and intent, like he meant it. Heat coursed through her as he stopped, nibbled her bottom lip, and then kissed her again.

When he started to pull away, she slowly began to realize that they were standing by her front door, where anyone in the neighborhood could see them, if anyone cared to look.

As she stepped away, the blinds moved.

Zella covered her face with her hands. "Oh no. My mother."

She didn't regret what had just happened. In fact it had been the greatest kiss of her life. But now that her mother had seen it, Zella had a feeling that it wouldn't be long before she started getting questions about wedding bells.

Trevor wrapped his fingers around her wrists and pulled her hands away from her face. He kissed the tip of her nose then smiled. "Don't worry about her. Let's just take this one day at a time. I'll see you tomorrow, I hope?"

Zella struggled to make her voice work. "Sure. But let's make definite plans."

Plans that didn't involve dark places with candles and music. Or kisses that he didn't have to work very hard to steal.

He'd once mentioned rock climbing, an idea that she'd rejected.

Suddenly rock climbing sound like a lot of fun.

Chapter 7

"Where are you going this time?"

Zella sighed as she sat on the couch to tie her sneakers. "It's Friday. I'm going to my book club meeting. I'm going to be late if I don't leave right away."

"Will you be seeing Trevor?"

"Yes."

"He certainly is a handsome man, isn't he?"

Zella's fingers froze halfway through the process of wrapping the bow on her laces. When they'd first met, the first thing that struck her about him was that he was, without a doubt, incredibly handsome. But besides his good looks, the thing she liked the most about him was his sense of humor. He was a very down-to-earth guy, taking everything in stride, chalking it up to experience—or when he was in writer mode, research.

Fortunately he didn't bruise easily, or else his arms and legs would be as blue as his eyes. When he'd fallen off the climbing wall last weekend, the staff had been ready to call for an ambulance. In the end he'd only had the wind knocked out of him, but she'd been terrified watching him struggle to catch his breath for those first agonizingly long seconds. When he'd regained enough strength to stand, he fought through his labored breathing, unable to wait, so excited to tell her about the incredible sensation of the freefall. Until he landed on the padded mat, which wasn't nearly as well padded as they'd been led to believe. Then he forgot all about complaining about the mat and went back to talking about the freefall and how the next thing they would have to try was skydiving.

Over her dead body.

But then, since he was writing a murder mystery, that was a phrase she could never use around him. Whenever she did, he waggled his eyebrows and laughed.

She cleared her throat and began again, tying the bow. "Yes, he's handsome." In fact, he was so handsome that when they were out in public, she noticed other women watching him, which she didn't appreciate one bit.

"And so tall. He's even taller than you."

Zella's fingers froze. She didn't need to be reminded of how much she stuck out in a crowd, even when she wore the flattest shoes she could buy that still looked half-dainty. Actually, nothing looked dainty in a size ten.

But on the other hand, along with his stolen kisses, Trevor had stolen a piece of her heart when he so gently kissed her on the nose.

No man had ever done that before. First, because no man she'd dated before had to bend down to kiss her nose when they were both standing, but mostly because he'd done it like she was delicate and special. He'd done it to calm her when she had been feeling agitated. That alone earned him points, whether their relationship was real or not.

"Yes, he's tall."

"Is he a keeper?"

Zella zipped her mouth shut. For this, there was no right answer.

"I have to get going; I'm going to be late."

She finally finished tying her sneakers and had almost made it to the door when her cell phone rang. The display showed it was Cindy, which meant it was an answer Zella was waiting for.

Zella glanced at the time as she flipped the phone open. "Hey, Cindy, sorry to bother you. Don't worry, my car is fine. I'm asking for a friend. I need to know how long before the brakes would fail if the brake line is punctured and dripping."

"Who's having brake trouble?"

She couldn't admit to Cindy she was writing a book. She hadn't told anyone, not even Annie. So far she was having fun, but unfortunately she hadn't written anything worthwhile because she'd found out that it was much harder than it looked. However, she was having a blast reading and commenting on everyone else's books and helping with the background research.

"I'm asking for a friend. He's not having trouble, actually, it's more of a hypothetical question. We were just talking about leaking brake lines and how bad it would be before an accident happened. If he was really having trouble with his brakes, you'd be the first to know."

Cindy laughed. "Thanks for the reference. I'm sorry I can't give you an exact answer on that. It really depends how fast it's dripping and if the hole is bad enough that dirt or water gets into the line, which can be just as bad as the brake fluid coming out."

"That helps a lot. I hate to be short but I'm on my way to see him right now. 'Bye."

Once again Zella checked the time as she flicked her phone shut and continued on her way to the door. She had just turned the knob and started to pull the door open when her mother's voice came from behind her.

"What time will you be home? Are you going out with Trevor again when your meeting is over?"

"Yes. Probably."

"Are you sure that's a good idea? I don't know. I'm thinking he seems a little"—she paused, seemingly thinking of the right word—"nefarious."

Zella blinked hard and turned to look at her mother. "Nefarious? What kind of word is that? Have you been reading my new T. J. Zereth book?"

"Of course not. I don't read that kind of junk. I know you and Annie like it, but I don't. I'm just not so sure about your

Trevor. Why were you talking to Cindy about brake lines?"

Zella struggled to think of something to say. If her mother was having thoughts that Trevor might be disreputable, she certainly wasn't going to tell her that she had asked Cindy about cutting brake lines on Trevor's behalf. "I think you're feeling nervous because Trevor is the first man I've dated who is actually taller than me when I wear shoes. Maybe he looks nefarious from down there, but from my height, it's a welcome treat. I really have to go; I'm going to be late. I'll probably be going out with Trevor afterward, so don't wait up."

Before her mother could ask any more questions, Zella dashed out to her car and was moving before she barely had the seat belt fastened. If she caught all the lights green, maybe she could still make it on time.

Trevor tapped his fingers on the tabletop, watching the door, ignoring the chattering around him, and especially ignoring Sheila as she flitted around the room.

For what felt like the tenth time, he checked his cell phone, but there were no missed calls. No new text messages.

But then again, Zella was too sensible to text and drive.

He looked up at the clock on the wall.

She was late.

His stomach churned.

She was never late.

Something was wrong.

If she wasn't coming because she'd somehow figured out that he was T. J. Zereth before he'd worked up the courage to tell her, he'd never forgive himself.

At first, he only wanted to get to know her a bit better before he told her, in case things changed. But then, the more they got to know each other, the more afraid he became, knowing things between them would indeed change. Every time he started to talk about his alter ego she got all starry eyed, like they were talking about a movie star or one of the all-time great mystery authors like Ellery Queen.

By then he didn't know if she would be angrier at him for not telling her or more disappointed that he wasn't special at all. He was just Trevor Jones, full-time windshield repair technician and part-time writer, who, by the grace of God, hit the bestseller list on a couple of slow weeks, and that brief success was what sold him as a series author.

His fear had become so great that for the last three meetings, as he was coming up on a deadline, he'd been too afraid to submit his chapters to the group for fear that Zella would recognize his writing as T. J. Zereth, part-time writer and full-time coward.

He nearly went into heart palpitations when she ran in the door.

"I'm so sorry I'm late. I hope you weren't waiting for me." Zella unceremoniously dumped the wad of everyone's chapters full of her meticulous red notes out of her purse and straightened the pile in front of her.

"I poured you a coffee," Trevor muttered and pushed the now-lukewarm mug toward her.

"Thanks," she said as she sipped it then turned to him. "I think I'm all caught up on reading everyone's chapters. I've got one of yours from a few weeks ago. It's really good. Has anyone ever told you that you write a lot like T. J. Zereth?"

Trevor had never been so glad that he wasn't currently sipping on his coffee. "Yeah," he muttered. "I've been told that."

She stared at him, waiting, but he had no intention of saying more.

Sheila settled down in her chair. "I've met T. J. Zereth."

Zella turned toward Sheila so fast her hair flapped then landed in her face. She swiped it away and stared at Sheila. "Really? Did he sign one of his books for you?"

Sheila grinned ear to ear. "He certainly did."

Trevor held his breath. He hoped Sheila wasn't going to show it to her because Zella had seen his handwriting. He had notes scribbled all over Zella's last chapter.

Zella's eyes widened. "What's he like?"

Sheila folded her hands in front of her on the table. "He's not like you think he'd be. He's not at all shy or quiet. He talks a lot about things that aren't important, and then when something needs to be said, he holds back."

Zella turned to Trevor and grabbed his forearm with one hand, squeezing so tight he was sure she was leaving the imprint of her hand. "Did you hear that? He's secretive. I bet he's just as mysterious as his books."

"And one more thing," Sheila said. "He doesn't really look like that picture on his website, unless he's trying to hide something."

Trevor glared at Sheila. "I know one more piece of information. I hear he's thinking of killing off Mrs. Rubenstein in the next book."

A hush fell around the table, and everyone turned to look at Sheila.

Zella squeezed his arm even tighter. "How do you know that?"

"I don't know. I just kinda get that feeling."

Sheila cleared her throat and tapped her pen on the table. "Enough. We don't want to run out of time. Let's start with Sasha's chapter."

The meeting seemed to drag on forever, and Trevor had never been so glad to see a meeting end as he was tonight.

This weekend he was going to tell her, before it got past the point of no return. If it wasn't already.

After they'd finished packing up, he walked with her to her car then stood in front of her door so she couldn't get away without talking to him first.

"How would you like to go to the corn maze at the Carpinito Brothers farm tomorrow? I need to do another chase scene, but chasing a woman through the forest and dodging trees is getting a little old. I need something different."

"That sounds like fun. I've never been to a corn maze.

It's supposed to be a nice day, so—"

Zella's cell phone stopped her words.

She muttered something he couldn't hear as she dug it out of her purse. "I can't believe how many times this stupid thing has interrupted me today. Why did we ever think cell phones were a good thing to have?" She checked the display then flipped it open. "Hi, Mom. What do you need?"

Trevor watched as her brows knotted and she raised her wrist and checked her watch.

"Now? Are you serious?"

She nodded and listened, her lips drawing into a tight frown.

"I suppose I could. I'll see you soon."

She flipped the phone closed with a sharp flick of her wrist and rammed it in her purse.

"I don't believe this. My mother picked now to bake a cake, and she says she's halfway through and just realized that she's out of eggs. I can't go out for coffee. I have to go to the Fred Meyer and hurry home. But what was even stranger was that she said that she wants me to meet the son of a friend of hers from bingo, and she said he's much more handsome and nicer than you. What have you done to my mother that she's trying to replace you?"

Trevor struggled to remember the only time he'd met Zella's mother. He'd thought everything went well. She'd even primped and tried to flirt with him, as if he would be interested in the mother of the woman with whom he'd already fallen in love.

His heart nearly stopped.

Love.

He'd finally admitted it to himself, even though he already knew that he'd given Zella his heart. He'd always thought love at first sight was just something that sold romance novels to women, but it really was true, because it had happened to him. Zella was his friend and soul mate, and it just occurred to him that he wanted her to be his wife. She was perfect for him in every way.

"You've got a strange look on your face. Don't let your mind wander. You do that a lot, you know. Think of what you said to my mother."

"Oops. Sorry. Give me a minute." While Zella stood before him tapping her foot on the pavement, Trevor searched his memory for the details of the short conversation he'd had with Melissa, or something that he might have done to make her think he wasn't good enough for her daughter.

Aside from not being entirely up front about who he really was, he couldn't think of anything. In fact if Melissa had found out before Zella that he was T. J. Zereth, then the opposite of what was happening would be more likely. Most people thought authors made much more money than they really did. So far, he was considered mid-list, but he was on the brink of reaching the big-time placement and royalty statements he could live on.

"I don't know. But whatever it is, I don't want to make it

worse. I'll go with you to the Fred Meyer because there's a few things I need for myself. Then I guess I'll see you tomorrow. Do you think it would help if I bought a dozen corn on the cobs for your mother as a makeup gift?"

Zella shook her head. "No. My mother really hates corn. Let's get going. I don't want to make whatever she's going through any worse."

Chapter 8

"Wow. This is a lot of corn."

Zella dragged one hand down her face and sighed. "We're standing at the entrance to a corn maze. What did you think we'd see here? Oats?"

Trevor's cheeks darkened, which Zella thought adorable. She didn't often see a man blush. "I guess that wasn't a very intellectual observation. I think what I was trying to say is that I hadn't imagined it being quite like this."

"I think the brochure said there were nearly four miles of paths. I forget how many acres, but it's a lot."

Trevor looked from side to side. "Yeah. This is totally a-maze-ing."

Zella didn't know whether to laugh or groan, so instead she reread the brochure. "There are two mazes here, and they're connected by a bridge in the middle. The rules basically say we're supposed to stay on the path, don't pick the corn, and no smoking. There are posts we're supposed to find that have paper punches to show we've completed the maze. And we should be prepared to get lost. But I can't see that happening." She stopped reading and looked at the other people near the entrance to the mazes. "There doesn't seem to be a lot of people here, but maybe that's because it looks like it's going to rain."

She glanced through the crowd, trying to guess how many people were doing the same thing at the same time. For a split second she saw a familiar pink, the same color as her mother's favorite sweater, but then it disappeared.

But that was ridiculous. Her mother would never come to a place like this.

Trevor shrugged his shoulders. "We had better get going if we're going to do both mazes."

As they trudged through, even though she expected to be following a crowd, the farther they went, the fewer people they saw.

They stopped at a fork in the path, unsure of which way to go. She waited for Trevor to decide, but instead he stood looking up at the top fluffy part of the stalks. "I'm surprised at how tall the corn is. I thought I'd be able to see over it, like in my mother's garden."

Zella also looked up. "I know what you mean. I thought this would be easy, but I don't think it will be."

Trevor broke into a laugh. "You were expecting to see over the corn and cheat!"

"I never said that."

At first the path seemed easy, but it wasn't long before

Zella realized that they'd taken many wrong turns.

She stopped at another decision to go right or left. "We are so lost." She held her palm up. "It's also starting to rain."

Trevor took the map from her and studied it, pointing as he spoke. "We're not lost. I think we're here. Or maybe here. Or we could be here."

She took the map back from him. "Or you have no idea. All you know is which maze we're in out of the two."

He took the map back, and his face turned into an evil grin as he tweaked an imaginary mustache. "Then the better to eat you with, my dear."

"What are you, the Big Bad Wolf? If you are, you're supposed to show me your teeth first. Or you could. . ." Her voice trailed off as she realized what he was doing. They'd talked about his villain chasing one of his female characters through the corn maze. In that case, she would play along, especially since there weren't many people here today. "Oh!" she squealed. "Don't hurt me, you cad!"

Trevor's smile dropped. "Cad?"

"You. . .uh. . .evil bad guy!" She almost called out the word *help* but realized they weren't exactly alone. If she called for help, someone actually might. In order to get a head start, she took advantage of him standing there, all perplexed trying to figure out a better phrase, and turned and ran.

Running through the short turns and small sections of path was harder than she thought, especially since the mulch on the paths had become slippery with the rain. A few times she passed small groups of people who stared at her open-mouthed then cleared the way when they saw Trevor running behind her.

Once, she did what the brochure told her not to do and hid in the corn off the path. Since she didn't want to damage the cornstalks, she didn't go in as far as she should have in order for him not to see her, and she certainly wasn't going to cut through. But when he saw her wedged in the corn row, he tried to stop too fast, sending pieces of mulch flying around him and causing a hole in the path.

"You'd better fix that," Zella called out as she ran away, knowing it would give her a minute's advantage. She could make a lot of distance in a minute.

She bolted past a few more groups of people, and just when she thought she had succeeded in escaping, she found herself in a dead-end path. Before she could get out, Trevor appeared, blocking her way.

"I win," he said as he walked toward her, slipped his arms around her, and pulled her in close for a hug. "Gotcha. You're dead."

"I guess I am. That felt strange. I felt like a human Pac-Man, running through the turns and short paths, trying to escape," she said in between pants as she caught her breath. The rain had picked up and it was now coming down hard. Her hoodie had blown off when she was running, and now her hair was quite wet and getting wetter. "I don't think running through a corn maze is going to work in your book.

If I was really being chased by someone who was really going to hurt me, I wouldn't have hesitated to go off the paths and break through the corn."

"Same. If I were really meaning to catch you, I would have run through the corn to where you were going. You would have made a lot of noise, and you wouldn't have been hard to follow."

When their breathing slowed to normal, Trevor didn't let go. Not only did the rain help cool her down quickly, she was starting to feel cold.

With Trevor holding her tight from head to toe, she felt him shiver. Then, in contrast to her cold skin, his warm lips pressed against her neck, just below her ear.

It felt nice.

Slowly he nuzzled a path to her mouth and gave her a gentle kiss on the lips. "The evil bad guy wouldn't do this, but Trevor Jones would." Not giving her a chance to reply, he settled in for a longer, deeper kiss.

Heat zapped through her, completely canceling out the cold of the water running down her back.

Until her cell phone rang.

"Don't answer that," he whispered against her lips and kissed her again.

She let it ring until it stopped, kissing Trevor back exactly the way he was kissing her.

Until a hard shiver racked his body, causing a mutual separation.

Zella swiped one hand over her hair in attempt to brush off some of the cold water. "It's really pouring. We should leave. Maybe we'll come back another day."

"If you're promising more of the same, you can count on it." He slipped his hand into hers, and they finished off the rest of the maze at a fast walk instead of running out, since they couldn't get any wetter. Just as they got to the car, a police car pulled into the lot with lights flashing.

Zella watched it go straight to the maze entrance. An officer got out and started talking to the attendants. "I wonder what that's about?"

Trevor shrugged his shoulders. "The brochure warned people not to steal the corn. It looks like they were serious."

As they drove out of the parking lot, a familiar blue car in the last spot caught her eye. "That's strange. That looks like my mother's car. When we first got here, I thought I saw her favorite pink sweater. I wonder if she's here, but I don't understand why. This isn't her kind of entertainment."

"Lots of people own blue cars, and lots of women have pink sweaters."

"I guess so. But while I'm thinking about her, before I left today, she asked me if I thought it was safe to come here with you."

Trevor grinned. "Why? Did she think you'd be forever lost in the never-ending labyrinth of killer corn?" He broke out into a full belly laugh. "Or maybe she thinks there's a corn monster, like Bigfoot, who might jump out and get you.

A monster tall enough to see over the corn. With big yellow eyes."

Zella glared at him. "Stop it. I have no idea what she was thinking. Maybe she knew it was going to rain and thought I would catch cold or something." She shivered again, giving the idea of catching a cold more credibility. "I think we both need to change into dry clothes before we have supper. Your place is closer. We can go there first."

They made good time, and before she knew it, Zella was standing in Trevor's living room, listening to the sound of his blow-dryer while he fixed himself up.

She'd never been to his house before, and it felt a little awkward to be left alone in his living room. The place was a mess, not dirty but untidy, made worse that he had books piled everywhere. He appeared to be reading three books at the same time, something she could never do, plus he had two nonfiction books on the craft of writing out, one on the corner of the coffee table nicely bookmarked, but the other hung haphazardly on the arm of the couch, facedown, marking his spot.

Zella shook her head and picked it up. She only had one of such books and had been amazed when she went to the bookstore at how many she had to choose from. She kept her finger in the page to hold his spot and started paging through. If he recommended it, she could buy herself a copy.

"Sorry about the mess." Trevor's voice came from behind her. "As you can tell, I wasn't expecting company."

"Don't worry about it. At least you don't have boxes of half-eaten pizzas lying around." She flipped a few more pages of the instructional book. "This is so overwhelming. I don't know how you do it. There's so much to learn."

He stepped beside her, removed the book from her hands, tucked in a napkin for a bookmark, and set the book on the coffee table. "Yes, there is, but you can do it. I know you said you haven't been writing long, but you've got a lot of potential. Your name would also look great on a book cover."

She glanced around the room. "Speaking of names on book covers, I've tried looking you up online and at the bookstore, and then I remembered you saying you didn't write under your real name, that you use a pseudo. What is it?"

"I...uh..."

She could barely believe that Trevor picked such a moment to be bashful. Instead of looking at him, she turned and stepped closer to his dining room wall, where he had a number of book covers framed and on display. She'd heard that since having a book published was such a major accomplishment, many authors had their covers framed, like a kind of trophy. "Don't be shy. I know you're quite good. You write almost like. . ." Her voice trailed off as she looked at Trevor's book covers. She'd read every single one of them, except for the last one, which she was only halfway through. "T. J. Zereth. All these covers hanging on your wall are T. J. Zereth books."

"It's not what you think."

Her own words that she'd said just the night before at their Friday night book club meeting echoed through her head. But Trevor didn't write merely like her favorite author, he wrote exactly like her favorite author.

She spun to face him. "It's *exactly* what I think. You're T. J. Zereth. Why didn't you *tell* me? I've even said a number of times, right in front of you that he's—*you're* my favorite author."

A mix of emotions flitted across his face, from surprise to embarrassment to confusion. "I"—he dipped his head forward and pinched the bridge of his nose—"I don't know."

"For someone who makes a living at words, you sure don't seem to be able to come up with any good ones right now."

"I don't make a living from it. I replace windshields."

Zella swung one arm through the air to encompass the display of covers on the wall. "You could have fooled me. Why did you lie to me?"

He stood straight, bringing himself to his full imposing height. Or at least a height that would have been imposing to most people. But not her. "I didn't lie to you. I just didn't tell you."

She stomped closer to him. "But everyone else knows, don't they? Sheila, Sasha, Jorg, Patty, all of them on Friday night know, don't they?"

"Well, yes."

Zella covered her face with her hands. "I look like an idiot with you stringing me along like that. Everyone must have had a good laugh when I said how much I wanted to have my picture taken with T. J. Zereth." She lowered her hands and glared at him. "You!"

"No, I don't think they did. I think—"

"Don't bother. I'm leaving."

She turned, grabbed her purse off the coffee table, and stomped toward the door.

"Wait. Don't go. I can explain. I didn't tell you because I wanted to get to know you first, before you found out who I was. I wanted you to get to know the real me first."

She skidded to a halt, spun around, and pointed at him. "The real you is a liar, and I don't want to know that person." She turned and continued to the door.

Trevor raced in front of her and splayed his palm on the back of the door to stop her from opening it. "We need to talk about this. Besides, I brought you here. I have to drive you home."

"No you don't. I will never get in a car with you again. Or a room. I'll catch the bus. If you try to follow me or stop me, I'll scream and someone will call the police."

He pulled his hand away from the door. Zella yanked it open and stormed out, leaving him standing in the doorway.

The second her foot touched the sidewalk, the tears she'd been fighting streamed down her face. She should have thought about it sooner. After reading Trevor's chapter, she knew the title—*Till Death*. And she'd seen on T. J. Zereth's website that same title was his next upcoming release.

Words that she'd heard very recently, twice, at Cindy's wedding and again at Annie's wedding, rang through her head. Wedding vow words. *"Till death do us part."*

She thought she had been falling in love with Trevor and that maybe one day in the future there could be a wedding. But not now. The words *till death* now had them parting for a very different reason, and maybe it was just as final.

She got on the first bus that came by, not caring where it was going, only that it was taking her away. Just like in every make-believe story, this was *The End.*

Chapter 9

Trevor sucked in a deep breath to gather his courage and knocked on the door.

He knew that the relationship between Zella and her mother wasn't great, but for the moment, she was his only connection to Zella.

He'd been a mental wreck all day Sunday, and even going to both the morning and evening church services hadn't helped. He'd nearly broken down and cried like a wuss, and the few people at church whom he'd told about his writing already thought he was a bit mentally unstable.

Every time he'd called, she hadn't answered. She hadn't replied to a single text.

It didn't take a rocket scientist to know she wasn't going to go to the book club meeting on Friday night. Even if she did, he couldn't wait that long.

He couldn't visit her at the pharmacy where she worked, nor could he wait by her car to try to talk to her in the parking lot. He didn't like being a public spectacle, and he knew she wouldn't either.

His only option was to talk to her in the privacy of her home. It probably wouldn't be all that private with her mother home, but her mother was the only way he was going to get in the door.

The door opened. Melissa gasped, and then her face hardened into a tight mask. "Go away or I'm calling the cops."

"The cops? But—"

Melissa stood back, with the obvious intent of slamming the door in his face.

Before she could do that, he went for the proverbial foot-in-the-door trick.

Often people were nervous around him because of his size, but he'd never thought anyone would be afraid of him to the point they needed protection from law enforcement. Especially a woman.

Especially the woman he loved and would die for. Or her mother.

He grimaced, waiting for the pain. He had just told himself he would die for her. A broken foot was nothing in comparison.

All he felt was a small nudge, but he heard a large string of curse words that would do any sailor proud spewing out of Melissa's mouth.

Trevor looked down and grinned. He'd forgotten that since he was coming straight from work, he was still wearing his steel-toed, CSA-certified, size fourteen safety boots. Not only good for falling windshields, they were also good for solid oak doors wielded by angry women.

Without moving his foot out of the doorway, he leaned forward. "I really need to talk to Zella when she gets home."

Melissa had the door gripped so tight her knuckles were turning white. "She's not going to talk to you. I don't know what you're up to or what you're trying to get Zella involved with, but I won't allow it. If you don't go away, I'm calling the cops."

"I'm not trying to get Zella involved in anything. Please let me in. We need to talk." From the look of Melissa, he needed to talk to her almost as much as he needed to talk to Zella.

"No. I don't allow criminals and hit men into my home. I'm warning you."

"Hit men? What are you talking about?"

"I don't know what you're up to, but I know you've been getting Zella to do your dirty work. I heard her asking about poisons and noxious compounds. Whose brake line are you planning to cut and make it look like an accident? I know you've been threatening her. I won't let my little girl get involved with a scumbag like you. Now go away."

"Dirty work?" Trevor's head swam. "I'm not a criminal. I'm a mystery writer. The world knows me as T. J. Zereth. I know you've got all my books in your house."

"No we don't. Zella threw them all in the fireplace last night and burned them."

Trevor cringed. Along with his books, he felt his heart go up in flames.

He cleared his throat then lowered his voice to sound as nonthreatening as possible. "If I wanted to I could push the door open and barge in right now, but I would never do that. I'll wait for you to voluntarily open it and let me in. I know I've hurt Zella. It's just a misunderstanding, but it's a pretty big one and I want to make it better. I need your help and your blessings. Please let me in."

He held his breath and waited. He felt himself about to pass out from lack of oxygen when slowly the door opened.

"Thank you," he said, inhaling deeply.

"How can you be T. J. Zereth? He's Annie's and Zella's favorite author. I thought you were her new boyfriend, the man she met at the book club."

"That's right. All of the above. I made a big mistake and didn't tell her everything about myself because I wanted her to get to know me first, just as the man from the book club."

"Didn't you trust her? Did you think it would make a difference?"

"At first, yes. I was afraid. I also didn't know Zella enough at that point. I know now it wouldn't have made any difference to her. Hindsight is a wonderful thing but most often ineffective. I need to tell her how sorry I am." He paused, which made Melissa look up, right into his eyes. With eye contact locked, he continued. "It all happened pretty fast, but I love your daughter and I need to tell her that.

I only hope that she'll forgive me for my poor judgment." He held out the special copy of his latest book that he'd brought. "I know she hasn't finished reading this one yet, and I want her to have this as a gift. When I give it to her, I would like it if you could give us some time alone to talk."

Melissa blinked. "Are you really T. J. Zereth?"

Trevor smiled. "Sometimes. But for now, I'm just plain old Trevor Jones. That's the T. J. part."

"I guess that makes sense." Melissa checked her watch. "She should be home any minute."

"I know." He squirmed and felt his cheeks heat up. He hadn't slept well, and then he'd gone into work early in order to take a long lunch break, and he'd fueled himself with far too much coffee, which was catching up with him. "Before she gets here, may I use the washroom?"

Melissa pointed. "Down the hall and to the right."

Just his luck, Zella came in while he was still washing his hands.

Her voice echoed down the hall loud and clear. "What's this? I thought I burned it."

He cringed as Melissa's voice came back even louder; he could picture her doing it on purpose so he would hear. "He brought it here for you, as a gift."

"Trevor was here? When?"

Trevor cringed. He'd parked down the street so she wouldn't see his car and know he was there. Now he wasn't sure he'd made the right decision.

He strode down the hall, stopping at the entrance to the living room.

Zella stood facing Melissa, her back to him, his book in her hand, her posture ramrod stiff.

He cleared his throat. "I got here about ten minutes ago, and I'm still here."

She spun around so fast her hair smacked Melissa in the face.

"I have something to do in the kitchen," Melissa muttered then turned and left the room.

Zella held the book out toward him at full arm's length. "I don't want this. Take it back and go home."

He approached her, standing close enough so she wouldn't throw the book at him, literally. "You have every right to be angry. I know I should have told you sooner. At first I was just feeding my ego, thinking that you'd treat me as if I were some big star or something, when I wanted you to get to know just the real me." He lowered his head and ran his hands down the sides of his pants. "I wasn't trying to deceive you. Or maybe I was, but not for the reason you think. As I got to know you better, things changed. I got scared that I wouldn't be able to live up to your expectations. Then you would have been disappointed that when you got to know me, you'd find out I'm just an ordinary guy with a day job." He swallowed. Hard. "I'm sorry."

"Oh." Zella lowered her head and stared at the book in her hands.

Suddenly doubts roared through him. He'd had two days of agony to sort his thoughts and make his plans, but now that it was happening, he realized that he was moving too fast. Just like him, Zella needed time to think, and he hadn't allowed her that.

Slowly she ran her fingers over the embossed lettering of his name on the cover. "I hate to say this, but you were right. I would have thought about you differently. I would have put you in a place that wasn't right, put you on a pedestal you didn't want to be on. But I'll always have the highest respect and even awe for what you've done. You've been blessed with a rare and special talent." She slid a couple of fingers inside the front cover in preparation to open the book. "I'm so sorry I destroyed all your books. Since you've brought this one, I was wondering if you can still fulfill one of my dreams and sign it for me. That would be really special."

Trevor's heart pounded in his chest. This wasn't going as planned. She was opening the book too soon. "No. Wait. I—"

As she flipped the cover, a sparkle of light flashed in her eyes.

Zella gasped.

"I love you, Zella, will you marry me?" he blurted as she stared at the engagement ring he'd put in the hollowed-out center of the book.

With shaking fingers, she pulled the ring out of its nest in the book.

And handed it to him.

Trevor gulped. He'd blown it again. But he would be a man about this. He would summon all his pride and dignity and walk out with his head held high. Then when he got home, if he didn't first run his car off the road, he would find something and break it into a million pieces, like his heart.

"Yes," Zella said, her voice trembling. "I love you, too, and I will marry you. But I can tell you don't do happily-ever-after endings. If that's what you want, I shouldn't put this on my own finger. You should be the one to do that."

Trevor didn't know how he did it without dropping it, but he managed to hold the ring in his hammy fingers, and despite his shaking hands, he slid the ring onto her finger.

"It's a little big, but they can fix that."

"Yes, they can. But you can't fix this book. You'll have to buy me another one. I never did get to finish it."

"It's got a happy ending," he said, grinning as he looked at the ring, his ring, on the finger of the woman he loved. "And now we've got one, too."

He started to close his eyes to kiss her, when he heard Melissa squeal and come running into the room.

"Mother. . ." Zella groaned as she turned around to face her mother. "We're getting married."

Melissa clasped her hands together. "Now I get to plan your wedding. The wedding of someone famous."

"No," Trevor said. "No media, no announcements. I want something quiet and simple. No one really knows who I am, and I want to keep it that way. I want a small wedding at either my church or Zella's church. Close friends and family only."

Zella's eyes lit up. "Or maybe you can pretend we never had this conversation, and then we can elope."

Her mother stepped back, her eyes wide. "Elope? But what about the party? You need a big send-off."

Zella crossed her arms. "Let them party without us."

"Yeah," Trevor said. "I don't do parties. In fact, eloping sounds like a great idea." He turned to Zella then whispered in her ear so her mother wouldn't hear. "Let's do that. How about next Saturday?"

Melissa sighed. "I heard you, but if that's what you want, fine." She shuffled out, and the room fell silent.

Zella giggled. "If this were one of your books, I'd call this a happily-ever-after ending."

"No," Trevor said, wrapping his arms around his bride-to-be. "This isn't the ending. This is the beginning of a new story. Ours. One that we're going to cowrite. Right?"

Zella smiled and snuggled into his chest. "Write. Er, right. Whatever."

NEVER
TOO LATE

Dedication

Dedicated to all the wonderful staff and volunteers
at Homeward Pet Adoption Center in Woodinville,
Washington (www.homewardpet.org). Thank you for your help,
and most of all thank you for giving so many homeless
pets another chance to share their love.

Chapter 1

Farrah Tobias waited as Cindy checked her watch. "Thanks again for housesitting for us," Cindy said. "And Kat-sitting. You don't know how much it means to us. It feels like I've been working ten hours a day, six days a week for months."

Farrah glanced at Kat, who very impatiently stood waiting at the door. "That's because you have. You need this weekend getaway. Especially on your anniversary. You and Luke go have fun. Hurry up or you'll miss your flight. We'll see you Sunday night."

Cindy glanced toward the bedroom, where Luke was still packing. "Still, I would think you have something better to do on a Friday night than making another trip to the animal shelter."

Farrah didn't, but she didn't want to tell Cindy that. In her grandmother's era, fifty was considered nearly over the hill, but in today's world, fifty-year-old women didn't spend all their time sitting in a circle sipping tea in their rocking chairs. Farrah had a rocking chair, but she wasn't ready to retire to it quite yet. Tonight a bunch of her friends had planned to get together to prepare for a shopping trip up to Canada on the next long weekend, but Susan had come down with the flu, so their planning party had been canceled at the last minute.

"Don't worry about it. Just think, when Kat gets her driver's license, she'll drive herself to the shelter."

Cindy's face paled. "That's something I don't really want to think about yet," she muttered.

"I remember when you got your license. The days your father took you out driving were some of the best, and worst, of his life."

Cindy raised one finger in the air. "It wasn't my fault when I hit that tree. Or wrecked that truck."

In the blink of an eye, Kat joined them. "You hit a tree when you were learning to drive? And you wrecked a truck? Maybe you shouldn't be teaching me. Maybe I'll go to that driving school after all."

Farrah burst out laughing. "It really wasn't her fault. Cindy and her father were driving beside a landscaping truck, and a tree fell out of the back of the pickup. It bounced, landed in front of her, and she hit it."

Kat stared at Cindy. Her eyes widened. "That must have been scary."

"Not as scary as the truck behind me," Cindy said as she shuddered. "When I slammed into the tree, I thought the truck behind me was going to squash us. It swerved at the last second and went into the ditch. Then it tipped. Watching it go over was like in the movies when all the bad things happen in slow motion. Except in real life it was terrifying. He couldn't stop because he'd been following too close. You know how traffic is around here. He wasn't badly hurt, but he blamed me for wrecking his truck."

"What about the guy who lost the tree? Did he come back?"

"No, but the car beside me chased him and had almost caught up to him when a police car caught him in his radar. Then the cop chased him while he chased the landscaper."

Luke joined them. "You never told me about that. It sounds like something that would happen in one of Trevor's books."

Kat grinned ear to ear. "Trevor gave me his autograph. I showed it to all my friends at school, and they want to know where I saw T. J. Zereth. I wish I could tell them that we're related." Kat turned to Cindy. "Am I related to T. J. Zereth? I mean Trevor?"

Cindy started counting the relationship jumps on her fingers. "Let's see. Luke is your uncle, and he's married to me, and I'm Zella's stepsister, only related by marriage, and Zella's married to Trevor. That wouldn't count as being related. Sorry."

Farrah shook her head. She couldn't believe that Zella had married so fast. Or Annie, for that matter.

Actually Cindy had married quickly, too. She barely had the engagement ring on her finger before the matching wedding ring joined it. Of course because of her job, she seldom wore either on her finger; instead, the rings hung around her neck on her mother's gold chain.

Farrah sighed. She'd been in love like that once, and she'd thought she would have one of the happily-ever-after relationships that Cindy, Annie, and Zella were all embarking on. But it hadn't worked out that way, and time kept marching forward. She'd turned thirty then forty, and a month ago she'd turned fifty, without ever having fallen in love like that again. She had come to accept that after what she'd been through, she no longer had it in her.

Of course she was happy that love had happened for her goddaughter, as well as Cindy's stepsisters, especially now that the three girls had become almost as close as real sisters. With Cindy married to Luke, Farrah spent so much time with Kat that it was like having a god-granddaughter, if there were such a thing.

"Come on, Kat. Let's let Cindy and Uncle Luke finish packing. I'll let you drive."

Matt Robinson double-checked the catch on the gate to the cage. Fortunately this dog hadn't been abused, only neglected.

He paused and lowered his head to rest against the cold metal fencing. *Only* neglected. Every time he saw what some of these animals had endured, it tore at his heart, and that was why he was there. He and his partner at the clinic, both veterinarians, each volunteered several days a month at the Homeward Pet Adoption Center animal shelter. As well, when a volunteer or the staff veterinarian called in sick or needed a day off, he frequently gave them extra time, as long as his appointments at his clinic were covered.

It was Friday night, and a small group of teens would be arriving soon—a kindhearted bunch who gave up part of their weekend to walk and bathe the animals at the shelter and clean and disinfect the cages. All of them would spend time petting and comforting the animals waiting to be adopted.

He sighed as he looked at the dogs, many with their noses at the front of their enclosures, waiting, watching him. Probably hoping that he would take them home.

This same sight, replayed with each visit, broke his heart. He wished he could take them all home, but he already had enough animals. He could only suggest that when someone lost a beloved pet, he or she might think about paying a visit to the shelter.

Matt straightened as he saw one of the teen volunteers approaching with her mother. He recognized this girl because she'd been part of the adoption of a dog he'd saved after a car accident. Not long after she adopted the dog, she began volunteering at the center.

Matt found it very amusing that a girl named Kat helped

her uncle adopt a dog. It was outright funny that she'd named a three-legged dog Tippy. He hadn't seen Tippy since the pooch had left the shelter, but he knew she was in a good home. In fact, from what he'd heard, it sounded like the dog was in Kat's home most of the time.

"Hi, Kat," he called out and waved. He liked to meet the younger volunteers' parents, to compliment the work that their kids did as a way of showing his appreciation.

When the two reached him, he extended his hand to Kat's mother. "I'm Matt. I'm covering for the staff vet today. It's a pleasure to finally meet you. Usually Kat's uncle drops her off."

Kat and her mother exchanged a strange look before the woman reciprocated the handshake. "My name is Farrah. It's nice to meet you, too."

Matt smiled. "I wanted to say how great it is to have Kat volunteering here. She's wonderful with the cats, and she does a great job helping in the cat rooms. How's Tippy been doing lately? On my last schedule, I heard that she was burying socks in the backyard."

Farrah turned to Kat. "She is?" Farrah started to laugh. "I hope she buried those ugly socks of yours with the toes."

Kat's eyes narrowed and her mouth tightened. "Those are my favorite socks." She turned back to Matt and smiled. "Where do you want me to start?"

"Since you're the first one here, how about you start at number one. I see Jeff and his dad coming into the lot. He

278

can start at the other end, and you can meet in the middle."

Kat grinned. "Sure, but first I want to see Muffy's kittens."

Before he could tell her that one of them had already been adopted, Kat grabbed her mother's hand and dragged her off to the cats' building.

As they walked away, Kat glanced over her shoulder at him and grinned then turned back to her mother, lowering her voice as they walked away.

"See? I told you Dr. Matt was a hottie."

Matt choked then thumped himself in the chest. He'd never been called a *hottie* in his life and certainly not since he was nearing forty years old.

He watched the two of them disappear around the corner, and when they were gone, he pressed one hand over his stomach, which wasn't bulging, but wasn't as flat as it used to be.

He couldn't help but be charmed by Kat's mother's smile. He knew Kat was seventeen, which made him guess her mother to be about the same age as he was, give or take a few years.

Not that he was interested in married women, but maybe there was still hope for him, after all.

Chapter 2

Farrah followed Kat to the cat room and stood to the side as Kat got ready to start cleaning the cages.

"What do you think of Dr. Matt?" Kat asked as she hung up her sweater in the closet.

"I really didn't have much of a chance to talk to him, but he seems nice."

"He's Tyler's uncle. That's how I found out about this place."

"That's nice."

"Tyler first started volunteering here because of his uncle Matt."

"It's really good of Tyler to do that."

Kat giggled. "My friends think he's so hot because he's doing this."

Farrah lost her smile. "Tyler should be volunteering here because he wants to help the animals, not to impress the girls."

"He does help the animals." Kat nodded her head so

fast her hair bounced. "He wants a dog and a cat but his mom won't let him. That's why he likes doing this. We get to hold and cuddle all the cats. It's really important to keep their cages clean, and we have to update the logs for food and meds if the cats need them. But the best part is holding them. The staff calls it socializing."

"Ah. Socializing. So that's what's going on here." Farrah smiled, but Kat just kept going.

"Tyler is going to be eighteen in a few months. After he goes through some training, he's going to change and be a volunteer to help the dogs. He says he wants to be a vet, just like his uncle. He'll make a really good vet."

It looked like Kat was quite taken with Tyler; maybe she should discuss that with Cindy. Farrah had never been a parent, but she'd loved her best friend's daughter like her own—and Dave needed help raising his daughter. It had been in the difficult year when Cindy was seventeen that Dave had first thought about getting married again, and not long after that he'd met Melissa, who was recently divorced and was looking for a husband after her ex left the country. Initially they thought it would be good for all the girls. But Melissa had never liked Cindy and only put on a show in front of Dave. Farrah had seen through Melissa's actions, but Dave hadn't believed her, and after they were married it was too late.

Now ten years later, she was more than happy to help Kat the same way she'd helped Cindy through those difficult years without a mother. However, Cindy had always been somewhat of a tomboy and never had trouble relating to the boys, especially once she had a hockey stick in her hand. But Kat was girlie through and through, down to her pink socks and Hello Kitty cell phone.

"Dr. Matt is single."

"Why did I need to know that?"

Kat scrunched her brows, tilted her head, and crossed her arms. "Because you're single, too."

Farrah pinched the bridge of her nose and shook her head. "My life is fine. I'm not looking to get married."

"Cindy said you need someone to love."

She would definitely have a talk with Cindy. "*If*"—she emphasized the word—"I need someone to love, I'll adopt a pet. In the meantime, I'm fine the way things are. After all, I have you to love."

Kat rolled her eyes. "Puh-leeze," she whined, "that's not what I meant and you know it. I think. . ." Kat's voice trailed off, and her eyes widened. "Speaking of adopting a pet—"

Farrah suddenly had the feeling her words were about to be used against her. "I don't know what you're thinking, but you can stop it right now. I work full-time, and I'm not going to leave an animal home alone all day, every day."

"Tiffany's sister's dog just had puppies, and they found out that their baby is allergic to dogs. Tyler's grandparents are fostering the dog and the puppies until they can find homes for them, but they need help because it's a lot of work. And it's going to be more work as the puppies are getting bigger. Can you help us with the puppies until we find people to adopt them?"

Farrah looked around Homeward Pet's facility. It looked like a very caring and professionally run place, but they probably would agree that it was best for new puppies to be with their mother in a loving foster home until they found new owners.

She didn't know how old Kat's friend's grandparents were, but she did know that looking after a litter of puppies was no small feat.

"How many puppies are there?"

"Eleven."

Farrah cringed. "What kind of dogs?"

"They don't know. The mom is mostly a fox terrier. They have no idea who the daddy was; they just say he was big. The youth group from church is helping, but none of us has a car."

"So in other words, you don't really need my help with the dogs. You want my help as a taxi service."

"Kinda."

That, she could do. She'd already met many of the teens in the youth group, and she'd never forget meeting Tyler. This would be a way to keep her eye on that one.

"I suppose I could." Farrah checked her watch. "I'll be back in three hours when your shift is over, and then I'll take you out for a burger."

Kat's eyes lit up. "Sweet!"

Matt watched as his nephew ate all of his own fries then started on Matt's. Both orders had been supersized. He couldn't imagine his sister's grocery bill. Which was one of the reasons he'd given Tyler a part-time job at his clinic. Of course the main reason was that Tyler simply loved animals, and he had a heart for the larger dogs that sometimes needed a stronger handler.

He stared as Tyler blatantly finished off the rest of his fries. "Now I see why you wanted to come here. Would you like the rest of my burger, too?"

Tyler glanced toward the door, and if Matt wasn't mistaken, the boy was nervous. "That's okay. Thanks," he muttered.

Matt leaned back in the chair. "You're hiding something. What's up?"

Tyler once again glanced over his shoulder and cleared his throat. "I know I ate your fries, but that wasn't the real reason I wanted to come here. Kat and Farrah were supposed to be here. Kat said you met Farrah today and she thought you were hot."

Matt frowned. "I met Kat's mother, and that wasn't exactly the way the conversation went."

Tyler's mouth dropped open. "You've met Kat's mom? When? I didn't know you knew Kat from before."

Matt shook his head. "Before when? I met her tonight when they came into Homeward Pet."

Tyler glanced at the door, scanned what he could see of the parking lot through the window, leaned forward over the table, and lowered his voice to barely above a whisper. "Uncle Matt, Kat's mom is dead."

What little appetite Matt had, vanished. He tried to recall the short conversation of earlier that evening, trying desperately to remember if he'd addressed Farrah as Kat's mother or not. He'd assumed but couldn't remember if he'd actually said it out loud. "I didn't know," he mumbled.

"Kat lives with her uncle, who married Cindy, who helps out with the youth group at my church."

Pieces of the conversation started falling into place. He'd been surprised that Kat's mother didn't know that their dog had been burying socks in the backyard. Now he knew why. It wasn't Farrah's dog or Farrah's backyard.

"Then who is Farrah?" In his mind, he pictured Kat's uncle and compared him with Farrah. While it was possible, it seemed like a rather large age gap between them to be brother and sister, although with blended families these days, anything could be possible.

"I'm not really sure. She's somehow related to Cindy, but I don't know how. Kat explained it all to me, but it's really complicated and I couldn't keep track. All I know is that she's not related to T. J. Zereth."

"Who?"

Tyler's eyes widened. "The author. I wasn't supposed to say anything. Pretend I didn't say that." Tyler glanced again to the door. "Here they come. Pretend this is a surprise."

"Why?"

"Because Farrah doesn't know that we're here."

"Why is that important?"

"Because we thought it would be good for you to meet her. She's not married either."

Matt squeezed his eyes shut. He'd suffered through many matchmaking attempts with friends and his sister, but never from the younger set and certainly not from a boy.

He opened his eyes and watched Kat and Farrah, whatever relation she was to Kat, as they stood in line to place their orders.

Because he was approaching forty, those who didn't know his reason for wanting to remain single kept trying to introduce him to women who were under thirty-five. Even his sister, who did know his reason, still kept trying. But Farrah wasn't under thirty-five. She looked like she could be anywhere up to forty—maybe forty, meaning she was possibly a few years older than he was.

In a way, he found the innocence of the teens trying to hook him up with an older woman refreshing. Unlike his adult friends, they weren't looking for someone who was still of childbearing age, but merely single—someone who could be a companion for him, not the mother of his children.

Because Farrah was probably past the point of her biological clock ticking loudly, he would humor Tyler. Matt had no intention of getting married, but he was always open to meeting a new friend.

"Okay, I'll cooperate and pretend I don't know what you and Kat are doing. But no more. After today, don't ever do anything like this again."

Tyler grinned ear to ear. "Of course, Uncle Matt."

Matt narrowed his eyes and studied Tyler. Why didn't Matt believe him?

Chapter 3

Look! There's Tyler and Dr. Matt!"

Farrah picked up the tray with their food and turned to watch Kat make a beeline to Matt and Tyler's table. Kat turned and waved. "Look! They even got a table with four chairs. We'd better sit with them."

Looking around the restaurant, there were many empty tables. Farrah didn't know whether to be amused or concerned at Kat's excitement to sit with Tyler and his uncle. If she had any doubts, it was now more than obvious the girl had a big crush on Tyler.

She lowered the tray to the table. "Hi, Matt, Tyler. Fancy meeting you here."

Tyler and Matt had been sitting across the table from each other. Naturally, Kat sat beside Tyler, so Farrah sat beside Matt.

Matt smiled at her as she divided up the burgers and fries between herself and Kat. "You might want to keep those fries a little closer if you value them."

Tyler's eyes widened. "Uncle Matt!"

Kat looked up at Tyler, all starry-eyed. "I'll share my fries with you if you're still hungry, Tyler."

Matt rolled his eyes.

Farrah bit her lip. She cleared her throat and turned to Matt. "Kat tells me that you're the vet who saved Tippy's life."

He shook his head. "I did the surgery, but it wasn't really me who saved Tippy. A young couple brought her into the clinic in tears after they'd hit her. They were the ones who really saved her by bundling her up and taking her to the nearest vet, which was me. I just did the technical stuff."

Kat fluttered her eyelashes at him. "Dr. Matt is a hero. He operated on Tippy even though her owners wouldn't pay. So he saved her life."

Matt shrugged his shoulders. "What's important is that she's in a good home. Sometimes it's hard for the shelter to place special-needs animals."

Kat narrowed her eyes and glared at him. "Tippy isn't a special-needs dog. There's nothing wrong with her. The only thing she needs is for us to walk a little slower. Tippy is fine."

Matt grinned. "See what I mean? A good home."

Farrah checked her watch. "Speaking of a good home, we shouldn't stay too long. Tippy's been home alone for nearly four hours."

Kat nodded. "That's right. Do you mind if Tyler and Dr. Matt come with us? I need Tyler to help me with my algebra.

Then you and Dr. Matt can take Tippy for a wobble."

"A wobble?"

Kat blushed. "That's what Uncle Luke says. But I really need Tyler to help me with my homework."

"On Friday night?"

Kat and Tyler nodded in unison.

Matt rolled his eyes again.

Tyler became very serious. "Kat and I can do our homework, and you two can take Tippy for a walk then maybe watch a movie or something."

Kat grinned ear to ear. "That's a great idea."

Farrah narrowed her eyes and studied the two teens. She had doubts that homework was what they'd planned to do.

"Or," Matt continued, "I have a better idea. I'm really good at algebra." He turned to Kat. "How about if I help you both with your algebra? I had to take a lot of math courses in veterinary college. Then we can all watch the movie together."

Kat's eyes widened. "I guess so."

Farrah bit her lip to hide her grin. It seemed that she wasn't the only one who didn't want Kat and Tyler left alone in the house.

She turned to Matt. "As long as you don't have other plans for the rest of the evening, I don't mind."

Matt shrugged his shoulders. "I'm good." He turned to Tyler. "Unless you had. . .plans. Tyler?"

Tyler's cheeks darkened. "Uh, no plans, Uncle Matt."

All Farrah could do was stare at Tyler. She didn't know why

the boy was blushing, but it seemed Matt knew something she didn't know or knew how to push the boy's buttons.

Farrah gathered the paper trash onto the tray and stood. "We have to go let Tippy out. Do you know how to get to Luke and Cindy's house?"

Matt and Tyler stood as well and scooped their garbage onto their own tray.

"Tyler can give me directions. I know the perfect movie. I'll pick it up and we'll meet you there."

Matt sighed, pausing before knocking on the door of Kat's uncle's house. He'd been the unwilling victim of many blind dates, but this was the strangest, if not the most well planned.

He turned to Tyler with his fist poised in midair. "Was this harebrained idea yours or Kat's?"

"We kind of thought of it together. Mom thought it was kinda funny."

Wonderful. Even his sister knew. He wondered how many other family members were having a chuckle at his expense tonight.

Although part of it, he knew, was out of guilt. But what was done was done. Nothing was ever going to change it. He'd accepted his lot years ago, even though he'd spent too much time being angry and bitter. Now he didn't know whether to speak to his sister and tell her to butt out, knowing full well that she would never stop, or again grit his teeth and let it go. But if he didn't let it go, he would only become bitter. Again.

So he raised his fist and knocked.

Farrah opened the door, smiled, and stood back for them to enter. "I thought I'd make a tray of nachos for the movie. I'm sure it won't take long before all the homework is done."

Matt looked into her striking green eyes. Eyes with cute little crinkles at the corners. Farrah really was an attractive woman. Not model thin, she had an extra pound or two that told him she had no issues with vanity and was comfortable with herself. He liked that.

And he could tell she really had no idea the teens were setting them up. She was only trying to make the best of unexpected company, when probably all she wanted to do was relax after a long week at work. He had no idea what kind of work she did, but he could see that she looked tired.

He followed her into the living room, where Kat already had her textbooks and notepaper spread over the coffee table. Tyler had come prepared with all the books he needed in his backpack.

Of course high school algebra was different than what he'd needed in veterinary college, but he'd always been good at math, so he was sure he could help them with whatever problem they were having. If they were having a problem. Which he doubted.

As suspected, the kids got more help from each other than from him. Matt excused himself and sauntered into the kitchen to see if Farrah needed his help, since Kat and Tyler didn't.

She didn't either. He found her seated comfortably at the kitchen table, her feet up on one of the chairs, reading not a book but an e-book reader. All the fixings of the promised nacho platter sat ready on the counter. Beside her, Tippy lay curled up on the floor, predictably between Farrah and the food.

"That was fast. I came in to see if you needed any help."

She extended one hand in the air to encompass the food. "Nope. All done. Kat loves nachos." She read a bit more, pushed the button to turn the e-reader off, and then put it down on the table. "Sorry. I had to finish the page. I hadn't expected to like this book because I've never read this author before, but it's really quite good."

Matt smiled. "No problem. I like to read, too." Again, he scanned all the fixings for their snack. He felt himself getting hungry just looking at it. He stepped closer and checked out the salsa, which unless he was mistaken, wasn't out of a jar but homemade. "This looks really delicious. Are you a chef?"

Farrah laughed. "Me? No. But I do like to cook. I made the salsa but not here. I always make a big batch and bring some over for Cindy because she likes it, too. No, I'm just a teacher."

Matt covered his face with his hands. "Please don't tell me you're a math teacher and I've embarrassed myself by telling them I could help."

"No. I teach elementary school. Grade five. I do teach math but nothing like what Kat and Tyler are doing."

"How long do you think we should give them to finish?"

"I'm not sure. They can call us when they're done."

"I'm pretty sure they won't be much longer." In fact, he was sure of it. Not only did they not need his help, they only had a few pages to do.

"We can get right into the movie. Tippy's been out already. What did you pick? Whatever it is, I probably haven't seen it. I don't watch many movies, I prefer to read."

Matt paused, now wondering if he'd made the right choice with the movie. He hadn't wanted to pick a movie that would in any way be associated with a date, for either himself and Farrah or for Kat and Tyler. But now he didn't know how he could rationally explain his choice. "It's an older movie, actually. I picked it for Tyler and Kat because of the characters and with them working at the shelter."

Farrah's eyebrows raised. "How old?"

He tried not to blush. "It was actually my sister's favorite movie. She—"

"Uncle Matt!"

Matt grinned at Tyler's outburst, loud and clear from the living room.

"It sounds like they found the movie."

Chapter 4

Tyler held out the movie toward him. "*Homeward Bound?* This is a kid's flick."

As Matt reached for it, Kat grabbed it from Tyler's hand and began to read the cover jacket. "This is *The Incredible Journey*. I had to read this in elementary school. I didn't know it was a movie."

Matt grinned. "This is the remake."

Farrah tapped his arm. "They're too young to know that. They wouldn't have seen the original movie. To them, this one *is* the original."

Actually, the only reason Matt had seen the original was because his parents had taped it for him off the television using a VCR.

Kat pointed to the list of credits of the main characters. "Who are these people?"

Farrah smiled. "The voice of the cat is Sally Field. Her first major credit was *The Flying Nun*."

Kat looked up. "The what?"

"I used to watch it all the time when I was a kid."

Matt looked at Farrah. He'd heard about *The Flying Nun* but never seen it. His parents hadn't got their first VCR until he was in middle school.

Kat looked down at the cover jacket again. "I've heard of Michael J. Fox."

Matt grinned. "He starred in my favorite movie series when I was a kid. *Back to the Future*. I think it was one of the first movies they made into a video game for NES."

"NES? What's that?"

Inwardly, Matt cringed. He wasn't quite forty, but sometimes the teens made him feel like he was fifty. "Never mind. It was state of the art in its day. Let's put the movie on. It used to be Tyler's mother's favorite movie." He neglected to add, "when she was little" on purpose.

Kat's eyes widened. "If it was your mom's favorite movie, I want to watch it. I don't know what my mom's favorite movie was." Her voice dropped down, and she spoke with a tremor. "I wish I had paid more attention to stuff like that. Now I'll never know."

Tyler's eyes softened. "I'm sure she would have liked it just like my mom did. Let's watch it."

Now Matt knew he'd picked the wrong movie. He hadn't meant to make Kat sad. He'd actually thought parts of the movie were pretty funny. The funniest was that his sister cried every time it looked like Shadow wasn't going to make it, regardless of how many hundreds of times she'd watched it. No matter how old he was, he always thought it was funny making his sister cry. But he hadn't wanted to make Kat cry.

Farrah tapped his arm again. "This was a good choice. It will be good for Kat to think of her mother watching this movie."

All he could do was stare at Farrah, wondering if she'd read his mind.

As the movie progressed, Matt was relieved to see that Kat and Tyler enjoyed it and amused that Farrah commented on certain parts she remembered watching with Cindy.

By the time the movie was nearly over, in exactly the part where his sister had always started to cry, so did Kat. He didn't know whether it was good or bad that Tyler slipped his arm around Kat while she sniffled. Since he and Farrah were watching, he wrote it off as harmless, but this was something he would tell his sister to keep an eye on. To give Farrah credit, she didn't sniffle, but she chose that very moment to clean up the remnants of the nachos.

They sat around and chatted for a little while, but it didn't take long for Matt to start feeling tired. He'd been up at 6:00 a.m. to do a surgery at the clinic, and after he'd worked all day, he'd gone to the shelter. It was now nearly midnight, and he was feeling every minute.

Beside him, Farrah stifled a yawn.

Matt stood. "Come on, Tyler. It's time for me to take you home. I'm tired; it's been a long day."

Farrah and Kat escorted them to the door. He kept an

eye on the two teens, as did Farrah, to make sure there were no parting smooches. Although, strangely, he wanted to give Farrah a little peck on the cheek.

He might have, too, if Tyler and Kat hadn't been watching him.

It had been a long time since he'd spent an evening in the company of a woman, and even though she didn't know it was supposed to be a date, it had almost felt like one. Actually, no, tonight hadn't been a date, it had been an entrapment. Except that he'd enjoyed himself and wished they could do it again.

He turned to Farrah. "This was good. Thank you. I guess I'll see you the next time we cross paths at the shelter."

She nodded, mumbled a good night, and the door closed as Matt and Tyler walked to the car.

"Well? Wasn't she nice? Did you like her?"

Matt sighed. "You promised me you were going to drop this. I'm not getting involved in any matchmaking schemes, so you can stop it right now."

"Sorry, Uncle Matt."

The trouble was, Matt was sorry, too. Farrah was a nice woman, and if he'd been in the market for a match, he had a feeling that Farrah would be a keeper. It was almost too bad that the chances of their crossing paths again at the clinic would be small. Probably for the best.

"Aren't the puppies cute?" Kat nearly purred as she picked up the runt of the litter and gave it a gentle squeeze.

Farrah couldn't help herself. She picked up one of the larger pups and hugged it. "Yes, they're adorable. And you're right, it's a lot of work to look after all these puppies. Tyler's grandparents were very generous to commit to taking care of all of them." Although Theresa and Bill weren't the frail old couple she'd been led to believe. They were only a dozen years older than she was and excited about all the fun things they were going to do when they retired. They'd clearly been active; Theresa looked every day of her sixty-two years, either from too much time in the sun or simply genetics.

Farrah had never been one to suntan, and she'd been lucky with her genetics. Like her own mother, she always looked ten years younger than her actual age—something she'd really grown to appreciate. She didn't have any wrinkles yet, and the last time she'd checked, she only had one gray hair, which she hadn't bothered to pull out, despite the mortification of her friends. And now that she'd turned fifty, Farrah had also been thinking of what she was going to do when she retired. Probably not much traveling, considering her teacher's pension, but she had good friends and family.

Theresa reached into the basket and also picked up one of the pups. "Are you and your daughter considering keeping one of these?"

Farrah smiled graciously at Theresa. The tragedy of losing Kat's parents and the complicated relationship between them was difficult to explain to strangers, so they'd both learned to respond politely rather than let the situation become awkward.

"No," Kat said. "I already have a dog. I'm just here to help."

"Good morning, ladies," a smooth male voice sounded behind them. "Fancy meeting you here. Hi, Mom. I see you've met Kat and Farrah."

Farrah turned to greet Matt. She shouldn't have been surprised to see him. Now that she thought about it, Tyler's grandparents were, of course, Matt's parents.

Theresa handed the pup in her arms to Matt. "I see Tyler is here. Where's Stephanie? Or did you bring him?"

"I brought him. He wanted me to have a look at one of the pups. He says that one's not gaining weight as fast as the others and I should have a look at it."

Kat jumped up. "That would be this one. She's so little."

Matt handed the large pup back to Theresa and took the small one from Kat. "This is the runt of the litter. She's probably getting outmuscled because she's outnumbered. Being the smallest, she has the least fight. Sometimes we have to help by giving the smallest ones a bottle."

Kat's eyes widened. "Can I do that?"

"You certainly can." He reached into his pocket and handed her his car keys. "There's a box on the backseat."

Kat grabbed the keys and was already on the run before Matt finished his sentence.

He smiled at her disappearing figure. "She's a good kid. I can see why Tyler likes her."

"She also likes Tyler, but I don't know Tyler well enough to comment."

"He's a good kid, too. Because he's so tall and the girls watch him, he plays the part in front of his friends, but he's really not like that. I keep telling him that if he acts like that in front of his friends, that's what everyone's going to think." Matt paused and tickled the little runt. "But he's only got eyes for Kat. Ever since she first joined the hockey team."

Farrah sighed. "Hockey. I'm afraid to mention hockey around Cindy, especially since her love of the game has rubbed off so much on Kat. I'm afraid I'm not really a fan."

"Me neither. I'm more into baseball myself."

Kat returned with the box Matt had instructed her to get, and Tyler followed close behind. Farrah stood aside and watched as Matt instructed them how to mix the formula ingredients, warm it in the microwave, and pour it into the bottle that was especially for puppies.

It made Farrah wonder why a man who was so gentle and caring with animals wasn't married and doing the same for children.

As he stood back to watch Kat feeding the pup, Farrah moved closer to Matt. "I know you see everyone else's pets all day long, but do you have any pets of your own?"

"Yeah. It's a proverbial zoo at my place. I have a dog, a cat, a lizard, and a rabbit. No birds, though. I couldn't stand the noise. Besides, I don't think a cat and a bird make compatible housemates."

"What about the cat and the rabbit?"

"It's a really big rabbit and a very small cat." He turned to her and grinned. "What about you?"

She shook her head. "No pets, just a couple of fish. I don't like to leave pets home alone while I'm at work."

"I leave the cat and the lizard and the rabbit at home all day, and they're fine. But I take Rex to the clinic every day. He thinks he's our mascot, and he gets really upset if he thinks I'm going to work and not taking him with me. Here, Kat, try this."

When he hunkered down to give Kat a little help with the pup, Farrah studied Matt. She couldn't count the times Kat had told her how hot Matt was for an older guy. She had to admit that he was a handsome man, and not so old, probably a decade younger than she was. But more than good looks, he had a soft heart for both pets and the teens. She wondered again why he wasn't married with a dozen kids of his own instead of spending so much time with his nephew and, now that she knew, a plethora of pets.

After Matt showed Kat how to burp the puppy, he once again stood and stepped back.

Still sitting on the ground and not looking like she wanted to put the puppy down, Kat looked up at Farrah with big, wide eyes. "I don't want to go home yet. Can I stay here? I also just thought of something. I think I forgot to let Tippy out. Maybe you and Dr. Matt should go back to Uncle Luke's and let her out. And I'm getting hungry. The two of you could stop somewhere for lunch and then bring back a couple of burgers or a pizza or something for me and Tyler."

Matt's eyes narrowed and he glared at Tyler, whose cheeks and ears turned a brilliant shade of red. "Tyler?" he muttered between his teeth.

Tyler cleared his throat. "I never thought of that. I really didn't. But I think it's a great idea. Can we stay with the puppies and Gramma and Grampa? You guys can come back later for us."

"You know Gramma and Grampa will give you lunch."

"Yeah, but maybe it would be a nice treat for you to bring them lunch, too. After all, they're doing a lot of work with these puppies. Don't you think?"

Matt slumped. Farrah could almost see the waves of guilt stabbing at him.

Then he sighed. "That's fine with me, what about you?" He turned to Farrah. "I don't mind driving you back to let Tippy out then picking up lunch for everyone."

Tyler grinned, and some of the color faded from his cheeks. "No rush. You two can take your time. Right, Kat?"

Kat nodded. "Right."

Farrah didn't understand why the two teens were trying to get rid of them, but she did know that they were in good hands with the puppies and Matt's parents watching them. Maybe she needed to talk to Matt about this, although she wasn't quite sure what to ask.

She turned to him. "That sounds good. Your car or mine?"

Chapter 5

Matt bit his bottom lip so Farrah wouldn't see him smiling and pretended to watch something out the car window as she drove to Kat's uncle's house.

He couldn't help himself. He couldn't remember the last time he'd felt so relaxed in the company of a woman—if he ever had—or if he'd ever enjoyed himself so much when they weren't really even doing anything. Of course, this situation was different than any he'd ever been thrust into. This was another blind date carefully orchestrated by Kat and Tyler, and again, Farrah appeared to have no idea that they'd been set up. But, unlike most women, it didn't matter if the meetings were planned or not. Every time he found himself alone with a marriageable woman, it soon became obvious that marriage was on her mind.

But not Farrah. So far the things she had on her mind were Kat and Tyler's relationship, the puppies, the gas mileage of her car, the rising price of gas, the parent-teacher meetings at her school, the upcoming Mariners season, the shopping trip to Canada she was planning with her friends, the possibility of snow this winter, and, of all things, that she was looking for a guitar so she could take lessons. All that in a fifteen-minute trip.

He turned to watch her as she reached for the switch to open the garage door and turned into the driveway. She was in no way a hermit, but she'd made no reference to seeing him again, nor had she expressed any desire to establish a relationship. She'd done nothing to try to impress him, and she'd even asked if he was aware he had a hole in his T-shirt. Then she pointed out that he'd missed a spot when he shaved that morning.

He followed her into the house then to the back patio door, where they stood side by side while waiting for Tippy to do her thing in the backyard.

"I had a feeling," Farrah muttered. "She's not doing anything except checking the last sock she buried." She pointed to a few raised mounds of dirt. "I don't know how she does that. How does she balance to dig?"

"You'd be surprised. With a little support, dogs adapt very quickly, even to tragedies. Unlike people." Although, part of the reason for that was that unlike people, animals didn't realize what they were missing. Matt lived with constant reminders of what he could never have.

But now that he was getting older, that cycle of life had passed him by, and a new cycle was beginning.

Maybe Tyler was right. He didn't have to marry Farrah. They could be friends, and, yes, he could even date her. If nothing became of it, that was fine. And if something did, it felt good to discover that would be fine, too. That she was three or four years older than he was didn't matter. All that mattered was she was past childbearing age, so he didn't have to think too far into the future.

For the first time in many years, he'd met a woman he liked. She was stable, responsible, and a firm believer with both feet on the ground, who was active in her church and even helped out at the youth group of another church, which happened to be his own. She treasured friends and family, and—if he had to fall back on an old cliché—she was both pretty and intelligent and knew how to do minor tune-ups on her own car. Plus she had a great sense of humor. And, apparently, a huge collection of shoes. He wondered if she had any of those strappy high-heeled things that looked so great when a woman wore a nice slim dress.

"Matt? Hello? Earth to Matt?"

Matt blinked as a hand waved in front of his face.

He felt his cheeks grow warm. "Sorry. What did you say?"

"I said Tippy is done checking on her secret stashes. We can go now. What do you want to do?"

He grinned. "I want to go to the music store and buy you a guitar. Then we can go back to my place, and I'll get my guitar out and get started on those lessons you want."

"Lessons?"

"I'm pretty good, and as far as lessons go, I'm cheap, too."

"How good are you?"

His smile dropped. When all his friends had been looking for the women they would eventually marry, Matt had stayed home and poured his energy and frustration into his guitar, when he wasn't studying for veterinary college. He wasn't just good, he was very good.

"I'm good enough to give you decent lessons."

"I guess that's okay, but I won't let you buy me a guitar."

"When's your birthday?"

"It was a couple of months ago. Why?"

"Consider it a late birthday gift. I know the store owner, and he always gives me a good discount. This is going to be fun."

"Wait. What about picking up some lunch for your family?"

Matt's grin returned. "I'll order pizza and have it delivered to the house. Come on. I'm starting to hear music in my head." He leaned closer to her then twirled an imaginary mustache. "Come, my dear. We're going to make beautiful music together."

Farrah mumbled something under her breath that he couldn't make out, turned, and headed for the car.

He followed, unable to stop himself from laughing. For the first time since he could remember, he was actually looking forward to a date, even if she didn't know it was one.

At least not yet. But it would be.

Chapter 6

I think this is enough. You've done well. You've learned some of the easier chords—E, A7, C, G, and D. You can now string them together to make a simple song."

"String them together? Is that a bad joke?"

He grinned. "Sorry," he said, but he wasn't really. "Seriously, you're doing great for a first lesson."

Farrah shook her left hand in the air to try to alleviate the stinging in her fingertips. "I can't do this. This hurts. A lot."

"That's normal. After a while you'll develop calluses and it will only bug you after you've played for a few hours."

"Hours?" After half an hour her fingers throbbed, and she was sure the lines were going to be permanent. She hadn't known it would be like this.

Yet Matt had played more than she had, and he was fine. All she wanted to do was run her fingers under icy cold water.

She stared at the aching, scored lines on her abused fingers.

Matt held out his left hand, palm upward. "See? One day your fingers will be slightly roughened, like this."

In her mind's eye, she pictured the rough hands of an old farmer, lumpy and knobby and scarred. Matt's hands were nothing like that. His hands were normal. Soft. Large. Masculine.

He smiled gently. "I meant for you to look at the tips of my fingers. See the calluses?"

Farrah shook her head. He smiled again. "Let me show you what I mean."

With his right hand, Matt reached forward and grasped her left. He started to reach forward to touch her sore fingers but stopped. "I wish I had some of that moisturizing stuff women put on their hands. That would probably help. But if you keep it up, your fingers will be like this."

Slowly, he brushed his fingertips over the soft skin of her wrist. "Feel how rough they are?"

All she could do was stare down at Matt's hands, touching her. His fingers weren't soft, but his touch was. From his tender movements she instantly knew he was very good at being a vet. She wasn't a nervous dog, but she already felt better, even without the hand lotion.

Rather than stare at their hands, she looked up to see him looking back at her with a goofy expression in his eyes.

He leaned forward, and as he moved slowly toward her, his eyes drifted shut—like a sappy romance movie, just before the handsome hero kisses the woman of his dreams.

Before her brain could process that this wasn't the movies, his lips brushed hers with a gentle kiss and it was over.

He straightened and smiled at her. "How would you like to have dinner with me tonight? I know you've got to keep an eye on Kat this evening, and I heard her and Tyler talking about a few of the new movies that are out. It's not raining, and I saw a barbecue out back at Luke and Cindy's house. How about we grill up some steaks and then the four of us catch a show?"

Farrah resisted the urge to press her fingers to her lips. She couldn't remember the last time she'd been kissed. Especially by. . .she wasn't sure how to classify him. She couldn't call him a boy; he was every inch a man. He'd graduated from college and had been running a successful business that had been established for years, so he wasn't young, but kissing someone his age certainly made her feel like an old lady. It made her wonder what he'd been thinking, but she really had no idea. "I. . ."

Before she could think of something to say, Matt stood. "We'll have to get back to my parents' place soon. First we can go to the supermarket and get everything we're going to need for supper. Then we have to go pick up Tyler and Kat and go back to Luke and Cindy's."

"I. . ."

He smiled, again sending her brain into a tailspin and once more leaving her unable to finish her sentence.

"It will give us a chance to keep tabs on Kat and Tyler, and it'll be fun."

Farrah nibbled her lower lip. She was an elementary school teacher, and accustomed to children coming up with things that stopped her dead in her tracks. Admittedly, she didn't have a lot of experience with teens, and even less with adult men ten years her junior trying to. . . She didn't know what he was trying to do. From what she could tell, he was flirting with her. She just couldn't figure out why.

For the rest of the weekend, she would probably see him as often as Kat saw Tyler, which she now knew would be a lot. After the weekend, her life would be back into the usual routine. Not that routine was bad, but she already knew she was going to miss him. Even though she couldn't understand his attention, it was flattering, and she enjoyed being with him.

"Well?"

She looked at Matt, who was looking at her like an expectant puppy dog.

"On one condition."

He blinked and his smiled faltered. "Condition?"

Farrah grinned. "For dessert, we get a nice chocolate cake."

He gave her a goofy smile. "I'll get you the biggest, richest chocolate cake you've ever seen, with real whipping cream and shredded chocolate and a cherry on top, but I have my own condition."

Her mouth watered and she gained a pound on her hips just thinking about it. "Name it."

"You come to church with me tomorrow morning."

She couldn't think of an easier condition. They'd talked enough that he knew she attended services faithfully every Sunday. To agree to such a condition would be almost cheating.

But there was chocolate involved.

"Deal."

Chapter 7

Farrah had never felt so disconcerted in church in her life.

The pastor's sermon had been both interesting and challenging. The worship and singing had been uplifting and inspirational. It had also given her a revelation into Matt's faith. She hadn't known he was so involved with his church that he played guitar for the worship team. Also, seated beside Tyler, not that she had been studying him, she noticed that Tyler paid rapt attention to the sermon. He'd also answered some of Kat's questions and easily found all the Bible references in his iPod. Tyler even convinced Kat to download the app so she could carry a Bible with her at all times to look things up or just read.

Everything had gone well until the service ended and she found herself in the foyer with Matt, chatting with his friends and other members of his church.

That was when things started to become strange.

It was like she was from another planet. Everyone stared

at her. There had been a few double takes. She'd gone into the washroom three times to make sure she didn't have something stuck in her teeth.

After being the target of much scrutiny, many people, especially women, kept asking Matt to introduce them to his friend, with a strange emphasis on the word *friend*.

By the time they finally made it out the door, Farrah's head was swimming with the number of people she'd met and the multitude of names she'd never remember. "You have a very friendly church," she muttered as Matt inched his car out of the parking lot. "Maybe a little too friendly. Does half the population of your church always want to be introduced to every new person who comes in the door?"

"Nah. They're not usually so overwhelming. They were all just curious about you."

"Why?"

"Because I've never brought a lady friend to church before."

A million different definitions of *lady friend* rushed through her head. One in particular flashed in red, and that was the kind of lady friend she knew she wasn't.

She watched him as he carefully merged into the traffic. "Why not?"

He shrugged his shoulders as he drove. "Don't know. I just haven't."

Unless she'd read the signals wrong, the ladies who asked about her didn't wanted to meet her, per se. They were checking her out.

From the backseat, Tyler piped up. "Aren't you glad you finally did?" Tyler leaned closer to Farrah. "And now because you're here, we get to go someplace good for lunch."

She turned to look at Tyler. "What about your parents? Where are they? You came with them, didn't you?"

"Yes, but I don't go home with them. Every Sunday me and Uncle Matt go get a burger after church. But not today. Today we're going to Green Lake. Uncle Matt packed a picnic."

Matt gritted his teeth. "Thanks for keeping it a surprise."

"Oops."

Beside Tyler, Kat giggled.

Matt sighed. "Guess what? I thought we could take advantage of the nice weather and have a picnic then go for a walk at the park at Green Lake."

"It's still a surprise. It just lacked a little on the delivery. Green Lake sounds nice. I haven't been there for years. Except we're headed in the wrong direction."

"We're going to Luke and Cindy's place so you can put on some jeans and comfortable shoes and get Tippy. Then we'll stop at my place to get Rex and the lunch I made before I left this morning, and we'll go."

"Yeah," Tyler said, "we're going to bring chairs to sit on and everything."

Matt checked his watch. "By the time we get to my place, a nice big pot of coffee should be ready. All we have to do is pour it into the thermos and go."

Farrah couldn't help but be impressed.

All the way to the park, she listened to Tyler telling what he thought were funny stories about Matt and his animals, especially the rabbit named Fluffball who was litter-box trained. She didn't want to tell Tyler that she'd already met all Matt's pets.

By the time they arrived at Green Lake, the sky had clouded over, and it felt like it was going to rain. However, in Seattle it often felt like that, so like most Seattleites they ignored it, hooked the leashes on the dogs, and began their walk.

Although Tippy was fast considering her handicap, she was much slower than Rex. Even though he was getting up in dog years, he was twice Tippy's size, and his pace matched his longer legs. To give the teens more freedom, they traded dogs and watched as Tyler and Kat ran ahead of them with Rex.

Automatically, Farrah reached to take the leash from Matt; after all, Tippy was her responsibility for the weekend. One of Matt's eyebrows quirked as she touched his hand, expecting the leash. He gave it to her freely but instead of simply handing it to her, he slid the loop around her wrist and then wrapped his fingers in hers and gave her a small tug to get her started walking.

Holdings hands.

Like a couple of kids. Or, as he'd called her in church, his *lady friend*. She really wasn't that kind of friend.

She gave her hand a slight pull, but he didn't let go.

"What are you doing?" she asked between clenched teeth.

"If you can't tell, then I must be doing something wrong."

She looked down at their joined hands. "We're not that kind of friends."

He gave her fingers a gentle squeeze. "But we could be."

She stopped walking, forcing him to stop as well, and looked into his eyes. Warm hazel eyes, sparkling with light and. . .something sappy.

"No. We can't be. Do you have any idea how old I am?"

The sappy look in his eyes was joined by a goofy grin. "My mama told me never to guess a woman's age, and I always listen to my mama."

"You forget, I've seen you with your mother, and you don't."

"I do most of the time. I respect my mama."

Actually, she had no doubt that he did. All teasing aside, she was certain that he was a good son and loved and respected both his parents.

But that didn't change the facts. She knew she looked younger than her actual age, but realistically she didn't think she looked *that* young. "You've got my permission to guess. How old do you think I am?"

He tipped his head to one side. "I'll use my Southern boy manners and say twenty-nine."

"Southern boy? I doubt you've ever been farther south than Portland or any more east than Montana."

"That's not true. I was at Disneyland once. Does that count?"

"No, that does not count."

"I'm still sticking to twenty-nine."

"Look at me, Matt. Look at my eyes. Really look. I haven't been twenty-nine for over two decades."

He laughed. Outright laughed. "I can't believe this. Most women try to undercut their age by five years, but I've never seen anyone do what you've just done. I wish I knew why."

He wiped his eyes with his left hand, not releasing her right, then laughed some more.

"What haven't you seen? A woman telling the truth about her age? Honestly, the birthday that I just had a couple of months ago was my fiftieth. How old are you? Forty?"

All his laughter dropped and Matt became very serious. "I'm thirty-eight. My birthday is in the spring. So I'm almost thirty-nine."

"You've got a whole winter to go. That's not almost. I'm twelve years older than you."

She watched the emotions run across his face. First bewilderment then concentration as he did the mental math then the shock that she knew would happen.

"You're serious. . . ," he said, his voice trailing off.

"I'm as close to your mother's age as I am to yours."

His hand went limp and dropped from hers.

"Wow," he stammered. "You look good. Really good."

She thought of the pizza and popcorn she'd been living

on all weekend and knew her butt was wider than it was a week ago. "Not that good." The only reason she looked good was because she was more careful with planning her wardrobe than she'd been a decade ago.

Matt cleared his throat and his voice dropped nearly an octave. "I still have to ask. How do you feel about babies?"

She opened her mouth but didn't say the first thought that popped into her head, which was that instead of thinking about babies, she was thinking about menopause.

"I'm fifty years old, Matt." She squeezed her eyes shut for a few seconds. "Many of my friends are grandmothers."

"Then—"

Farrah held up her hands to stop him from saying any more. "You need to find someone your own age."

"But—"

She shook her head. "It's not open for discussion."

His eyes widened. "I'm—"

She backed up. "I said this discussion is closed."

His eyes widened even more. His mouth hung open, but fortunately he didn't speak.

Farrah stared into his eyes. She'd heard the expression that a person's eyes were the window to his soul, and in Matt's case that was certainly true. Depths of conflicting emotions warred in his eyes. He looked absolutely stricken.

Thinking about what could have been but now would never be, her heart probably ached as much as his.

The years most people spent searching for their life's

mate, she'd spent in mourning. Like most of her friends, she had met the man who was her other half. They fell in love and got engaged, just like a storybook romance. But they never got married. Just after they'd set a date, Ed was diagnosed with hepatitis B. After a transfusion, he'd been infected with tainted blood and became terminal. So she wouldn't be held liable for his escalating medical expenses, especially when his workplace benefits were reduced, he'd stopped the wedding, but they never stopped loving each other. She'd been with him when he died and thought his funeral would be the hardest day of her life. But it wasn't. The day after the funeral, her best friend, Cindy's mother, had been diagnosed with cancer and then lost the battle after three painful years. After that, the only way Farrah could deal with losing the two biggest loves of her life was by pouring her soul into helping Dave raise Cindy and teaching the children who came and went in her classroom the best she knew how.

Now at fifty, she couldn't be what Matt needed in his life—which was a wife who would be his soul mate. With the way the economy had gone in the last decade, she was thinking of ways to secure her retirement—not raise children. Since Matt was nearly forty, if men did indeed have a biological clock, his time was running short. He had a tender heart, and he needed to share that with a wife and children he didn't have yet, not his herd of pets. In order to bond with the woman who would be his other half, he needed to meet and date women slightly younger than he was, not waste his time with her.

Farrah looked around the park. They were surrounded by families and couples who looked like one day they would be families.

That was the way Matt should be. Matt wasn't even forty and had so much of his life ahead of him, while she was now officially middle aged, when most people started to wind down. She couldn't be, as he'd called her earlier, his lady friend. Still, she didn't want to stop seeing him. The more time she spent with him, the more she was growing increasingly fond of him.

If only she were two decades younger.

Farrah shook her head. She wouldn't dream of things that would never happen, nor would she dwell on things she couldn't change. But she could dwell on what she could have. Now that Matt knew and understood the parameters, things would be fine.

Matt cleared his throat. "At church, I introduced you as my lady friend. You—"

Farrah held her palm up to stop him from putting his foot in his mouth. She hadn't wanted to embarrass him then, and she didn't want to embarrass him now.

For just a moment, she thought of what it would be like to really be his lady friend and to have more than the quick brush of a kiss he'd given her on Saturday. But that wasn't going to happen.

"You don't have to explain. I know you didn't know that

I was so much older than you. It's okay. I understand. I can't be your lady, but I can still be your friend. After all, with something blossoming between Kat and Tyler, I think we're going to be seeing a lot of each other." Perhaps by saying they could be friends, the awkwardness would be gone, and they could make the best of things.

To save both of them from an embarrassing conversation she was sure neither of them wanted to have, she secured Tippy's leash around her wrist and motioned her head to the right. "Let's go find Tyler and Kat and dig into that picnic you packed before it starts to rain."

At her words, the first drop landed on her nose and the skies opened up.

As people around them scattered, Tyler, Kat, and Rex appeared in the distance, running toward them at full tilt as the rain began to beat down.

Matt hunkered down to unclip the leash from Tippy's collar then picked the dog up. Cradling her, he tensed, ready to run.

"I think we're going to be eating in the car. Let's go."

Chapter 8

Matt stared up at the ceiling in the darkened bedroom.

The glowing numbers on his clock radio told him he had to be up in four hours to get to the clinic, and he hadn't yet fallen asleep.

His body was exhausted but his brain was racing.

She wasn't that close to his mother's age. He didn't know exactly how old his mother was without checking his contact list on his iPad, but he knew she was two or three years from retirement.

Farrah wasn't close to that point. She was only closer than he was.

He flipped over and buried his face in his pillow. Beside him, Rex made a disgruntled snuffle, kicked him, and started to snore.

Matt wished he were snoring, but instead when he closed his eyes, visions of Farrah danced through his head.

Farrah petting the puppies. Farrah reminding Tyler about

his manners. Farrah driving her car just a little above the speed limit then pretending to act guilty when he pointed it out. Farrah promising to practice her guitar lessons even when her fingers hurt.

He'd liked her before he found out her age, and now that he had time to think about it, her age didn't really matter. He still liked everything about her. Her smile. Her sense of humor. The way she protected Kat and cared for Tippy. She loved her job and was good to others. From her comments following a short discussion on an article they'd read in the paper, he knew she didn't cheat on her taxes.

All his life he'd prayed for God to send him a woman like Farrah who didn't want to have children, but that hadn't happened. Something about him naturally gravitated to that type. But every woman he started to develop feelings for had either told him or shown him in other ways that one day she would want to become a mother. As he reached his thirties, most single women outright asked him how he felt about having children, some even on the first date—making it also the last date.

So Matt had stayed single.

But now when he'd given up and resigned himself to being single and alone for the rest of his life, he met a wonderful, sweet woman.

He'd never believed in love at first sight—he usually scoffed at such things. But now that it had happened to him, he wanted to shout it from the rooftops.

Except he would be shouting alone.

He rolled over and stared at the ceiling again.

He wouldn't have thought of seeking an older woman for a life's mate. He couldn't help but feel that finding Farrah was a gift.

If all she would commit to was being friends, then even though he didn't know how to be just friends with a wonderful woman like Farrah, he was going to be the best friend she ever had, and then some.

Matt rolled onto his side and closed his eyes. As his body finally started to relax, he smiled, thinking of the dreams he would have and drifted off thinking of how he would make those dreams a reality.

Just as Farrah removed the casserole dish from the oven, the doorbell rang. She lifted the lid, inhaled deeply, set it on the counter, and went to see who it was.

"Kat? What are you doing here?"

Kat checked her watch then hugged her purse. "Uncle Luke dropped me off. I have to go to Tyler's grandparents' place to help give the runt puppy her bottle right away."

"Why couldn't he drop you off there instead of here?"

"Because you know where it is."

Kat also knew where it was. All she had to do was give Luke directions. Kat's answer didn't make sense or at least it didn't to Farrah. Maybe to the teenage mind it did.

"You keep checking your watch. Are you in a hurry?"

"Yes."

Farrah waited but no explanation was forthcoming.

"Why?"

"Because she's going to be hungry. I have to show Tyler how to feed her. Dr. Matt is dropping Tyler off."

"If Dr. Matt is going to be there, I'm sure he can show Tyler how to do it because he's the one who showed you."

Kat's eyes became wide. "But I want to do it."

There. Now the reason was stated. Because Kat wanted to feed the puppy.

Farrah pressed her palm over her rumbling tummy. If that puppy was half as hungry as she was, then the puppy had all her sympathy.

She hurried back into kitchen to tilt the lid so the casserole would cool, said good-bye to her supper, and led Kat to the car.

They had barely pulled out of the driveway when Kat turned to her. "I'm sorry for interrupting your supper. Maybe you can go have supper with Dr. Matt while Tyler and me feed the puppy."

"While Tyler and I feed the puppy."

"You're going to feed the puppy? But I don't want to go have supper with Dr. Matt. He's so. . .old. He's like, almost forty. Ish."

Farrah sighed. "So old."

"Yes, but he's really nice." Kat's voice lowered to a whisper. "I think he likes you."

The typical response would have been to say that she

liked him, too, but that wasn't something she was going to say to a hormonal teenager who was in the early ravaging stages of her first love. Farrah could only guess where the conversation would go once she said such a thing, and she wasn't going to go down that road. "I'm not going to feed the puppy. I was correcting your grammar."

Kat mumbled something Farrah couldn't hear and hung her head just like one of her primary students after she'd corrected their grammar in the classroom.

"I don't think I'm going to go out for supper with Dr. Matt. I'm sure he's already had supper by now. How do you know he's going to be driving Tyler to his grandparents' place?"

Kat pulled her cell phone out of her pocket, opened it to a text message, and held it up. "Tyler said so. He also said that Dr. Matt is hungry because he came right from his clinic to pick Tyler up. So if both of you are hungry, you can go eat something while we feed the puppy."

"That's a lot of info for one little text message."

"It wasn't one. It was more like ten." Kat grinned. "Uncle Luke got me unlimited texting."

Before Farrah could comment more on the alleged plan for the evening, Kat's phone played a short melodic tone. "Eleven," she muttered, with her thumbs typing at the speed of light.

Farrah gave up.

It appeared she was going to have supper with Dr. Matt. She wondered if Dr. Matt knew.

Chapter 9

"How do I look? Is this okay?"

"It would be better without the tie, Uncle Matt."

Matt checked himself one last time in the rearview mirror and yanked off the tie just as the light changed to green and the cars ahead of him began to move.

The boy was probably right. Matt was trying too hard and he knew it. Besides, the tie was crinkled from being squished in the pocket of his smock all day.

"They're almost there."

"Tell me, when you're actually with each other, face-to-face, do you talk or still text each other?"

"You're so not funny, Uncle Matt," Tyler mumbled as he typed furiously with his thumbs, hit SEND, and waited.

Matt shook his head. He did all his typing the old-fashioned way, with all his fingers and one thumb. Plus, he actually used his cell phone to. . .phone people. Go figure.

"Kat says they're in the driveway." He typed some more,

hit SEND, and waited for ten seconds. "They're getting out of the car."

Matt counted to ten.

"They're knocking on the door." Tyler hit a few more letters, hit SEND, and had a beep in seconds. "Gramma answered the door."

"Enough," Matt grumbled between his teeth. He wondered if Kat's texting got on Farrah's nerves as much as Tyler's got on his.

Of course, as annoying as it was, it would make a great conversation starter.

"What are they doing now?" he asked as they turned onto his parents' street.

"Gramma is taking them downstairs and Gramps is already there."

Matt turned into the driveway. "Why don't you text them and tell Kat to tell Gramma and Grampa that we're letting ourselves in?" Which was the first useful thing he could think of that Tyler had ever texted.

"Kat says Farrah is really hungry. She left her supper on the counter to take Kat to Gramma's house."

Another bit of useful information. Maybe the constant texting was good for something after all.

He opened the door and Tyler followed him inside.

He found everyone in the basement, kneeling in front of the box of puppies huddled against the mother dog.

As if right on cue, Farrah's stomach made a loud grumble.

Even from the side, looking down at her while she knelt and he stood, he could see her cheeks turn red. Her ears, too.

"Anybody want supper?" he asked.

"Farrah does!" Kat called out, causing Farrah's face to turn even redder.

He held out his hand as she scrambled to her feet, but she didn't take him up on his offer to help. "Guilty as charged," she mumbled, the color in her cheeks fading just a bit.

"I know the perfect place to go." They would get a basket of warm garlic bread sticks to nibble on until the main course was delivered, which was always a long time at this place. He could make the time last even longer with a good appetizer. He already knew Farrah loved chocolate cheesecake, and they had one that was absolutely magnificent. With little chocolate chunks and gooey sauce.

While they took their time, from bread sticks to closing coffee, he'd be sitting across the table from her, staring into her sparkling emerald-green eyes.

Or better yet, he could sit beside her, so he could hold her hand when they weren't eating.

But in order for that to happen, someone else had to come to give him an excuse to sit beside her. That would make the night perfect, sitting side by side with Farrah in a dimly lit restaurant at a nice secluded corner table, with a romantic little candle in an amber-colored glass thing flickering to heighten the mood.

He cleared his throat. "Anyone else want to come?"

Tyler and Kat both turned their heads and gave him the strangest look, like they couldn't believe he'd asked such a stupid question.

Maybe it was stupid. He wasn't going to try to hold Farrah's hand in front of Tyler and Kat. He didn't want to give them any ideas or, worse, encourage them. It would be worse if his parents wanted to come. Even at his age, there was something about sharing a meal with a girl in front of your parents. They weren't at that meet-the-parents stage. He didn't know what stage they were at. All he knew was that they weren't there. But the invitation had already been extended. He couldn't uninvite his parents. He'd been raised better than that.

His parents turned and smiled. "We'll pass," his mother said.

Matt didn't know what he felt more, relief or guilt or a combination of both.

His mother turned toward him. "We have a pot roast in the oven and it's almost done. Why don't you stay and eat with us? You're all invited."

Matt's stomach sank into his cowboy boots along with his appetite.

Farrah turned and smiled back. "Are you sure? I don't want to impose."

His mother smiled. "You're not imposing if you promise to help with the dishes."

Matt rolled his eyes. "Mom, are you trying to save

electricity by not using the dishwasher again?"

"Not really. I just—"

His father didn't let his mother finish her sentence. "Yes," he said with no hint of remorse that he'd let out her secret.

"I would love to help with the dishes."

Matt forced a smile. "Me, too."

Both his parents turned to him. "Really?"

"Yes, really."

"I'm going upstairs to get everything ready. Matt, would you like to set the table?"

"Sure."

Apparently tonight was meet-the-parents night, after all. Except they weren't dating. Yet.

In order to make that happen, he needed help, and he knew where to get it.

Cindy nudged Farrah in the ribs. "I think he likes you."

Farrah gritted her teeth as she reached up to get the big bowl from the storage cupboard of the church's kitchen. "I don't know what you're talking about."

The youth group's hockey team had just finished practice, so it was time to get the snacks together while the teens put the sports equipment away.

Usually Farrah prepared the snacks alone, but today Cindy was helping. Typically she helped the teens stow the nets, sticks, and vests, but for two weeks in a row, Luke had been unable to come, so they needed another referee. Both times, Matt had volunteered. Now it was Matt who was helping put everything away.

"During the halftime break, everyone noticed how he sat beside you."

"That's because the only empty chair was beside me."

Which was odd. Usually there were lots of empty chairs. Tonight there had been exactly the number of chairs for the number of people present, almost like they'd been counted. As well, everyone had sat very quickly. The flurry had been like of a game of musical chairs with her elementary school class, except that everyone got a chair. In the commotion of everyone finding a seat at once, the only empty chair remaining was beside her, which was where Matt sat.

She had no idea what the joke was, but after everyone was seated, a group of the girls sat huddled together, all firmly planted on their chairs with their heads together, giggling.

Farrah suspected that something was rotten in the state of Denmark. Or at least in a certain suburb of Seattle.

Cindy dumped the last bag of chips into the bowl. "I heard rumors that you were going out on a hot date to Jazz Alley Saturday night."

Farrah's hands froze in the middle of tugging the lid off the dip container.

"I'm not going anywhere all weekend. I have papers to grade."

"What?" Cindy stared at her, her eyes wide. "But I heard

him telling the boys that he got tickets for a great show and he had a special evening planned."

"Don't look at me like that. If Matt's going out on a date tomorrow night, good for him."

Farrah tried to tell herself that she truly was glad Matt was finally going out with another woman. For the past two weeks, she'd spent almost every evening with him. Almost every day, Kat had summoned her to take her to Matt's parents' home with some excuse about why neither Cindy nor Luke could drive her. She'd helped Kat and various members of the youth group tend to the puppies and their ever-increasing appetites and energy, and every time she was there, so was Matt. She'd ended up not spending much time with the puppies but sitting back with Matt, talking and supervising and directing all the helpers.

She didn't know how they'd done it, but Kat and Tyler convinced her to volunteer one evening a week at the animal shelter. It was an amazing coincidence that it was the same evening as Matt.

Or not.

The approaching din indicated that the teens had finished putting everything away and were coming in, hungry. This time, instead of just the girls, nearly the whole group crowded into the kitchen, removing all the food, plates, cups, and both punch dispensers in one trip, like a wake of vultures.

She gave the counter one last wipe then joined the crowd in the meeting area, where there was one empty chair, exactly beside Matt.

The room was almost eerily silent as she walked toward that chair, feeling the heat of every eye on her. She wondered if it was her imagination, but a couple of the boys gave Matt a brotherly punch in the shoulder, and one of them, in what was probably supposed to be a hushed tone, wished him luck.

As she sat, a few of the teens started talking, but the room was nowhere near the usual volume or excitement levels after a practice game.

Matt shifted his body toward her, picked up her left hand, and brushed his fingers over her developing calluses. "You know how we've been doing guitar lessons on Friday nights lately."

She nodded. "I've been meaning to talk to you about that. This weekend I have to—"

He raised one hand to stop her from finishing. "I hope you don't mind, but I thought we could skip the lesson on Friday because I got tickets for Jazz Alley on Saturday. There's this great ensemble playing, a guitarist, a bass player, and a drummer. I haven't seen them, but a friend said the guitarist is great. I think being up close to him would be a great learning experience for you."

Her mouth opened but no sound came out. She'd heard one of the other teachers talking about the same show, and she knew the tickets weren't cheap.

As she thought about it, the room fell silent.

If she wasn't 100 percent sure then, she was sure now. Everyone was watching.

Cindy's words about the tickets echoed through her head. Cindy, Kat, Tyler, and likely the entire youth group, had already known. Now everyone was watching, waiting for her answer.

"I—I don't know," she stammered.

"Aw, come on, Farrah!" one of the boys called from across the room. "It'll be fun."

"My mom says the food is great," one of the girls resounded from the other side.

The boy beside her began to play air guitar then moved his hands as if playing a double bass. "I downloaded a few of their songs. The bass player is awesome."

She turned to Matt. "There isn't any way I can say no and save face, is there?"

His ears turned red. "I'm sorry. At first I only told a couple of the boys, and before I knew it, things got kind of out of control."

She glanced around the room. Everyone was staring at them. A few of the girls looked like they were holding their breath. "Ya think?" she asked, making no attempt to keep the sarcasm out of her voice.

Instead of turning to Matt, she turned to the group. "Sure," she said loudly so everyone would hear. "That sounds like fun."

Everyone cheered. As the ruckus died down, a few of them started texting, including Cindy.

"I think she's telling Luke," Matt whispered in her ear.

Farrah covered her face with her hands. "This can't be happening," she muttered.

"Why not? We'll have fun."

She stood, grabbed his arm, hauled him to his feet, and dragged him into the kitchen.

"Kiss! Kiss!" the teens yelled. In the background, she could hear Cindy telling them to calm down and mind their own business.

As if that were likely.

"Contrary to popular opinion, this is not a date. I'm only doing this to not disappoint the teens. I'm not going to date you."

"Why not? Everyone's really happy for us."

Farrah waved one hand in the air. "This is ridiculous. Look at us. When I retire, you'll still have over a decade left to work."

"I run my own clinic. I set my own hours and hire staff. I don't have a regular nine-to-five job."

"No. In running your own business, you work twelve-hour days, six days a week. I've already seen the way this works with Cindy and Luke."

"But I have more staff than they do. I work like this because I have nothing better to do with my time. Now I do."

Farrah didn't want to guess what he was leading up to. "I meant that I'll be retired, and you'll be out working."

"So? Lots of women work part-time or stay home while their husbands work. I wouldn't care if you stayed at home and I worked."

"But what if I wanted to travel? Do things? Go places?"

"Like I said, I'm self-employed. I have staff. I can arrange any time off I want."

Farrah waved one hand in the air . "But by the time you finally do retire, I'll be ready for a nursing home."

"I doubt that. I don't understand what the difference is between that and the other way around, where the man is older than the woman and he retires first and she keeps working."

"Because, uh. . ." She didn't know. Her friends were all her age, and even though all of them had husbands who were older, they weren't that much older and both were still working. She didn't know how it was going to play out when one of them reached retirement.

"Then let's not worry about it and take it as it comes. Besides, we can't disappoint our fan club out there."

"Fan club?"

"They all want this to happen. You heard them."

Unfortunately she had. And if she was honest with herself, she did like him. She just couldn't help but feel that the large age difference was wrong, and nothing was going to make it right.

"It will be fine to have fun together, but aren't you looking for something permanent?"

He reached forward, grasped her hands, and smiled. "Yes, I am. I'm so glad you feel that way."

Farrah yanked her hands away from him. "Not me. You need to meet someone else, to get married and have a family."

He stiffened from head to toe. "I'm not going to have a family. No children for me. So if you aren't going to want children at this point in your life, then there's nothing stopping us."

"But..."

He held up his hands. "Let's not think about it. All I want to think about is Saturday night. We're going to have a great time. Now let's get back and show everyone that they're cheering for the right team. This show is preassigned seating, and I got great seats. I'll pick you up at six, but I'm counting on seeing you before then at the animal shelter."

Farrah sighed. This was against her better judgment, but at the same time she could hardly wait. But until then, she had to face the masses.

"Okay, let's go back. But remember, if I have a rotten time, you're going to have to face the consequences with them."

Matt pressed both palms over his heart. "I'm ready."

He was, but was she?

Chapter 10

I changed my mind."

Matt's heart sank. So far they'd had a wonderful time—at least he'd thought so. They'd had a relatively traffic-free drive, considering the usual downtown Seattle mayhem, Saturdays included. As happened every time they got together, when she forgot about their age difference they had a great conversation, and, of course, he fell just a little more in love with her. If that were possible.

As promised, their table was close to the stage with a good view of the performers. The meal was superb and the show fantastic. He'd bought the tickets because he knew Farrah was a hard-core jazz fan. He wasn't, but this band was different than he'd expected—there was no brass, just strings and the drummer. When he got home, he would go online and buy a selection of this band's music. He liked them that much.

When the band had first started up, she'd agreed with him that it was a great performance in a small venue. Matt didn't know what had changed. He tried to smile but knew it came across as strained. "I'm sorry. I thought you'd really enjoy the guitarist."

She beamed ear to ear, and he could have sworn his heart skipped a few beats.

Farrah waved one hand in the air. "Yes, of course he's good, but look at that bass player." Her eyes went a little starry, her smile turned a little crooked, and she sighed.

Matt turned toward the stage. The bass player was an older gentleman with gray hair at his temples, a good start to a bald spot, and a few lines showing at the corners of his eyes. Overall he was quite a handsome man for his age, which Matt figured was in his early fifties.

His fine meal turned to a lump in his stomach.

The bass player was about the same age as Farrah.

She sighed again. "That's what I want."

Of course it was. "Oh," was all he could say.

"How much do you think it is? Is it expensive?"

"What?" He shook his head. "Excuse me?"

"That electric stand-up bass. Just look at it. Doesn't it look fun to play? I want one like that."

His heart picked up in double time. Just like the last song the band had done. She wasn't going to dump him after all. "Y–yeah," he stammered. "It looks great for a stage performance, but it's probably not practical. I mean, it's big and maybe heavy. Might be awkward to carry around."

Farrah shrugged. "Then I'll get a regular bass guitar. I've

been thinking about it for a while and now I know for sure. I want to play both bass guitar and regular guitar. What do you think? Have you ever played bass guitar?"

"I have one, but I don't play it often."

"I wonder if. . ." Her voice trailed off as she turned to face him. "Are you okay? Your face is awful pale. Do we need to leave?"

He felt the paleness change to a blush, hoping she wasn't going to ask what he'd been thinking. "I'm fine. But since you mention it, they'll be asking everyone to leave soon so the second performance can get started."

She sipped her coffee, set the cup down on the saucer, and checked her watch. "You're right. The time sure went fast. This was really nice. Thank you."

They leisurely made their way out to the car. As Matt opened the door for her, he said, "It's still early. Instead of calling it a night, how would you like to take Rex out for a walk with me? My street is well lit, and I live in a safe neighborhood."

She smiled. "I'd like that."

♋

Farrah waited on the porch with Rex while Matt went inside to check his other animals.

Tonight she'd done something she promised herself she would never do. She'd known going out on a real date—which it was, no matter what she called it—would be a mistake.

341

And she was right, but the youth group had goaded her and she'd fallen for it.

Or rather, she was falling for him. Which was wrong... so wrong.

"All locked up. Let's go."

Unlike her walks with Tippy, Rex stopped often to check out all the landmarks and poles along Matt's street. Of course she was in no hurry and neither was Matt. His neighborhood was safe and busy. Besides, Rex was pretty fearsome, and Matt had taught him to growl on command. The display of teeth and the noise would frighten off any potential attacker.

Somehow, Farrah couldn't imagine Tippy scaring off a mugger, but the thought amused her.

When they arrived at the park, Matt unclipped Rex from the leash to let him run, and the dog took off across the field. Before she could think of what was happening, Matt's fingers became entwined with hers. "We can just stay here and wait. Rex knows his way in the dark. He won't be long."

Her heart sped up. Part of her had seen this moment coming, and part of her didn't want to deal with it, but part of her wanted him to never let go.

In the muted light of the streetlamp, she watched Rex circle his favorite tree.

Holding hands with Matt was wrong. He should have been holding hands with someone his own age. But for today, Farrah chose to turn back the clock.

He gave her hand a gentle squeeze. "I really enjoyed

myself tonight. How would you like to do the same thing next weekend? Well, something similar. There's so much to do around Seattle."

No. She couldn't. She hadn't wanted tonight to be a date—it was an obligation. Or something. If they went out again, without the youth group cheering in the background, that would be another date, and she couldn't do that to him when this wasn't right.

Matt turned and smiled at her. "Actually, next weekend there's a dog show I wanted to check out. Would you like to go with me?"

A dog show wasn't a date. "Sure."

"Then we can go out for dinner afterward. There's a great seafood place near the arena. How about it?"

Dinner afterward at a fancy restaurant was a date. But if they were already in the neighborhood, then it was only half a date. So that didn't count. "Sure."

"Great. When we get back to my place, would you like to have a try at my bass guitar? Maybe we can have a jam session."

Farrah laughed. "I can barely play a handful of chords on the guitar. What makes you think I'll be able to play anything coherent in one day?"

"I have great confidence in you. Even if all you do is play the bottom note on the first beat, it will be fun."

She looked up into his eyes, never having felt so pulled apart in her life. This couldn't go on. She had to cut loose and spare them both the agony. It wasn't fair to him and it wasn't fair to her.

Matt tugged her hand, and before she realized what she was doing, he'd led her a few steps off the sidewalk and onto the grass, where he stopped and nudged her under a tree, giving them as much privacy as they could have in a dark public park.

"What's wrong?" he asked.

Amazing how he could tell. Or maybe not so amazing.

"I don't really know. I just feel so strange about this. What's happening between us?"

He dropped her hand then cupped her cheeks with his palms and bowed his head. "This is happening." He closed his eyes and kissed her. Not just a little peck this time. If she'd thought that his first kiss had rocked her, this was earth shattering. Her heart pounded and her knees turned to jelly. His hands drifted down to her waist then her back, and he pulled her close to him, enveloping her in his kiss.

She wrapped her arms around his back and embraced him as fully as he embraced her, sharing a closeness like no other.

At the sound of a *woof* and a cold nose prodding her, she forced herself to separate from him. "It's late," she muttered. "We should go."

He didn't speak; he only nodded and bent to clip Rex to the leash. They walked back to his house in silence, only this time instead of holding hands, his arm remained around her waist, just as one of her arms remained around his.

So many years ago, when she'd been engaged, it hadn't felt this intense. Even though with age came maturity, she didn't know what to do or in which direction to turn. It was too late to turn back, but she couldn't move forward.

When they got back to his house, she couldn't go inside. Her brain was spinning, and she couldn't concentrate on a guitar lesson or anything right now. Instead of walking to the door, she stopped at his car in the driveway. "I think I should go home."

Without a word, he pulled his keys out of his pocket and hit the button to unlock the car. While she opened her door, Matt opened the back door and Rex hopped in. "I hope you don't mind," he said before he closed the door.

"Not at all." In fact, she thought it was rather sweet that he'd asked.

Just like everything he did. Thoughtful and always mindful of others.

They chatted about all sorts of things she knew she'd never remember discussing.

Like a gentleman, he turned off the car and escorted her to the door.

Before she could open it, Matt's hand covered the doorknob. "I think we have to talk," he said.

She didn't know whether to laugh or scream. A man needing to talk. She didn't know if she could handle a talk right now, but since his hand was on her doorknob, she didn't have a choice unless she broke a window and jumped in.

"I love you, Farrah. I know it's been fast, but that doesn't change the fact that it's true. This probably feels awkward for you, so I didn't want to leave you at loose ends. I know what you're thinking."

She would have laughed if the whole thing hadn't been so pathetic. "I don't think you do."

His lips narrowed and his head tilted a bit to one side. "I think I do. I know our age difference is really bothering you, but I'm okay with it. More than okay. I think what's bothering you the most, though, isn't retirement or traveling or anything like that, but that you're past the point of having children. That's okay. I'm never going to have children, and I've adjusted my life knowing that. This can work."

Farrah shook her head. "You can't say that. If you met and fell in love with a woman, say, five or six years younger than you, you're not too old to be a father. I know a few men at my church who became fathers after they turned forty, and they're good fathers."

"I don't think there's any way for me to say this without being really blunt, so please forgive me. I'm never going to have children because I can't."

"Can't?"

"When I was in my late teens, I had what could be loosely defined as a sporting injury, and we'll just say that when people talk about a man getting hit hard in a sensitive area and say he'll never have kids, it's not a joke."

Farrah felt all the blood drain from her face. "I didn't know that was true."

"It's true. I didn't get medical attention because everyone was too embarrassed, including me, and I've paid the price for it for my entire life."

"What about adoption?"

"The frequency of adoption in today's society isn't what it was a couple of generations ago. I couldn't do that to a woman who wanted kids of her own. Every woman who wants kids should be able to, so I've stayed single. But you... please forgive me if I'm out of line, but if you don't want to have kids at this point in your life, then I don't think there's anything stopping us from seeing where this will go. And I hope you know where I want us to end up."

Farrah felt her mouth drop open, but she couldn't form a single word.

Matt pressed a kiss to her forehead. "I know I've hit you with a big one, so I think it's best for me to go home and give you time to think. Can I pick you up for church in the morning?"

All she could do was nod.

"Good. See you then."

She stared at him as he returned to his car without completing the words to finish his sentence.

See you then, ready or not.

Chapter 11

Matt sucked in a deep breath and knocked on Farrah's door.

This was it. He hadn't intended to hit her with the soap opera of his life, but it had all tumbled out of his mouth before he could stop himself. For years he'd been bitter, but he'd managed to fill the holes in his life with other people's children—especially his sister's oldest son, Tyler—and he'd filled in the rest with his work at the Homeward Pet Adoption Center. He knew he was okay, but he wasn't really happy. But now that he'd met Farrah, he could be, and even though he knew she'd suffered some serious losses in her life, he would do his best to make her happy, too.

The door opened and there she was. Beautiful as always, dressed in a nice blouse and matching pants, ready for church. Except, like him, she had dark circles under her eyes, like she hadn't slept very well either.

"Hi," was all he could say.

She looked up at him. "Do you want to talk now or later?"

He was glad he hadn't eaten breakfast because if he had,

he would have lost it. "Now, I guess." He certainly wouldn't have his heart in the worship service or the pastor's sermon if he left this conversation hanging over his head, and he doubted she would either.

"I guess you've been thinking about this"—she waved one hand in the air—"whatever thing is going on, all night, too, right?"

"Yeah."

"It's probably pretty obvious that I'm not going to want a baby at this point in my life."

All he could do was nod, and hope.

"I've told you before that I was engaged, but he died before we got married. And then my best friend died not long after that."

"I'm in good health. I can get a doctor's note for you."

She rested one hand on his arm. "I don't think that will be necessary. I want to ask you something, and I want you to be honest."

Now he felt really sick, even with the empty stomach. "Go ahead."

"Have you ever considered fostering an older child? You're good at helping older pets find good homes. There are many older children and teens who know it's not realistic that they'll ever be adopted but really need a good foster home."

His mind spun. "I've never thought about that before."

"That could be because when we're younger, everyone only thinks about babies. But we're both older now, and even though I'm older than you, we're at different places in our lives than ten years ago. I'm thinking, for example, about Kat.

The only family she had was Luke, and he gladly took her in, but what about all the other kids like her who don't have someone like Luke?"

Matt thought about Kat and Tyler and how his being involved with both of them helped everyone. He could do that. "I like that idea."

Farrah slid her hand from his forearm to his hand and gave it a squeeze. "I do, too."

His heart sped up. "So this means?"

She smiled. "This means that yes, this relationship—even though we're off to a late start, just as you said last night—can go where you want it to go."

He gulped. "Just in case I wasn't 100 percent clear, where I want this relationship to go is to the altar."

"Matt, are you proposing to me?"

"What a great idea! I'm glad you thought of it." He couldn't stop his grin. Still holding on to Farrah's hand, he dropped to one knee. "Farrah, I love you. Will you do me the honor of becoming my wife?"

"Yes, of course I will. And speaking of late, I hope you know that now you're going to be late for your worship team practice time at church."

Matt jumped to his feet, grabbed Farrah by the waist, twirled her around, and then planted a fast but firm kiss on her lips. He wanted to do more, but she was right about the practice. Not only that, he was busting to tell his friends and family that God had given him the perfect woman he'd prayed for all his life.

He'd waited a long time, but with someone as special as Farrah, it was never too late for a happily-ever-after.

Gail Sattler was born and raised in Winnipeg, Manitoba, and now lives in Vancouver, BC (where you don't have to shovel rain), with her husband, three sons, two dogs, three lizards, and countless fish, many of whom have names. Gail and her husband were baptized together in 1983. Between acting as a referee for her three active boys and half the neighborhood, her day job as office manager for a web design company, her evening job as Mom's Taxi Service, and being the bass guitarist for her church's adult worship team, Gail loves to glorify God in her writing. Gail also writes for Barbour's Heartsong Presents line, where she was voted as the Favorite Heartsong Author three times. Gail has also written a number of novellas for Barbour's fiction anthologies.

A Letter to Our Readers

Dear Readers:

In order that we might better contribute to your reading enjoyment, we would appreciate you taking a few minutes to respond to the following questions. When completed, please return to the following: Fiction Editor, Barbour Publishing, Inc., P.O. Box 719, Uhrichsville, OH 44683.

1. Did you enjoy reading *Seattle Cinderella* by Gail Sattler?
   ❑ Very much. I would like to see more books like this.
   ❑ Moderately—I would have enjoyed it more if

   _____

   _____

2. What influenced your decision to purchase this book?
   (Check those that apply.)
   ❑ Cover   ❑ Back cover copy   ❑ Title   ❑ Price
   ❑ Friends   ❑ Publicity   ❑ Other

3. Which story was your favorite?
   ❑ *Cindy and the Prince*   ❑ *Till Death Do Us Part*
   ❑ *Love by the Books*   ❑ *Never Too Late*

4. Please check your age range:
   ❑ Under 18   ❑ 18–24   ❑ 25–34
   ❑ 35–45   ❑ 46–55   ❑ Over 55

5. How many hours per week do you read? _____

Name _____

Occupation _____

Address _____

City_____ State _____ Zip _____

E-mail _____